Kimberly Brubaker Bradley

Jefferson's Sons

A Founding Father's
Secret Children

Dial Books for Young Readers an imprint of Penguin Group (USA) Inc.

Descendents of
Thomas Jefferson

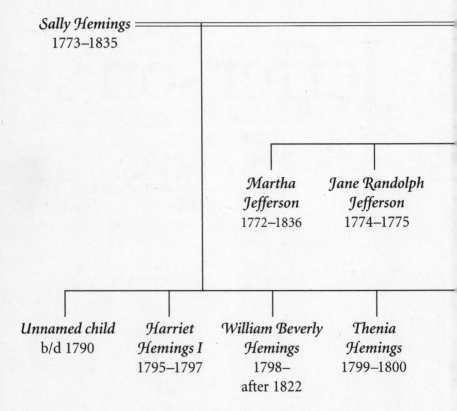

Sally Hemings
1773–1835

Martha Jefferson
1772–1836

Jane Randolph Jefferson
1774–1775

Unnamed child
b/d 1790

Harriet Hemings I
1795–1797

William Beverly Hemings
1798–
after 1822

Thenia Hemings
1799–1800

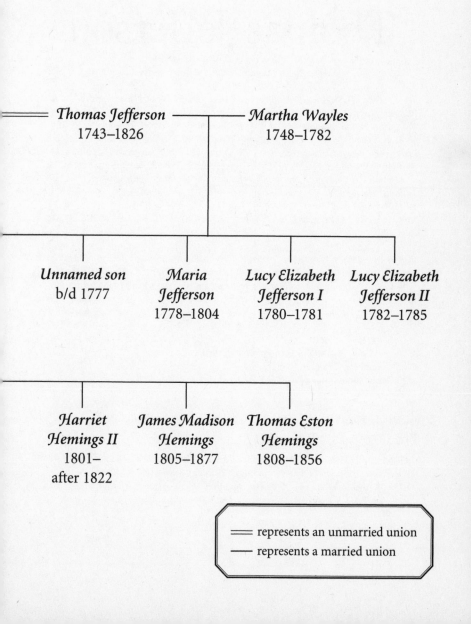

| Thomas Jefferson | | Martha Wayles |
| 1743–1826 | | 1748–1782 |

Unnamed son	Maria	Lucy Elizabeth	Lucy Elizabeth
b/d 1777	Jefferson	Jefferson I	Jefferson II
	1778–1804	1780–1781	1782–1785

Harriet	James Madison	Thomas Eston
Hemings II	Hemings	Hemings
1801–	1805–1877	1808–1856
after 1822		

═══ represents an unmarried union
─── represents a married union

To Bart, Matthew, and Katie

DIAL BOOKS FOR YOUNG READERS
A division of Penguin Young Readers Group · Published by The Penguin Group

Penguin Group (USA) Inc., 375 Hudson Street, New York, NY 10014, U.S.A. · Penguin Group (Canada), 90 Eglinton Avenue East, Suite 700, Toronto, Ontario, Canada M4P 2Y3 (a division of Pearson Penguin Canada Inc.) · Penguin Books Ltd, 80 Strand, London WC2R 0RL, England · Penguin Ireland, 25 St. Stephen's Green, Dublin 2, Ireland (a division of Penguin Books Ltd) · Penguin Group (Australia), 250 Camberwell Road, Camberwell, Victoria 3124, Australia (a division of Pearson Australia Group Pty Ltd) · Penguin Books India Pvt Ltd, 11 Community Centre, Panchsheel Park, New Delhi - 110 017, India · Penguin Group (NZ), 67 Apollo Drive, Rosedale, Auckland 0632, New Zealand (a division of Pearson New Zealand Ltd) · Penguin Books (South Africa) (Pty) Ltd, 24 Sturdee Avenue, Rosebank, Johannesburg 2196, South Africa · Penguin Books Ltd, Registered Offices: 80 Strand, London WC2R 0RL, England

3 5 7 9 10 8 6 4

Library of Congress Cataloging-in-Publication Data
Bradley, Kimberly Brubaker.
  Jefferson's sons : a founding father's secret children / by Kimberly Brubaker Bradley.
    p. cm.
  Summary: A fictionalized look at the last twenty years of Thomas Jefferson's life at Monticello through the eyes of three of his slaves, two of whom were his sons by his slave Sally Hemings.
  ISBN 978-0-8037-3499-9 (hardcover)
  1. Jefferson, Thomas, 1743–1826—Juvenile fiction. 2. Hemings, Sally—Juvenile fiction. [1. Jefferson, Thomas, 1743–1826—Fiction. 2. Hemings, Sally—Fiction. 3. Slavery—Fiction. 4. African Americans—Fiction. 5. Monticello (Va.)—Fiction. 6. Monticello (Va.)—Fiction. 7. Virginia—History—1775–1865—Fiction.] I. Title.
  PZ7.B7247Je 2011
  [Fic]—dc22
                                                    2010049650

Chapter One
The Violin

It was April and all Monticello was stirring, but in their cabin Mama had just put baby Maddy down to sleep and she told Beverly and Harriet to be still.

Beverly did not want to be still.

Harriet reached under the bed for the box where she kept things and pulled out the sampler Mama was teaching her to sew. Beverly knew what would happen next. Harriet and Mama would talk sewing, and ignore him. He aimed a kick at his little sister. "Don't do *that*," he said. "Let's do something fun."

Harriet sat down on the stool beside the hearth. She beamed at Mama with what Beverly called her good-girl smile, like she was trying to show off how sweet she was. Harriet was almost four years old. She was not a sitting-still little girl, but sometimes she took a mood to act like one. Beverly reached out with his foot again. His toe grazed the end of one of Harriet's braids. Harriet screeched.

"Beverly," Mama said, not even looking up, "don't wake your brother."

"I didn't yell," Beverly said. "Harriet did."

"You're the one looking for trouble," Mama replied. "Do you need something to do?"

Beverly knew better than to say yes. Mama would make him do chores. "No, ma'am," he said. "I guess I'll go visit Uncle Peter."

"Don't you bother him, neither," Mama said, but she let him go.

Beverly went out the cabin and down Mulberry Row. The spring wind whipped the still-bare branches of the mulberry trees. The packed dirt road felt cool and firm beneath his bare feet. Beverly spread his arms into the wild wind. He felt wild too.

The kitchen was halfway down the row, in the basement of a little brick guesthouse. Uncle Peter, one of Mama's brothers, was the cook. Uncle Peter didn't hand out treats very often, but you never knew. It was midmorning. If the folks in the great house hadn't been hungry at breakfast, there might be muffins left over.

Beverly slid through the open door. On the hearth, Dutch ovens steamed in a row over piles of coals. Uncle Peter and the two girls that helped him stood behind the long table, chopping vegetables. Uncle Peter gave Beverly an eye. "What do you want?" he asked.

"Nothing," Beverly said. He edged closer to the table. There *were* muffins left, and slices of ham too.

Uncle Peter whapped Beverly's hand with the end of a towel. The girls laughed. "Get out of here, Beverly!" Uncle Peter said. "Two hours since breakfast, you can't be hungry yet!"

"Can too," said Beverly, but he went.

Outside, the wind still howled. Beverly stopped and thought about what he wanted to do. He was too little to have a real job. Most days he helped Mama while she sewed in the cabin, or visited his aunts and uncles, or ran around the gardens or the orchards. Sometimes he walked with Mama to the great house, where she checked to see that everything in Master Jefferson's room was all right. Master Jefferson spent most of the year in Washington. When he was gone the great house stood empty. Besides taking care of Beverly and Harriet and Maddy, Mama didn't have much to do.

Now Master Jefferson was home for a month and everything had changed. He'd brought his grown-up daughter and all her children with him, and invited friends to visit, so the house was full to bursting. Mama worked and worked. What's more, she stayed up at the great house every night.

Beverly didn't mind the bustle. But whenever he thought about Master Jefferson, his stomach gave a little twist, almost like he was hungry. It twisted now. He wished Uncle Peter had given him a muffin.

He looked to his left, toward the woodshop. His uncle

John worked there, learning fancy carpentry from a white Irishman named Mr. Dismore. Beverly loved Uncle John, and he loved watching him make things out of wood, but he wasn't sure how he felt about Mr. Dismore. Unlike the overseers, Mr. Dismore was cheerful and funny, but he also sometimes said things like, "I don't want you pickaninnies hanging around my shop."

Beverly hated the word *pickaninny*. It sounded like something you'd stomp on if you saw it running across the floor. He was not, he thought, a pickaninny.

Straight across the road was the smokehouse, locked so the hams couldn't grow legs and wander away. To the right was the blacksmith's shop. Beverly often went there to watch the nail boys work. He knew he'd be a nail boy himself when he was older. The nail boys made nails all day long, *tap, tap, tap!* They cut nail rod into short pieces, then hammered one end of each piece long and pointy and the other square and firm. The nail boys' muscles stood out on their arms. Master Jefferson was proud of them.

The only problem with visiting the blacksmith shop was Mr. Stewart. He was head blacksmith, a white man, and mean when he was drunk. Lately he stayed drunk all the time. Only yesterday, Master Jefferson's daughter, Miss Martha, said it was about time she took matters into her own hands and showed Mr. Stewart the door, before he grew careless in his inebriation and burned the blacksmith shop down. She said it was a good thing they had Joe Fossett, or that place would be a ruin.

Beverly'd heard her. He was good at hearing things. "If you're smart," Mama often told him, "you'll keep your mouth shut and your ears open. You're a smart boy, aren't you?"

"Yes, ma'am," he'd say, proud that it was true.

Beverly loved the word *inebriation,* even though Mama said it was just a fancy name for *drunk.* Beverly savored beautiful words. They were like music in his head. He didn't care what words meant nearly as much as how they sounded. He loved it when Mama and Miss Martha spoke French together, even though they only did it so no one else could understand them.

"Teach me," he begged Mama. "Teach me how to talk like that."

Mama taught him a song in French, and how to say "I love you, Mama," but she said she didn't have time to teach him more, and besides it would upset Miss Martha. No good ever came from upsetting Miss Martha.

Miss Martha's full name was Mrs. Martha Randolph. She was the only one of her mama's children still alive. She loved to come to Monticello and act like the boss of everything. But she wasn't the real boss—Master Jefferson was—and she wasn't there very often. Beverly didn't care if he upset her or not. When he said so, Mama shook her head. "Trust me," she said. "It's better to stay on her good side."

"Does she have a good side?" asked Beverly.

For a moment Mama looked like she might laugh, but then she set her lips together and told Beverly not to act like he was too big for his britches. She said everyone had a good side, even if with some folks you had to look mighty hard to find it. She told him again that smart boys kept their mouths shut, was Beverly listening?

Beverly was. He wondered where Miss Martha kept her good side. On the sole of her left foot, maybe, safe inside her shoe.

Miss Martha was two years older than Mama. Once upon a time, after Master Jefferson's wife died, but when Miss Martha was still just a girl, Master Jefferson and Miss Martha went to live in France. After a few years they sent for Master Jefferson's other daughter, Miss Maria, who was still alive back then, but little and scared. Beverly's mama was just fourteen years old, but she got the job of taking Miss Maria on a ship across the wide ocean to France. They all lived in Paris for three more years. That was where Mama learned French.

Miss Maria grew up, married a nice man, had a son, and died. Mama told Beverly that. Miss Martha grew up, married a loud, angry man, and had too many children. She walked around looking like she'd just tasted sour milk. Mama didn't have to tell Beverly that; he could see it for himself.

Beverly had two dead sisters and one dead brother. He couldn't remember any of them, but Mama told him and Harriet about them because she said it was important to keep their stories alive. Family counted, living or dead.

Baby Madison seemed healthy, Mama said, but you never knew for sure. One of the dead sisters had lived for over a year, walked and talked and everything.

Beverly looked out over the blacksmith shop, past the gardens and down the mountainside. He sighed. There was only one place he wanted to go. He knew it, and he might as well go there. He lifted his chin and tried to look like a boy with an important errand to do, not one sneaking off where he didn't belong.

He went to the great house.

It was in pieces. It had been a fine big house, but not fine or big enough to suit Master Jefferson. He'd hired workmen to rip the walls open and add rooms off the long sides, and remove the roof to add a third floor. Right now the work was about half-finished; to live there you had to not mind dust and dirt and no roof and holes in the walls. Master Jefferson didn't mind. Miss Martha did, but she was there anyway, because she preferred a house with no roof away from her husband to one with a roof and her husband inside.

Beverly's grown cousin Burwell was the butler whenever Master Jefferson was at home. Burwell hated mess even more than Miss Martha did, but he didn't have any say. He just had to cope the best he could. Master Jefferson expected a fancy dinner on a clean tablecloth with china and silver and lots of good wine, every afternoon at exactly three o'clock, whether there was a roof over the house or not. Burwell always managed to make everything right.

I'll go see Burwell, Beverly told himself. *He'll let me polish spoons.* But he knew Burwell wasn't the person he wanted to see.

He slipped between the poplar trunks supporting the unfinished porch roof and through the back door into the great house. Upstairs a baby wailed. Beverly heard footsteps hurrying across the hall. Burwell's dining room was to the left, but Beverly turned right.

There in front of him stood a wide-open door.

Beverly stared. His breath came quick with happiness and surprise. It was open—the door to Master Jefferson's room was open! Beverly'd been inside many times with Mama, but never, ever when Master Jefferson was home. When Master Jefferson was home, he kept the door locked. He did not want his papers or books or self disturbed. Only Burwell and Beverly's mama had keys to the door. Even Miss Martha had to stay out.

Beverly peeked inside. Nobody. The fire had burned down, but a new pile of wood waited by the swept hearth, so Beverly knew Burwell had come and gone. The curtains at the open windows fluttered in the breeze.

Beverly took a cautious step. The room sure looked different with Master Jefferson home. When he was gone Mama kept the desk swept bare and all the books shut up safe in cabinets behind glass. Now piles of books covered the floor and tables. Some had scraps of paper or ribbon sticking out of their sides, and one lay upside down on the polished wooden desk, with half its pages cut, and the paper knife lying beside it.

Then Beverly saw, beside the half-cut book, the violin.

He sucked in his breath, fast. His heart hammered. Oh, that violin! How he loved the sound of that violin! Master Jefferson had brought it with him from Washington, and sometimes in the evenings Beverly could hear its music all the way down Mulberry Row, sharp quick notes, long dancing bits, ta-dum-dum-ta-dee. He had never heard anything like it. Better than *inebriation* or the sound of words in French was the glorious music from Master Jefferson's violin.

Beverly crept forward. He'd never seen a violin up close before. Now he stood over it, admiring the shiny honey-colored wood. Next to it was the stick thing you drew across the strings. Beverly reached out and touched the stick, just once. His fingers kept moving and brushed the smooth wood of the violin itself. He thought he could feel the music inside.

Right on the bottom was the dark spot where you were supposed to put your chin. He'd watched Mr. Jefferson through the open windows one night.

Quick as a flash, before he could think hard enough to make himself stop, Beverly tucked Master Jefferson's violin beneath his chin. He pushed on the strings beneath the fingers of his left hand, and curled his right hand around the stick. He told himself not to make a sound. Burwell would hear—Miss Martha would hear—he would be in a heap of trouble, and Mama would be upset. But he couldn't stop. He raised the stick in the air.

Right behind him a soft voice said, "You're not holding the bow right."

Beverly jumped. His hand clutched the violin. He knew that voice. *Master Jefferson.* Beverly's heart beat faster; his mouth went dry from hope and fear. He wanted to set the violin down, tell Master Jefferson he was sorry, and run home as fast as his legs would go, but he couldn't move. His feet had frozen to the floor.

Master Jefferson's smooth, long-fingered hand came from behind Beverly, and carefully covered Beverly's hand on the stick—on the *bow.* Master Jefferson plucked at Beverly's fingers to loosen their grip, and then curved around them. Master Jefferson held the bow like it was something alive.

His other hand covered Beverly's hand on the strings. Softly he drew the bow across the strings. It made a sound.

Master Jefferson said, "Hold it gently. You've got to coax the music out."

Beverly turned and looked up at him. The last time he'd been close to Master Jefferson had been at Christmas, months ago. Master Jefferson was tall and thin and loosely put together, his joints floppy like the ones on Harriet's wooden doll. His gray hair hung untied around his shoulders. He wore old gray breeches and a red waistcoat Beverly's mama had made last year.

"Hello, Beverly," he said.

"Hello," Beverly whispered.

"How old are you now?"

"Seven," Beverly said. "Seven years and one day. Yesterday was my birthday. April first, that's the day I was born."

"I remember. Happy birthday." Master Jefferson smiled. The lines around his eyes crinkled. "It's good to see you again. I like having children around. In Washington Miss Martha's been keeping house for me, and her children stay with us there."

"They're here now," Beverly said.

"Yes," said Master Jefferson. "Aren't I lucky?"

"But Miss Edith and the new baby had to stay behind."

Master Jefferson raised an eyebrow. "Miss Edith?"

"Miss Edith," Beverly said, "that went with you to Washington." Master Jefferson looked puzzled, so Beverly explained. "Miss Edith that's married to the blacksmith, Joe Fossett. Miss Edith that lives with you. She just had a baby, right before Mama had Maddy, and it was a boy and they named him James."

"Oh. You mean Edy? The cook? My apprentice cook?"

"Yes, sir." Beverly nodded. "Joe Fossett's real sorry they didn't come home with you. He understands, 'cause the baby's so little, but he wanted to see them. He misses them. We all do."

"I see." Master Jefferson pulled a chair closer and sat down. He turned Beverly around to face him and held him lightly between his knees.

Beverly smiled. He touched the side of Master Jefferson's face. "Your eyes are gray," he said. "Just like my baby brother's. Maddy has eyes just like yours."

"Is that what you're calling him?" Master Jefferson sounded amused. "Maddy?"

"Yes, sir."

"His name is James Madison. He was named after the patriot James Madison, a good friend of mine."

"Yes, sir. Mama said so. But she calls him Madison so we don't get him mixed up with Miss Edith's baby James, and Harriet and I call him Maddy because Madison's too long to say."

"I see. And do you call Harriet Harry?"

"No, sir," Beverly said. "She smacks me if I do."

Master Jefferson laughed. "You don't smack her back, I hope."

"No, sir," Beverly said. "Mama said I can't 'cause she's littler than me, and a girl. But it's not fair. She's little, but she hits hard."

"Little sisters are never fair," Master Jefferson said.

Beverly thought about this. "Do you have a little sister?" he asked.

"I do. I had four of them when I was growing up."

"Did they smack you?"

"I don't recall." Master Jefferson poked the top of Beverly's nose. "But I do know that I never, ever smacked them back. Neither must you. A gentleman never hits ladies. Nor sisters either."

Master Jefferson had patches of sunburned skin on his cheeks, and a dark spot on his waistcoat that looked like ink. Beverly touched it.

"Mama'll have a job getting that out," he said.

Master Jefferson looked at the spot too. "I write so many letters, I'm always covered in ink." He looked back at Beverly. "So, why are you here? Did your mama give you a message for me?"

Beverly bit his lip. He wished he could say yes. "No, sir."

"Did Burwell, or someone else?"

"No, sir. I just sort of came by myself."

"My bedroom's private. Do you know what that means?"

"Yes, sir. It means I'm supposed to stay out." Beverly took a deep breath. "I just wanted—I wanted to see—" He looked around. How much could he say? His hand came down on the violin.

"You wanted to see the violin?"

"Yes, sir," Beverly said. It wasn't all of the truth, but it was a piece of the truth. "I love this violin."

Master Jefferson looked surprised. "You do?"

"Yes, sir," said Beverly. "I like—I sure like to listen to you play."

Master Jefferson held up his right hand and slowly flexed his fingers. "I used to play for hours on end," he said. "A long time ago. I played in string quartets before the war. But I broke my wrist; it doesn't bend very easily, and it aches after a while. So I don't play as often or as well. You know about the war, don't you? The Revolution? How we started a new country?"

"No, sir," Beverly said.

"You must learn about it. It's important. We broke away

from England and . . ." Master Jefferson paused, and smiled again. "You're young, I forget. My grandchildren don't understand it yet either."

He lifted the violin and set it into place beneath Beverly's chin. "But seven years old might be old enough for this. Give it a try. Be gentle."

Beverly didn't know which strings to push or how hard to push them, but he moved the bow the way Master Jefferson had. The violin screeched. Beverly stopped. "Did I break it?" he asked, alarmed.

Master Jefferson laughed. "No. It always sounds like that at first." He seemed to be thinking about something. After a moment he asked, "Are you a hard worker? Would you work to learn to play the violin?"

Beverly's eyes widened. "Oh, yes! Yes, sir!"

Master Jefferson smiled. He cupped his hand around Beverly's face, so quickly Beverly barely felt it, then rose and went to a cabinet built into the wall. He came back with a small wooden case. "I have several violins," he said. "The one you're holding is my best. Italian. It's not an instrument for a boy. But this one"—he took the Italian violin away and put the case he was holding into Beverly's hands—"this is what they call a kit violin. You can strap this onto the back of a horse to travel and bounce it around without hurting it. It doesn't sound as pretty as the Italian violin, but it's a good deal harder to break. Mind, you'll still have to be careful.

"I'm going to give you this violin," he continued. "Do you know Jesse Scott, down in Charlottesville?"

Beverly nodded. Jesse Scott's wife was Joe Fossett's sister.

"He's a good fiddler, and a good teacher," Master Jefferson said. "You go down to him with this violin, and tell him I said he's to give you lessons. Once a week. And in between you practice. I'll expect to hear progress by the time I come back here this summer. All right?"

Beverly clutched the wooden case tight to his chest. He swallowed hard. "Sir?"

"What's wrong? You need lessons, in order to learn."

"Yes, sir, but—" Beverly bit his lip. "Couldn't you teach me?"

Master Jefferson looked away. "No," he said. "Jesse will suit you better."

"Yes, sir." Beverly knew he shouldn't have asked.

Master Jefferson patted his back. "Go on home. Your mama will be wanting you, and I have work to do."

Beverly was halfway to the door when Master Jefferson spoke again. "Beverly—"

Beverly turned.

"Do you know who I am?"

"Yes, sir," Beverly said. He smiled. "You're the president. President of the United States. Mama says it's a very important job."

An odd expression flitted across Master Jefferson's face. For a moment he almost looked sad. Beverly wondered if he'd said the wrong thing. But the look faded. Master Jefferson said, "That's right. You go on home."

Beverly walked quietly out of the great house, but as soon as his feet hit dirt he ran. He tore into the cabin and didn't care if he woke the baby, not one bit.

"Mama, Mama!" he shouted. "Papa gave me a violin!"

Chapter Two
Papa

Mama wheeled about, angry. She said, "Don't you call him Papa."

"But—" Beverly danced up and down, waving the violin. "I'm going to take lessons, from Jesse Scott, and he gave me the violin, Papa, he really did, and when he comes back in the summer—"

"Don't you ever call him Papa," Mama said. "Do you hear me?" She shook her finger at him. Mama never messed around.

"Yes, Mama," said Beverly. "But—"

"But nothing," Mama said.

Beverly looked at the floor. "But you said he's my father. You said so." Mama had, a week ago. Beverly'd had that buzzing feeling in his stomach ever since. He had wondered if it could possibly be true. Now he had a violin to prove it.

Mama said, "What you know in your head and what you can say out loud are not always the same. You know that—"

"You're not stupid," chimed Harriet. Beverly glared at her. Mama had told Harriet about their father too. Beverly wished she hadn't.

"I don't *ever* want to hear you call him Papa," Mama said. "Not to me, not to Harriet, not to *anybody*. Is that clear?"

"Yes, ma'am."

"Good. Now, show me this violin." She took Beverly on her lap and helped him open the case.

Beverly snuggled against her. "He gave it to me," he said. "To keep."

Mama kissed him. "It's a fine thing, to learn to play the violin."

"He wants me to," Beverly said. "He said."

When Mama told Beverly that Master Jefferson was his father, she called it a secret everybody knew.

"Everybody in the world?" he asked.

"No," Mama said. "Everybody at Monticello. The folks in Charlottesville whisper about it. Some people spread talk farther away, but we don't need to worry about them."

Beverly nodded because he thought Mama expected him to, but he didn't understand.

Mama said Master Jefferson was president of the entire country, which was so big, a single person could never see it all, not if that person traveled all his days. She said Master Jefferson was a very important man. Beverly already knew that. He was proud to learn he had an important man for his father. He didn't understand why it had to be a secret.

"Because I say so," Mama said. She sighed, and brushed his hair back from his forehead. "You're maybe too young to know. I shouldn't have told you, maybe. But if you're old enough to ask, I figure you're old enough to hear the truth."

He wouldn't have thought to ask about his father if not for Joe Fossett. A few days before Master Jefferson came home, Davy Hern, the wagon man, arrived with a load of goods from Washington. Davy always brought Master Jefferson's heavy luggage ahead. As he made the last turn onto Mulberry Row, Davy let out a big halloo, and folks came running from everywhere to hear his news. Beverly dashed out his cabin door. He saw Joe Fossett come out of the blacksmith shop and take three big steps toward the wagon, and then Beverly saw the light go out of Joe Fossett's face. It was like somebody snuffing a candle.

"She didn't come?" Joe Fossett said. He ran up to the wagon and grabbed Davy's arm. "Where's Edith? Why didn't she come home? Is she all right? What about the baby?"

"They're all right," Davy said. "They're fine. Baby's healthy. Nursing fine. Edith thought four days of travel might be too much for them, though, in this wet weather. She said to tell you she's sorry, and she and James'll see you in July."

Joe shook Davy's hand, and went back to the shop before

old Mr. Stewart could kick up a fuss. Beverly helped unload the wagon. He thought about that look on Joe Fossett's face, that joy snuffed cold.

He waited until nighttime, when Harriet was asleep and Mama was stroking his back. Then he told Mama all about it. "Why was Joe Fossett sad?"

"He misses Miss Edith," Mama said. "He wants to see his baby boy. He expected they'd come home." After a pause she said, "It's hard for families and mamas and daddies to be apart."

Beverly thought of his family—Harriet snoring beside him, and Maddy making little baby noises from the cradle. Mama sat on the chair beside the bed, but later, when she got tired, she'd crawl in with him and Harriet. It was such a nice night, the fire crackling low. Beverly didn't think they needed a daddy.

"Anyway," he said, "I haven't got one."

"Haven't got what?" Mama asked.

"A daddy," he said.

Mama laughed. "Of course you do. Everybody's got a daddy."

"Do not," said Beverly.

"Every living thing," Mama continued. "Every cow in the field. Every chicken's got a daddy. So do you."

"Well, who is it, then? He doesn't live around here. Is he dead?"

Mama's hand stopped stroking Beverly's back. "He lives

here sometimes. He's not dead." After a pause she added, "Your daddy's Master Jefferson."

Beverly sat straight up. "Mama! Are you sure?"

She laughed again. "Yes. I'm sure. Hush, you'll wake Maddy."

"Who's *his* daddy? Who's Harriet's?"

"Master Jefferson. All my children have the same daddy." Mama pushed him back down. "But you listen, Beverly. It's a secret. You mustn't talk about it, except to me. Not to anybody. If you have questions, you ask me and I'll answer you, but I don't want you talking about it outside this room. Promise."

"Why?" asked Beverly.

"'Cause I said so," said Mama.

"He got more children around here?" Beverly asked.

"No," Mama said. "Just you three. And the ones I had that died. And Miss Martha, of course. And Miss Maria, and the other babies his wife had, but they all died a long time ago."

"Can I tell Joe Fossett?" Beverly asked.

"No, sir. You may not."

"Uncle Peter? Uncle John?"

"No."

"Nobody?"

"Nobody, Beverly. You promise me."

"What about Miss Martha?"

Mama pushed her lips together. "I'm not joking, Beverly. I told you this, and I'm telling you not to speak about it. Especially not to Miss Martha. You've got no business talking to Miss Martha anyhow."

Beverly considered. He had never thought much about his father before. Some people had daddies around, and some didn't, that was all. He'd never thought his daddy could be Master Jefferson. "Doesn't nobody know?"

"Doesn't anybody," Mama corrected. "Yes. Lots of people know, but we can't talk about it."

"Mama," Beverly said, "that doesn't make sense."

"It will when you're older," Mama said.

Beverly thought hard. He'd heard people say how sad it was that Master Jefferson had only old Miss Martha left, out of all his children. Now here was Beverly, and Harriet, and Maddy. That wasn't sad at all. "Mama? Why don't we tell people? Maybe some people would be glad to know. Miss Martha—"

Mama sighed. "Miss Martha and Miss Maria were the children of Master Jefferson's wife. I'm . . ." She paused.

"Won't he marry you?" asked Beverly.

"He can't," Mama said, after a second silence.

"Why not?"

Mama sighed again. "A black person can't marry a white person. A slave can't marry at all."

This was news to Beverly. "Are you a slave, Mama?"

"Yes."

"Am I?"

"We'll talk about that later," Mama said.

"Are Harriet and Maddy—"

"Later," Mama said. "You've had enough talk for the one night."

Beverly tried to hold silent, but finally he had to say, "Then Joe Fossett, he's not a slave."

"How do you figure?" asked Mama.

"'Cause he's married," Beverly said. "He's married to Miss Edith."

"Yes and no," Mama said. "Joe and Miss Edith pledged to each other. They're married, but not by law. They're married in their hearts. Joe and Miss Edith—they're both slaves. We'll talk about it later, all right?"

"Are you married to Master Jefferson in your heart, Mama? Like Joe and Edith?"

"Oh, Beverly," Mama said.

"Are you?"

"Of course I am," Mama said. "Now go to sleep."

In the morning Beverly thought of another question. "Does he love me, Mama?" he asked. "Does he love me like Joe Fossett loves baby James?"

Mama smiled at him. "Of course he loves you," she said. "He named you. William Beverly, after a friend of his father's. And you'll see. Someday you'll have a fine life, because of him."

The very next day Master Jefferson came home. Beverly hoped Master Jefferson would come to their cabin right away, but he didn't. He hoped Master Jefferson would let them all sit down to dinner with him and Miss Martha, but he didn't.

But then Master Jefferson gave Beverly a violin. So Beverly knew what Mama said was true.

Mama spent nights in the great house with Master Jefferson. A big girl named Fanny Gillette came each evening to stay with Beverly and Harriet and Maddy. Maddy was an easy baby and usually slept until morning; when he did wake before Mama returned, Fanny dipped a cloth in sugar water and let him suck on it. Maddy always woke up hungry, but other than that he was too little to mind Mama being gone, and Harriet slept so hard she barely noticed, but, after he got his violin, Beverly didn't like it at all.

"I wanted to sleep in the great house with you," he told Mama.

"Can't," Mama said, without a trace of a smile.

"I don't see why not," Beverly said. "Even if the bed up there is little. I wouldn't mind." He stomped his foot. Throwing a fit didn't usually budge Mama, but you never knew.

Mama grabbed his arm, hard. "Don't go down that road," she said. "I told you it was a secret, about you and Master Jefferson. It's a secret about me too. That I go up there at night. What kind of secret would it be if I took you and Harriet and Maddy along?"

"It can't be a secret," Beverly argued. "Fanny comes here— everybody on Mulberry Row knows that. And Burwell lights the fires every morning. And Miss Martha sleeps right upstairs."

"Miss Martha doesn't know anything," Mama said. "Nor Burwell neither. Master Jefferson lights his fire himself in the morning. Burwell's not allowed into the room until after breakfast."

Beverly knew this didn't make sense. Burwell was sure to know about Fanny even if he didn't know anything else. But Mama looked so fierce Beverly kept quiet. Mouth shut, ears open, that was what Mama said.

A few days later, Beverly said, "I've been studying Miss Martha, Mama. She's not stupid."

Mama shook her head. "Don't study her. She's not stupid, but she only sees what she wants to."

Beverly thought about this. "She doesn't want to be my sister, does she?"

"No," Mama said. "She does not."

"But she is my sister, isn't she?"

"She is," Mama said. "But she won't ever admit it, not this side of heaven. If you're smart—and I know you are—if you're smart, you'll leave Miss Martha alone."

"Doesn't she like you, Mama?"

Mama sighed. "She likes me fine. She doesn't like—I don't know the words for it. She'll never admit she's kin to us, let's leave it at that."

. . .

Beverly tried to play his violin on his own, but he couldn't make it sound right and he was a little afraid he might break it. He thought he'd die of impatience before Mama finally took him down to Charlottesville to see Jesse Scott.

Mama waited for a day when Davy Hern had business in Charlottesville, so she and Beverly could get a ride in the wagon. It was a pretty morning, soft and warm, and all the leaves on the mountainside were just popping out. In the woods the redbuds bloomed. The wagon circled slowly down, and Beverly, his violin on his lap, felt too happy to speak. He would learn to play beautiful music. He would make his father proud.

Jesse Scott was a kind, friendly man. When Beverly made the violin squawk and screech, Jesse laughed. He taught Beverly four notes, one for each string. He told Beverly to practice a little every day. "But not too much," he said, "or you'll drive your mama crazy."

"Master Jefferson used to practice for hours," said Beverly.

"When you're older you can practice for hours," said Jesse. "Right now you can practice a little each morning, and a little each night. Come back for a lesson next week if you can."

Mama told Jesse to keep track of Beverly's lessons and send Master Jefferson the bill. Beverly beamed.

He practiced as much as Mama would let him. He played for Mama, Harriet, and Maddy. He played for Joe Fossett in the blacksmith shop, Uncle John in the woodshop, and

Uncle Peter in the kitchen. More than anything, he wanted to play for his father. He waited for Master Jefferson's door to be open again, but it never was, and pretty soon both Mama and Burwell started shooing him out of the great house every single time they saw him there. They sent him on errands to the stables or gardens and kept him busy all day long.

"You need to stay away from the great house," Mama told him.

"I need to see Papa," Beverly said. "I need him to hear me play."

"Don't call him Papa," Mama said. "You call him Master Jefferson, you hear me? Same as everybody else."

"I'll only call him Papa to you."

"No, you won't," she said. "You'll forget and let it slip sometime."

Beverly said, "I don't see why it has to be a secret."

Mama bent over him, sparks of anger flashing in her eyes. "I don't care whether you understand it or not," she said. "I care whether or not you obey me. You keep your mouth quiet or I'll give you something to help you remember. Now put that violin down and go help Uncle Peter with the dishes."

Beverly didn't move. Mama pointed to the door. "Go."

"I need him to hear me," Beverly said. "Please."

"Go," she said.

Beverly went. But later, after dinner and just before Mama left for the night, she called him over to the cabin door. "Stand just here, in the doorway, and play your notes. Master Jefferson said he'd stand by his bedroom window and listen."

Beverly could see the open window, and the thin white curtains softly fluttering against it, but he couldn't see through the curtains into the dark room.

"Is he really there, Mama?"

"This is the only chance I'm giving you. Play."

Beverly played his best. It sounded like music, even though it was only four notes. Then he waited, watching the curtains. They fluttered once more. Maybe Master Jefferson was waving to him.

"Did he like it, Mama?" Beverly asked the next morning.

"He did," Mama said.

"What did he say?"

Mama sighed. "Let it go, Beverly. Let it be."

A week later Master Jefferson returned to Washington. Mama stayed home at night. Everything went back to normal, until one of the nail boys, James Hubbard, ran away.

Chapter Three

Run

James Hubbard was a big boy with heavy arms and a fierce temper. He was smart and hardworking, and Beverly admired him. So did Master Jefferson. A few years back Master Jefferson gave James Hubbard a fancy red suit of clothes as a reward for making the most nails of all the nail boys over an entire year. James Hubbard still wore his red shirt sometimes.

Joe Fossett broke the news. It was dinnertime. Beverly was sitting on one of the long benches in the kitchen, between Harriet and Fanny, eating a bowl of stew. Field hands cooked for themselves in their own cabins, but mountaintop people ate their meals in the kitchen in one big noisy group.

Joe Fossett came through the door, looked around, and cleared his throat, loudly and on purpose. Suddenly, before Beverly could understand why, the entire room went still.

Uncle Peter raised an eyebrow. Joe Fossett turned and checked that the kitchen door was latched tight behind him.

You never knew when an overseer might come in. Then Joe turned back and said, "James Hubbard's run."

Nobody moved. Beverly stopped his legs swinging. He heard Fanny catch her breath. Joe said, "He didn't come to the shop this morning. Stewart sent a boy to fetch him. Cabin was empty. All his things were gone." Joe shrugged and took a bowl of stew from Uncle Peter. "That's what I know. He's gone."

Beverly started to ask where James had gone, but Fanny smacked him. "Hush," she said, so fiercely that Beverly obeyed.

All afternoon he felt sick and strange. If he hadn't known James Hubbard was gone, he probably wouldn't have noticed, but he did know, and he couldn't stop thinking about him. What did it mean, "run"? Where had he run to? Why?

In the cabin that night, Mama said, "The less said, the better."

"Why?" Beverly asked. Harriet wanted to know too.

"Might be some folks know more about James Hubbard than they're letting on," Mama told them. "Might be some folks around here helped him. We don't want to know. It's better if we all stay quiet."

"But, Mama," Harriet said. "Where'd he *go*?"

"To freedom," Mama said.

"Where's that?" Beverly asked.

"Depends," Mama said. "For James Hubbard, it's pretty far away."

All that week no one so much as whispered James Hubbard's name. It was as though he'd never even lived. The silence made Beverly feel quivery inside. Then one of the overseers, the new one, came up through Mulberry Row. He called all the workers together, even making Harriet fetch Mama from the great house. "Jamie's in jail," he said. "He didn't get far." The overseer held up a scrap of paper. "Which one of you wrote this?"

Nobody moved. "Anybody? Any of you all? I know some of you can read. Some of you must be able to write." The man waved the paper in the air again. "This here is a forged pass," he said. "Jamie was carrying it. Too bad he can't read, because he'd have known what a piece of trash it was. It's the worst-spelled mess of a fake pass I ever saw. Wouldn't have fooled a white man's dog. Just so you all know. I find out one of you wrote this pass, I'll have you whipped alongside Jamie. You hear?"

He crumpled the pass in his hand, dropped it onto the ground, and strode away.

Harriet pulled Mama's skirt. "Who's Jamie?" she whispered.

"James Hubbard," Mama said. "Jamie's just what the overseer calls him."

The overseers nosed around Charlottesville and pretty soon the details came out. Beverly learned them in bits and pieces, by listening in the kitchen to Davy Hern and Joe Fossett and others who traveled and could pick up news.

James Hubbard had worked for pay on his own time, which meant Sundays and late at night. He'd cleaned out privies and burned wood for charcoal, nasty jobs, but the only work he could get for cash. He spent some of the money on real breeches, a fancy shirt, and a coat, to replace the loose pants and long shirt that would have identified him as a slave. He spent the rest—five whole dollars, Joe Fossett said—to bribe one of the overseers' sons to write him out a fake pass. The boy was a poor scholar. He spelled the words on the pass wrong. The first person James Hubbard showed his fake pass to had had him arrested.

Five dollars! A year of cleaning out privies earned six. Beverly imagined working that hard for a piece of paper the overseer could just crumple in his hand. He didn't know anything about passes. He'd never heard of them before.

Mama explained in the cabin that night. If you were a slave, you were not supposed to travel anywhere without either a white person or a pass. When Davy Hern went by himself to Washington, he carried a pass signed by Master Jefferson that said who he was and what he was doing. "What about in Charlottesville?" Beverly asked.

"In Charlottesville everyone knows Davy Hern," Mama said. "They won't bother him. Anywhere else he goes, he'd better have a pass."

A slave caught without a pass was thrown in jail. Black people who weren't slaves had to carry papers saying they were free.

Beverly stared at Mama. He'd never heard of free papers either. "Even Jesse Scott?" he asked.

"Even Jesse Scott," Mama said.

"Mama," Harriet said, "why are we slaves?"

Mama looked at Harriet. Then she did something strange. She lifted Maddy from where he was playing on the floor, took off his shirt, and set him in the middle of their bed. Maddy waved his hands at them. He was a pretty baby, with soft brown curls, big gray eyes, and cheeks as round as apples. Harriet bounced the bed a little, and Maddy laughed.

"Look at Maddy," Mama said, "both of you, and tell me, does he look like a free baby or a slave baby?"

Beverly looked at Maddy, then back at Mama. "A slave baby," he said. It made his heart sink a little. He'd figured it out—the people who lived on Mulberry Row, and the people who worked in the fields—they were slaves. The overseers and the people who lived in big houses were not. Maddy was a slave, and so was Beverly; when they were older they would need a pass.

Harriet nodded. "Slave baby."

"How do you know?" Mama asked.

"'Cause he is one," Beverly said.

"But how can you tell?" Mama persisted. "Look at him. What do you see?"

"He's a boy," Harriet said, after a pause.

Mama pounced on that. "Yes. He's a boy. If we took off his diaper we could see he was a boy. So. Since he's a boy, he must be a slave, right? Because all boys are slaves?"

"No," Beverly said. "Plenty of boys aren't slaves. Miss Martha's boys aren't."

"Ah," said Mama. "Then why would this boy be a slave?"

Beverly didn't know what Mama wanted them to say. He took Maddy's hand and rubbed it. "He's kind of dark," Beverly said. "I mean, not really, but his skin is a little bit darker than mine."

"So, dark skin is what makes you a slave?" Mama said. "Everyone with dark skin is a slave."

Well, that wasn't right. "No," Beverly said. "Jesse Scott's got dark skin, and he's not a slave."

"That's right," Mama said. "So here's a baby, and he's not a slave because he's a boy, or because of the color of his skin. Why do you say he's a slave?"

"Because we just know," Harriet said.

"Pretend you don't know," Mama said. "Pretend you're walking down a road you've never been on before, so you don't know who lives on it, and you see this little baby sitting on the side of the road. This boy, our Maddy, only you've never seen him before. How would you know whether or not he was a slave?"

Beverly looked at Mama. She waited. "You wouldn't know," he said, thinking it out. "You couldn't ask the baby. He can't talk. So you wouldn't know until somebody else came along and told you."

"That's right!" Mama said. She swooped down and kissed

Beverly, then took Maddy back on her knee and dressed him. "You remember that, both of you. Nobody is a slave on their own. There is nothing inside either one of you, or anyone else—Joe Fossett or Uncle John or me or anyone—that *makes* you a slave, that says you have to be one, that says you're different from somebody who isn't a slave. The difference is other people—people who make laws and put other people into slavery and work to keep them there."

Mama's eyes blazed. "But you aren't really slaves either," she said. She rocked Maddy back and forth in her arms. "You remember that. You'll never be sold and you'll never be beaten, and when you turn twenty-one you'll be free. Both of you, and Maddy too. That's a promise. A promise your father made me about all the children we might have. You'll be *free*."

"How can he promise that?" Beverly asked. "He can't just make us free."

Mama paused, frowning. "He can," she said.

"Because he's the president?"

"Because he owns us," Mama said. "He owns all of Monticello. The buildings and the farms. The people too."

Harriet asked, "You mean, because he's our daddy?"

Mama shook her head. She said, "Because he's Master Jefferson."

Chapter Four

James Hubbard's Back

When Uncle Peter slapped him for dipping into the sugar jar, Beverly thought Mama had lied when she said he wouldn't be beaten. He told her so. Mama said there were smackings and then there were beatings, and if he didn't understand the difference now, he would someday, most likely someday soon. Mama was right. Beverly was up on the new roof of the great house when word came that James Hubbard had been brought back to the mountain.

It was September. The heat of the summer was over, and the air was cool and clear. Master Jefferson had come and gone. Once he'd called Beverly into his room and listened to him play, and twice he'd happened to stop by Jesse Scott's house just when Beverly was taking a lesson. Master Jefferson had stayed until Beverly was done. He'd smiled at Beverly and said he was glad to see him working hard. Beverly thought Master Jefferson's smile was his favorite thing in the world.

Now Master Jefferson was gone, and the great house was shut up again, except for the workmen finishing the new rooms.

Beverly loved being on the roof. He could see for miles down the mountain on all sides, to mountains beyond mountains making ridges against the sky. The new roof had a dome in the center, and Beverly's uncle John had built a fancy wooden railing all around it. Now Burwell was painting the railing white. Beverly was helping. Burwell always painted things when Master Jefferson was away; he knew just how to mix paint, any color you could wish.

Harriet brought the news about James Hubbard. Beverly saw her dashing across the great house lawn, her skirt hiked up and her braids blowing behind her. She shouted, "Burwell, Burwell!" and then she scrambled up the ladder three stories to the roof and plopped herself over the edge.

"Easy, missy," Burwell said, grabbing her arm.

"James Hubbard's back!" Harriet said. "They brought him back from jail. He's in the wagon. An overseer's driving. James Hubbard is all skinny and he's got handcuffs on." She took a gulping breath. "Overseer said James Hubbard's getting whipped tomorrow, and everybody has to watch." Her eyes shone big and frightened. She said, "James Hubbard looks *bad*."

"Well," said Burwell. "So would anybody who's been locked

up months in jail." He patted Harriet's cheek. "Don't fret. We don't worry about tomorrow today. You get down and go play. And don't you climb this roof again without asking me, hear? You could fall."

Harriet smiled. She was a wonderful climber, always in and out of trees. "I never fall."

"See you don't." Burwell held the top of the ladder while she climbed down. He yelled, "Tell your mama."

Burwell went back to the railing and picked up his brush. Beverly sat cross-legged beside him. Burwell didn't speak. Finally Beverly whispered, "What's going to happen?"

"He'll be whipped," Burwell said. "Maybe that's all, this time."

"Will it be bad?"

Burwell smoothed white paint over the golden brown wood. He covered three pieces before he answered. "Yes."

The overseers brought the field workers to the mountaintop for the whipping, dozens and dozens of people Beverly didn't know. The mountaintop people, the workers from Mulberry Row, all had to be there too. Beverly asked Mama if he could bring his violin. He thought James Hubbard might like music to take his mind off being whipped, and he thought too that if he was playing he could shut his eyes and only hear the music and not have to think about James Hubbard.

"Nonsense," Mama said. "You and Harriet will stand still and behave, just like everyone else."

"But I don't want to," Beverly said.

"What you want doesn't matter," Mama said.

The overseers—four of them, all white men—prodded everyone into a sort of half circle around a post. James Hubbard stood with his hands tied to the top of the post, his back toward them. Mama moved to the front of the crowd, and as she did Harriet stepped behind her and hid her face in Mama's skirt. Beverly tried to do the same, but Mama grabbed his shoulders and held him facing forward. One overseer ripped James Hubbard's tattered shirt from his back, and a second stepped forward with a long black bullwhip in his hand.

The whip whistled through the air and came down with a crack against James's back. James jerked, but didn't yell. A red welt formed on his skin.

Beverly turned his face away. Mama pushed it back. "You watch," she whispered. *Crack!* Another jerk. Another welt, and a trickle of blood. *Crack!*

Beverly wanted his violin. He wanted to run away, back to his cabin or to Master Jefferson's room with all the books and chairs. *Crack!* Blood ran down James Hubbard's back. It soaked into his breeches, the real breeches he'd bought to run away in. They were going to turn red, just like the red suit he'd won for being the best worker in the nail factory.

Beverly turned his head and vomited down the side of Mama's skirt.

. . .

Afterward, in the cabin, he cried and cried. Mama rinsed her skirt. She seemed sad, not angry. She patted Beverly's back and held Harriet in her lap, and when Beverly's sobs slowed to hiccups she said, "There's a reason I made you watch that."

"'Cause the overseer said so," Beverly said.

"No. I could have let you hide your face. I wanted you to watch because I wanted you to understand. *That's* slavery. Not this nice life you children have, because of who I am and who you are. That. James Hubbard didn't do anything wrong. All he wanted was to live his own life, to earn money for himself and make his own choices.

"I love you children more than life, and I'm going to get you out of Jordan, do you hear me?" Mama's eyes blazed up, fierce but still not angry. "I'm going to see you live free. What happened to James Hubbard will never happen to you. But you've got to understand it. You've got to know how things are. When you're grown you'll be able to go anywhere you want in this world. *Anywhere*. Do you understand me?"

"No, Mama," Beverly said. The look on her face frightened him. He didn't understand anything at all.

"James Hubbard did too do something wrong," said Harriet in a thin, trembling voice. "He did too. He ran away. Master Jefferson had to punish him. Because he ran away. He wasn't supposed to—"

"Master Jefferson didn't punish him," Beverly cut in. "The overseers did."

Mama looked grave. "The overseers only do what Master

Jefferson tells them to," she said. "Master Jefferson ordered the whipping. It was his responsibility. No one else's."

"That's not true," Beverly said. He thought of Master Jefferson's gentle hands, his soft voice, his warm smile. "He would never do that. He wouldn't. He'd never whip anybody. He's not mean like the overseers."

Mama said, slowly and deliberately, "All James Hubbard did was try to get free. Running away is against the law, but it's not *wrong*. Sometimes laws are wrong. Master Jefferson told the overseers to whip James Hubbard. They wouldn't have done it otherwise. They wouldn't have dared."

"You're lying," Beverly said. "I know you are." He put his hands over his ears and refused to listen anymore. His father, whip James Hubbard? Beverly knew it couldn't be true.

Chapter Five

Great-grandma
and the Sea Captain

Cold weather came. The garden froze and died. Beverly and the other mountaintop boys covered its beds with deep layers of horse manure from the stables. The great house seemed asleep, except for the faint sound of Uncle John's hammering, hard to hear behind the sounds of the nail boys at their anvils.

Dawn to dusk was the master's time; dusk to dawn belonged to the slaves. In winter, days were short enough that folks had time to relax together in the evenings, before they fell asleep, and with Master Jefferson in Washington, Mama stayed with them every night. Usually, after she rocked Maddy to sleep, she told Beverly and Harriet stories.

"Tell about Great-grandma and the sea captain," Harriet

said. Beverly stretched out on the floor in front of the hearth, close to the dancing flames. Mama's chair creaked as she rocked in time to her knitting. Harriet drew Mama's shawl over her head until only her nose peeped out.

"Once upon a time," Mama began, "your great-grandma lived free with her family in a place called Africa, over the ocean and far, far away."

"Like France," said Beverly.

"Farther away than France," Mama said. "Warmer too. She wasn't a slave, your great-grandma. She was a free woman, with beautiful ebony skin and beautiful black kinky hair. She didn't need to carry papers. Everybody in her village, her mother and father and brothers and sisters, her uncles and aunts and her friends, all of them were free.

"Then evil men came to her village. They kidnapped your great-grandma. She was strong, and she fought them, but they had guns and no one in her village did."

"Were they white or black?" asked Beverly.

"Who?" Mama said. "The villagers?"

"The kidnappers."

Mama paused. "I don't know," she said. "Might have been either, or both. Evil comes in all colors. They kidnapped hundreds of people, from all up and down the coast of Africa. They chained them into the belly of a horrible ship, and sailed them all the way to the city of Williamsburg, right here in Virginia."

Mama paused before she went on. "And they sold all those

people into slavery. Your great-grandma, she was bought by a man named Mr. Francis Eppes."

"Who got the money?" Beverly asked. "Who did Mr. Eppes pay?"

"The kidnappers," Mama said. "And the people who owned the ship."

Beverly bit his lip.

"Your great-grandma wasn't born a slave," Mama said. "She didn't have something wrong with her turned her into a slave. She didn't do anything wrong. She didn't deserve to be captured. You remember that." Mama paused again, then went on with the story.

"Mr. Eppes called your great-grandma Parthenia."

"But that wasn't her real name," Harriet said.

"No," Mama said. "Parthenia was what Mr. Eppes called her. Her real name was the one her parents gave her, in Africa. We don't know what it was."

Beverly wished somebody had known his great-grandma's real name.

"Some time later, your great-grandma formed an attachment with a sea captain—"

"A *different* sea captain," Harriet cut in. "*Not* the captain of the slave ship."

"A different one," Mama agreed. "A white man named Captain Hemings, who was captain of a merchant ship from England. He was a fine man, and Parthenia was a woman of uncommon beauty, and together they had a beautiful little girl named Elizabeth Hemings, and that was your grandma."

Grandma lived down the hill, in a cabin by herself. She was old, old. It was hard for Beverly to imagine her as a little girl.

"The captain was at sea when Elizabeth was born," Mama continued. "He didn't come back for years. But when he did, he tried to claim his daughter. He wanted to take care of her. But the law said Elizabeth belonged to Mr. Eppes, and Mr. Eppes wouldn't sell her to the sea captain. She was pretty and smart, and Mr. Eppes wanted to keep her."

Mama smiled. "Everyone always loved your grandma."

"Tell us about France," Beverly said. He was sick of hearing about Great-grandma and the sea captain. Why couldn't Grandma Elizabeth belong to her daddy, the way Beverly belonged to his? "Tell us about the French soldiers," Beverly said.

So Mama told them about the French soldiers, who wore feathers on their helmets and guarded the city gate near where she lived in Paris. She told them about the fancy people who lived in France, lords and ladies and even a king, and how she used to watch them when she was lady's maid to Miss Martha.

"You saw a king?" Beverly asked. He knew kings were like presidents, only with crowns.

"No," Mama said. "Master Jefferson met the king, but Miss Martha never did, so I never did, either. I went to parties with Miss Martha, as her chaperone. That's how I got to see things. The maids had to stay off to the side, but we used to sit together and laugh at all the fancy goings-on."

"Did she go to lots of parties?" Harriet asked.

"Not at first," Mama said. "At first she was away at school. But when she grew up and had her come-out, our last year there, she went to parties two or three times a week."

"Were they fancy?" asked Harriet.

"Fancier than you can imagine," Mama said. "Fancier than anything that's ever happened in Charlottesville. Silk dresses and silk ribbons, and everyone with powdered hair." She tweaked Beverly's hair. "Wouldn't you look fine with your hair dusted white? Should we ask Uncle Peter for some flour?"

"Mama," Beverly protested.

Mama laughed. "That was the fashion. Even the soldiers powdered their hair. The skirts of the ladies' dresses stuck out sideways on wooden hoops, so wide they could barely get past the door."

Harriet giggled. "Did your dresses do that?"

"No," Mama said with a smile. "Maids' dresses weren't *that* fancy. But I did have beautiful silk dresses. Maids had to dress fine, to be a credit to their employers."

"What's an employer?" asked Beverly.

"A person that's paying you to work for them," Mama said. She bit her lip. "Servants are paid in France. There are no slaves there."

Beverly said, "You were paid?"

"I was," Mama said.

"But not anymore," Beverly said. "Not here."

"No," said Mama.

"But Mama," said Beverly, "why—"

"Here," Mama said, getting up from the rocker. She opened the trunk Beverly and Harriet weren't allowed to touch. "I kept one of my old dresses. I'll show you." From the bottom of the trunk she pulled out a real dress, like Miss Martha wore, made of shiny, bright-colored cloth. Harriet rubbed it between her fingers. Beverly just stared. He tried to imagine Mama wearing such a dress.

"Did you buy that?" he asked. "With your pay-money?"

Mama shook her head. "I could never have afforded silk," she said. "Master Jefferson bought it for me, once I needed clothes to be a proper chaperone. He took me shopping. He had wonderful taste. Still does." She smiled.

Beverly stiffened. "He never takes you shopping here." Mama got cloth for their clothes at the give-out time, same as everybody else on the mountain.

"Of course not!" Mama said sharply. "It's different here, you know that."

Beverly didn't know it. He knew what it was like here, but he didn't know what it had been like in France. Sounded pretty fine.

"Maybe we should have stayed there," he said.

"Master Jefferson had to come back," Mama said. "His term there was over.

"I could have stayed," she continued softly, almost as though speaking to herself. "I knew it too. I spoke French, and I knew how to find a good job. But my family was here, my mama and my brothers and sisters, and I was expecting a baby—your brother, the first one, that died." Mama sighed. "I was only sixteen."

She smiled at Beverly. "It's a good thing I came back. Otherwise, you wouldn't have been born. Nor Harriet, nor Maddy."

Beverly nodded. "You would have been lonely."

"I would have," Mama said.

"Did Miss Martha like France?" asked Harriet.

"She loved it," Mama said. "She wanted to stay forever. She told Master Jefferson she felt a vocation to become a Catholic nun. He didn't like that!" Mama shook her head. "Miss Martha was happier there. She was happier then."

"How about you?" Beverly wanted to know. "Were you happier then?"

"Of course not," Mama said. She reached down and scooped him into her lap, and rocked him like he was the baby, not Maddy. "Look at my beautiful children. I'm happier now."

Chapter Six

Home for Christmas

In late December Miss Edith came home in Davy Hern's wagon. James was a beautiful baby, bigger than Maddy, and just as bright-eyed. Joe Fossett couldn't take his eyes off them, James or Miss Edith, either one. He held Miss Edith on his lap and kissed her neck, and she laughed and smiled. He bounced baby James on his knee.

Beverly wished Master Jefferson would come to their cabin, hold Mama on his lap, and bounce Maddy on his knee. He wished Master Jefferson would smile at him as often as Joe Fossett smiled at baby James. It was hard, knowing Master Jefferson was right there in the great house, and not getting to see him at all.

Of course the great house was full of all kinds of people, not just Master Jefferson. Miss Martha, who had lived with him in the President's House all fall, came to Monticello for

Christmas, instead of going to her own farm only three miles away. She brought her grumpy husband and all six of her children with her, and a slew of maids and nurses. Friends of Master Jefferson came too. They filled the great house, top to bottom, side to side.

Field hands didn't work on the days around Christmas, but up at the great house there was more to do than ever. When Mama came back to the cabin at dawn, she prodded Beverly awake. "Get up and help Burwell," she said. "Fetch firewood."

Beverly groaned. All the bedrooms in the great house had fireplaces. Beverly hauled armload after armload from the woodshed to the house, up the narrow twisting staircases to the second and third floors. He took wood to Master Jefferson's room, the parlor, and the dining room. After that he carried armfuls to the kitchen, where Uncle Peter was stirring and chopping and cooking fit to bust. Then he ran errands, to the stables where the guests' horses were, or to the big storeroom or the smokehouse. Then Uncle Peter told him to wash the dishes and dry them and stack them up without breaking one, as though he weren't almost eight years old and didn't know how to stack a dish.

All the time, all he could think about was Master Jefferson. He longed to see him. Sometimes he imagined conversations with him. They could talk about violins or music or France. Maybe Beverly could tell him how awful James Hubbard's whipping had been. Then Master Jefferson could explain that the overseers had made a terrible mistake, and that Master Jefferson would never let it happen again.

But no matter how hard Beverly hoped, he never got to speak to his father. He hardly even saw him from afar.

The guests at Christmas ate so much that Master Jefferson didn't have enough food in his cellars to feed them. That was good news for the slaves. On the Saturday before Christmas, Uncle Peter sent word all over the mountain that Miss Martha was buying for the great house.

All year long, everyone except Beverly's mama grew vegetables or raised chickens for their own. The field hands did it so they'd have something to eat besides the cornmeal, fatback, and salt fish that was all the overseers gave them, but even they saved extra to sell. Now they slit the throats of the oldest of their chickens, or dug into their store holes for sweet potatoes or turnips or eggs. They stood in a long line by the back door of the great house, holding whatever they could scrounge for sale.

Miss Martha stood on the porch, pursing her lips while she chose. She took coins out of her purse and dropped them into people's hands. Beverly collected whatever she bought, and carried it to Uncle Peter in the kitchen.

Uncle Peter was feeling fine. "Some turkeys would be tasty, did anybody catch any," he told Beverly. "And I'd never say no to possums or nice fat raccoons."

"I didn't see any turkeys," Beverly said. You could catch

them sometimes in snares. Raccoons and possums were hunted at night, but they were hard to find in winter when they holed up in their dens. "I saw lots of folks with sweet potatoes," he said.

Peter grunted. "You tell Miss Martha I need a whole bunch. Tell her to buy every sweet potato she can." He grinned at Beverly. Beverly grinned back. He knew Peter already had all the sweet potatoes he could use, but Miss Martha didn't know it. "Whatever you see people holding, you tell Miss Martha that's what I need," Uncle Peter said. "Got that?"

"Got it," Beverly said. Everybody ought to have a little money at Christmas.

"Good heavens!" Miss Martha said, when Beverly reported back. "How can Peter possibly need more sweet potatoes? You tell him I don't want them on the table every meal!"

Beverly rubbed his nose and looked away. Sometimes Miss Martha sounded exactly like Harriet. "Lots of extra folks around," he said.

"Well, sure," Miss Martha said, more calmly. "He must want them for the servants. I forget how you people like your sweet potatoes."

That comment stuck in Beverly's head. He couldn't puzzle it out. He couldn't imagine anyone not liking a sweet potato. "Which people was she talking about?" he asked Mama at night.

"Enslaved people," Mama said. "That's what she meant. Don't worry about it."

"But I'm the same people she is," Beverly said. "I'm her brother."

Mama sighed and rubbed her hand through his hair. "Don't say that," she said.

"It's true," Beverly said.

"A lot of things are true," said Mama, "but that doesn't mean we say them out loud."

After the excitement of Christmas was over and most of the visitors had gone, Beverly asked Mama, "Will you get Papa to listen to me play again?" He was still with them for another week.

Mama swooped Beverly under her arm. She pulled Beverly's pants down and walloped his bare bottom hard. Beverly howled.

"That's for calling him Papa," she said, shoving him onto the edge of the bed. "Quit crying. Next time it'll be a switch, and if there's a time after that it'll be Joe Fossett and a big leather strap."

"But it's true!" Beverly said, between sobs. "He is my papa! He *is*!"

"It's also true you're not to call him that. Not *ever*. Do you hear me?"

Beverly sniffled and sobbed. He got down on the floor and wriggled under the bed to fetch his violin. Mama took it from him. "That's mine until he goes back. Maybe if you worry less about who's going to hear you play, you'll remember to mind your tongue more."

Three days later Beverly finally saw Master Jefferson alone. Beverly was just leaving the great house after delivering still more firewood when Master Jefferson returned from his daily ride. Beverly hurried to the edge of the porch, and took the horse's reins while Master Jefferson dismounted. He looked at his father. Suddenly, he couldn't speak. "Hello," he whispered, looking away.

"Hello, Beverly," Master Jefferson said, as though they spoke every day.

Beverly smiled. He liked it that Master Jefferson called him by name.

"I haven't heard any music lately," Master Jefferson said. "Aren't you practicing?"

"Oh, yes—" Beverly kept his eyes on the ground. "Mama took my violin away. For punishment."

"I see. What was your transgression?"

Transgression. That was a lovely word, but Beverly didn't know what it meant. "Sir?"

"What did you do?"

Beverly studied his feet. "I'd rather not say. Sir."

Master Jefferson put his hand under Beverly's chin and lifted it, so that Beverly had to look at him. "Then I won't ask. We'll leave it between you and your mother."

"Thank you," Beverly said. Master Jefferson put his hand down and started to walk toward the house. "Sir?" Beverly asked quickly, trying to make Master Jefferson stay. "Do you like the sound of words? Like—like *inebriation* or *transgression*?"

Master Jefferson stopped walking. He laughed. "Yes," he said, turning back toward Beverly. "Yes, I do. Those are fine-sounding words. But their meanings, perhaps, leave something to be desired. What about—let's see—what about *tranquility*. There's a word that's beautiful in meaning and in sound."

Tranquility. Beverly loved it. "What does it mean, sir?" he asked.

"It means peacefulness."

Tranquility. Peacefulness. Beverly smiled. He watched Master Jefferson walk into the house, then led the horse to the tranquility of the stables.

When Master Jefferson returned to Washington, Miss Martha and all her people went with him. Mama shook her head. "If I were Miss Martha," she said, "this time I'd stay home." Miss Martha was about to have another baby. "Four days in that jolting carriage," Mama said. "She'll be lucky if she doesn't give birth on the side of the road."

Miss Martha was lucky. It wasn't until January 27 that she had her baby boy. Uncle Peter got word of it in a letter. "James Madison Randolph," Uncle Peter said.

James Madison was Maddy's name. Beverly didn't think Miss Martha should be allowed to take it for her own baby. He said so.

"It might have been Master Jefferson's doing," Mama said. "He likes naming babies, and James Madison is his particular friend."

"But we had it first," Beverly said.

"Families often use the same names over and over," Mama said. "Maybe someday you'll have a son, and you'll name him James Madison too."

Beverly doubted it. "If I have a daughter," Beverly said, "I won't name her Martha, that's for sure."

In spring, Miss Fanny married Davy Hern. Not long after that, Master Jefferson made her go to Washington, to take cooking lessons alongside Miss Edith. Davy was sad when she left, but he knew he'd be going to Washington in July to bring Master Jefferson's luggage home. He planned to bring Fanny, Edith, and baby James home for the month too.

Everyone knew what day to expect Davy, and when they heard the wagon coming up the last part of the mountain they all came out to Mulberry Row to say hello. But when the wagon rounded the corner only Fanny sat beside Davy on the seat. Miss Edith and baby James weren't there.

Everyone stared. Joe Fossett ran up to the side of the wagon. He grabbed Miss Fanny's arm. Miss Fanny leaned over, took him by the shoulder, and said something to him, low and hard. Beverly couldn't catch the words.

Joe Fossett's face closed up like somebody'd snapped a shutter over it. He turned on his heel and walked away. He didn't go to the blacksmith shop, even though he had a horse waiting to be shod. He walked to his cabin on Mulberry Row, went inside, and slammed the door.

The look on Joe Fossett's face made Beverly's stomach hurt. He ran for Mama.

"What's wrong?" he asked her, after she'd had a chance to speak with Miss Fanny. "Did Miss Edith die? Did baby James?"

Mama looked troubled. "Nobody died," she said. "Nobody died, and the rest is none of your business. It's grown-up business. You leave it alone, do you hear me?"

Beverly had to find out. But, before he got a chance, word came. Joe Fossett had run away.

Chapter Seven

Joe Fossett

Beverly thought he would vomit. He thought of Joe Fossett with his arms tied to the whipping post, Joe Fossett with blood running down his back. Joe Fossett working in the fields, the way James Hubbard did now. Joe Fossett bowed down, the smile gone from his eyes.

"Quit crying," Mama said. "Nobody's going to hurt Joe Fossett."

"Why not?" Beverly said. "James Hubbard was the best nail boy, and they still whipped him."

"Joe isn't running away from Master Jefferson," Mama said. "He's running toward Miss Edith. There's trouble between them. Joe's gone to make it right."

"What kind of trouble?"

"The kind that's none of your business."

"Does Master Jefferson know about it?" asked Beverly. "Does he know Joe isn't running away?"

Mama pursed her lips. "I'll see that he does." She went to the great house. When she came back she looked upset. Beverly and Harriet saw her walking down the path to the kitchen and ran to catch up.

Mama sat down on the bench inside. "I told him," she said to Uncle Peter and Miss Fanny. "I told him Joe just needed to see Edith and he said, 'Why Edith?' "

Mama sank her face into her hands. Beverly grabbed Harriet's hand and shrank back against the door. "Like he didn't realize who her family was," Mama said. She shook her head. "I think it'll be all right. As long as he doesn't take Joe's leaving personally, I think it'll be all right."

Mama caught sight of Harriet and Beverly. "You all get out of here!" she said. "This is none of your business."

Harriet scurried back to the cabin, but Beverly hightailed it to the great house instead. He crept along the corridor until he could peek inside the half-closed door into Master Jefferson's room. Master Jefferson sat at his desk, his back toward Beverly, writing. Beverly wondered what he was writing about, and to whom.

Burwell grabbed the back of Beverly's neck and hauled him away from the door. "Go home," he whispered. "And be glad I'm not your mama, catch you spying like that."

For over a week, nobody heard a word about Joe Fossett. Without him the blacksmith shop fell apart. The drunken white blacksmith, Stewart, couldn't control the nail boys, who cracked jokes and acted foolish instead of making nails.

Stewart lamed one of the farm horses brought in for a shoe— lamed it bad, with blood spurting and the horse thrashing around. He reeked of cheap brandy and let the forge go cold.

Mama said, "Joe'll get caught or he won't. He'll have seen Miss Edith first or he won't. We can't do anything to change what happens, so we just have to wait."

Beverly asked, "What if he can't fix it?"

Mama gave him the eye. "Fix what?"

"Whatever's wrong that you won't talk about."

Mama sighed. "That's not our business either. The only part that was my business was making sure Master Jefferson understood why Joe went away."

The next night after dinner, Beverly heard violin music wafting on the sweet summer breeze. Master Jefferson was playing on the porch outside his bedroom. Beverly stood outside the cabin door, listening. Mama came out behind him. "That's a French song," she said. "Isn't it lovely?" She kissed Beverly good night, then hurried up the path.

Beverly ran for his violin. He stood in the doorway and tried to match the music Master Jefferson was playing. His tune was simpler, and slower, but it sounded a little like Master Jefferson's tune.

Beverly felt a wave of peace—of tranquility—wash over him. When Master Jefferson stopped, Beverly kept playing, until Miss Aggie, who watched them now instead of Miss Fanny, said she'd heard enough, and made him go inside.

. . .

Always before, Beverly could find out whatever he wanted to know by asking Mama, or by listening to talk in the kitchen or the blacksmith shop or somewhere else along Mulberry Row. With Joe Fossett it was different. Grown-ups shut their mouths tight whenever any child came around. Beverly knew there was trouble between Joe Fossett and Miss Edith, but he never learned more about it than that.

Before long word came up the mountain. Joe Fossett was caught, and coming home. Beverly buried his face in the bed to hide his tears. He couldn't bear to think of Joe coming back like James Hubbard, bent down in a wagon bed, hand-cuffed, with his face like stone. Harriet came in and lay down beside him. "Maybe we won't have to watch," she whispered.

But they didn't hear any shouts or commotion. Eventually they got up and walked out of the cabin, hand in hand. One of the overseers strode down Mulberry Row. Harriet shrank back, but Beverly made himself follow the man. The overseer went to the blacksmith shop and talked in a low voice to Mr. Stewart. That was all.

In the kitchen Uncle Peter said he was too busy cooking to talk. "But Joe—" said Beverly.

"Get me some wood," snapped Uncle Peter. "And shut your mouth. It don't concern you."

The next day Joe Fossett rode up the mountain straight and unbound on the wagon seat beside an overseer. He looked perfectly calm. He went into the great house and spoke with Master Jefferson, and then he went to the blacksmith shop and shouted at the nail boys, just as though he'd never run away.

Beverly was amazed. He and Harriet and some of the other children hurried to the shop. The nail boys were pounding nails as quick and hard as they could. Joe Fossett shoveled charcoal onto the fire. Already his arms gleamed with sweat.

"You all want something?" he asked them.

"No, sir," Harriet said.

"Then run back out of here," Joe Fossett said. "I got work to do."

Beverly had seen all he needed to. Joe Fossett's face looked stern, but his eyes were smiling.

"He went to Washington," Mama said, later on. "He saw Miss Edith. Now he's home and everything's fine."

"So he really wasn't running away," Beverly said. "That's why he didn't get whipped."

Mama started to answer, but paused. A small smile came to her lips. "I don't know," she said. "I doubt we'll ever know. Joe won't be whipped because he's Joe Fossett, and because they found him in the President's House with Miss Edith, and because he came back without a fight. But if they hadn't found him when they did—maybe he and Edith would have taken baby James and run. Maybe. I hope so."

Beverly scowled. He couldn't picture Monticello without Joe Fossett. "I don't," he said. "I'd never run away."

"You will," Mama said.

"Of course I won't."

"Of course you *will*," Mama said. "I've told you. When you grow up you'll be free. You won't have to run, but you'll go away. Free, Beverly. You'll never be a slave."

"If I'm free," Beverly argued, "then I'll be free to stay here with you. I'll never leave Monticello."

Mama pulled him close and stroked his head. "I love you. Don't worry. Everything will turn out fine."

Beverly hid his face in the folds of her skirt. "*Never,*" he said.

Chapter Eight

Hidden in Plain Sight

Joe Fossett worked hard in the blacksmith shop. At Christmas, Miss Edith and baby James came home with Davy Hern and Fanny, and neither Miss Edith nor Joe Fossett acted like anything had ever been wrong. Beverly didn't understand. He supposed he never would.

For Christmas Joe gave Miss Edith a big piece of Turkey red cloth. Miss Edith cut it up and made it into a headscarf for herself, a neck-scarf for Joe, and a tiny little coat for James. She said that way everybody could see they were all one family. Beverly liked that. He wished his family could do the same—him, Mama, Harriet, Maddy, and Master Jefferson. But Mama didn't say anything about it, so Beverly kept quiet too.

Baby James and Maddy were both just two years old. Both of them were learning to talk. James said Maddy's name first.

He pointed his finger at Maddy and said, "Mah! Mah!" while Beverly and Harriet cheered. Maddy took a few days longer. He was sitting on the floor of the cabin one morning when Miss Edith came in carrying James. Maddy looked up and said "Hi, James!" like he'd been saying it for months already.

The great house was packed full for the holiday. Miss Martha came, of course, and her crabby husband and her horde of children, and so did aunts and uncles and cousins, and guests whose names Beverly never learned. He stayed busier than ever, hauling wood and water, taking ashes away and poking up fires.

Burwell spent half the day fetching wine and French cheeses out of the fancy cellar storerooms. Those rooms were kept locked, and only Burwell had a key. Beverly wasn't sure why. There were rules about what you could take and what you couldn't. Taking anything out of the great house, including the fancy storerooms, was stealing. It was flat wrong and you would be whipped for it. Taking things out of the cabins, or swiping the vegetables folks grew on their own, that was stealing too. But helping yourself to a bit of extra salt pork from the smokehouse, or a handful of corn from the stables for chicken feed, or a spare potato or two from the main gardens—that wasn't stealing. That was justice. The enslaved workers grew the crops. They tended the gardens, the fields, the orchards, and the animals. Anything they put into their own pockets was no more than what should have been theirs already.

Beverly asked Mama once why they didn't raise chickens

or grow vegetables. Everyone else did, even Joe Fossett and Uncle Peter. Mama lifted her chin, proud. "I don't sell things to Master Jefferson," she said. "If we need money he will give us some."

Beverly couldn't remember Mama asking for money, but he was glad to know she could have some if she needed it. "Maybe you could buy a piece of fancy cloth," he said, "and make Master Jefferson a shirt from it, and then make me something out of the scraps."

"Oh, Beverly," Mama said.

"Just the scraps," said Beverly. "So we look like—"

Mama cut him off. "If we looked like all one family," she said, "what kind of secret would it be?"

Master Jefferson—or Papa, as Beverly still called him in his heart—went back to Washington like always. Beverly missed him. Even if his father didn't talk to him, Beverly felt like he had a father when Master Jefferson was nearby. Now the quiet mountaintop seemed lonely and forlorn. Some days clouds hung down so far upon the mountain that the cabins and the great house poked out the top of them. The tip of the mountain, with the house and cabins, looked like an island on a sea of cloud. "Is this like the ocean?" Beverly asked Mama.

She drew her shawl around her shoulders. "Very much like the ocean," she said, "only you don't get seasick here."

That night Mama told them again about her trip to France. "When Mrs. Jefferson died," she said, "Miss Martha was ten years old. I was nine, Miss Maria was four, and little Miss Lucy had just been born.

"The little girls were so small that when Master Jefferson went to France, not long after, he only took Miss Martha with him. He sent Maria and Lucy to live with their aunt, Mrs. Eppes, and he sent me along to help take care of them.

"Two years later, Miss Lucy died. Master Jefferson wrote that he wanted Miss Maria sent to France. She didn't want to go. She didn't remember her daddy, and she was afraid of the ocean. Since she trusted me more than anyone else, they made me take her."

Beverly had heard this story over and over. Now he tried to imagine Master Jefferson an ocean away, gone for years. Beverly would get on that ship. He would be glad to. "How old were you then, Mama?"

"By the time everything was settled, I was fourteen," Mama said. "Miss Maria was eight, going on nine. I didn't speak a word of French and had never been to any city at all."

"Were you afraid?" asked Beverly. He wouldn't be.

Mama laughed. "I didn't know enough to be afraid!" she said. "Sometimes it's better to be ignorant. To me it seemed like nothing but an adventure. Miss Maria was so scared and seasick, she about cried the entire trip, but I used to stand on the deck sometimes watching the wind carry the ship—and I loved it. I loved Paris too."

Harriet said, "I think I like Miss Maria better than Miss Martha."

"You would have liked Miss Martha then," Mama said. "I did." She paused before she continued. "She married Mr. Randolph two months after we came back from France. She'd known him less than five weeks. She didn't take time to think. I wouldn't want to walk in her shoes."

Beverly wouldn't want to walk in her nasty shoes either. They probably smelled. But how he wished he could take her place! He could live in the President's House. Master Jefferson would introduce him to people with a proud smile, saying, "This is Beverly, my son."

"If you and Master Jefferson got married," he asked Mama, "would you make Miss Martha stay away?"

"Beverly!" Mama said. "What a thing to say!"

"I would," Harriet said.

"There's no sense discussing it," Mama said. "No sense even thinking about it. It can't happen, not ever, not this side of Paradise. Put it right out of your heads."

Beverly did until the next day, when he and Harriet were alone. Then they talked about it some more. "We'd travel in the carriage to Washington City," Beverly said. "Think about it. We'd be with Mama and Papa both, all the time."

"We'd eat in the big dining room," Harriet said. "Roast chicken off china plates. Miss Edith would cook for *us*." Harriet stopped. She clapped her hand over her mouth.

Beverly understood. "We'd *pay* Miss Edith," he said. "We'd pay her good for all her fancy cooking. And we'd let Joe Fossett come to Washington and be blacksmith there, and he could live all the time with Miss Edith and James."

"And we'd invite them to dinner," Harriet said, "like Mr. and Mrs. Madison come to dinner now."

She and Beverly looked at each other.

"No," Harriet said softly. "That can't happen."

"We'll just make them not slaves," Beverly said. "We'll make everybody free, and everybody equal, and then Mama can marry Master Jefferson and everybody can do what they want."

But, he thought, what if Miss Edith didn't *want* to be a French cook? What if Joe Fossett didn't *want* to move to Washington? If Joe and Edith were free, would they want to work for Master Jefferson?

When he asked Harriet about it, she frowned. "These are just stories," she said. "We're making them up. They're not real like Mama's stories. They're pretend."

Beverly knew that. "I only like pretending things that can happen," he said.

In the spring, Master Jefferson arrived at Monticello with plans for new dependencies. That was what he called them. What he meant, Beverly learned, was more construction— not on the great house this time, but all along Mulberry Row.

Right now the little brick guesthouse with the kitchen in its basement was a long way from the great house, so food was always cold by the time it reached the dining room. Master Jefferson wanted the kitchen closer to the house. He wanted the kitchen to be bigger too, and he needed more stabling for guests' horses. But what really bothered him was that anyone standing on the back porch of the great house got a clear view down Mulberry Row, of the double row of cabins, the stables, blacksmith and woodshops, smokehouses and garden sheds. Master Jefferson was tired of looking at all that.

He decided to dig out part of the great house lawn, and put a row of buildings—the dependencies—halfway underground, disguised by fancy walkways covering their roofs. He would hide a new kitchen, a smokehouse, and some rooms to live in—including one for Beverly's family—on one side of the lawn, and a new stable, icehouse, and laundry on the other. Then he could tear down the part of Mulberry Row that was most visible from the great house.

"He wants to hide us?" Beverly asked. He felt grumpy. Papa had been home two days, and Beverly hadn't even caught a glimpse of him.

Mama sighed. "It's nothing to do with us," she said. "It's to make the mountaintop more beautiful."

"Our house isn't ugly," argued Beverly.

Mama gave him an eye. "A log cabin or the great house," she said. "Which one would you rather look at?" She picked up a piece of her sewing.

He could just make the cabins look better, Beverly thought. He wandered outside, still grumpy, and found Uncle John standing near the garden shed, sharpening a hoe.

"What're you doing?" Beverly asked. Burwell's brother Wormley was in charge of the gardens, not Uncle John.

"Wormley's covered up," said Uncle John. "Didn't you see that wagonload of trees Davy Hern brought? Master Jefferson wants new flower beds laid out this morning, and since Wormley's setting the trees, I told him I'd dig the beds." Uncle John straightened and smiled at Beverly. "Master Jefferson's coming out to show me where to put them. Want to help?"

Beverly's grumpiness evaporated in an instant. "Sure," he said. He grabbed a spade and followed Uncle John.

Master Jefferson was waiting for them at the front of the great house. Beverly saw him and started to smile, but the smile froze on his face. His grumpiness came flooding back. One of Miss Martha's girls stood beside Master Jefferson, holding his hand. She was all decked out in big ribbons and a crisp white dress and shoes, and she swung Master Jefferson's hand and beamed at him. "I love flowers!" she said in a happy, chirpy voice Beverly instantly despised. "I can't wait to see them bloom!"

Master Jefferson smiled down at her. He didn't even glance at Beverly.

Beverly dropped his eyes. He didn't know the girl's name— all Miss Martha's girls looked alike to him—but he hated her just the same.

Master Jefferson and the girl laid string on the ground to mark the space for two big oval beds. Beverly and Uncle John cut out the edges of the ovals with their spades, then stripped the sod inside the ovals while Master Jefferson and the girl stood and watched. The girl chattered constantly. Beverly thought her voice sounded like a horsefly buzzing.

It was hot work for a warm morning. Sweat ran down his back until his shirt stuck to him. He wished the girl would go away. If Harriet were here, little as she was, she would grab a spade and help. She wouldn't just stand and giggle. He stomped hard on the edge of his spade. It hurt his foot.

Uncle John noticed. "Take the hoe and strip the sod," he said quietly. "I'll go get a wheelbarrow of old manure. We'll mix it in before we set out the plants."

A big piece of Master Jefferson's hair came loose from its tie. The wind blew it in front of his eyes. He pushed it back with an irritated gesture.

"I'll fix that, Grandpa," the girl said. She untied Master Jefferson's queue and combed his hair with her fingers.

Beverly slashed at the sod. He hated this. Then Master Jefferson said, "You're getting stronger, Beverly."

It wasn't much, but it made Beverly feel better. "Yes, sir," he said, straightening. "Mama says I've grown."

"I can see."

The girl finished Master Jefferson's hair, then tugged his shirt sleeve. "Are we done here? I want to go look at the strawberries. I want to see if they're ripe."

"Certainly," Master Jefferson said. He took her offered hand and they walked away. Beverly waited for something else, for Master Jefferson to turn back, or wave or say good-bye. Surely he wouldn't just leave, not after starting a conversation.

He did. As he and the girl walked past Uncle John, who was

pushing the barrow of manure, the girl said, "Oh, Grandpa, aren't we lucky to have John to help us?"

I'm invisible to her, thought Beverly. She doesn't see me.

John set the wheelbarrow down. Beverly said, "Did you hear what she said? Like she did the work, and you and I just helped a little."

John shrugged. "She's young," he said. "She doesn't know better."

"She's older than me," protested Beverly.

Uncle John shook his head. "Don't let little things bother you. If you do, you'll be nothing but bothered, all the days of your life."

But Beverly *was* bothered. He shouldn't be invisible. His house shouldn't have to be hidden. He ought to have just as much right to talk to Master Jefferson—his father—as that girl had to talk to her grandfather.

Mama wouldn't take his side. "You listen to Uncle John," she said that night, when Beverly complained. "People in our position don't have the luxury of being upset. You'd best learn to ignore all you can."

"What's my position?" Beverly said.

Mama looked stern. "You're Sally's son," she said. "Sally's oldest son."

"But I'm *his* son too," Beverly said. "I'm family. That girl acted like she couldn't even see me. I'm her *uncle,* and she acts like I don't matter at all."

"You matter," Mama said.

"Not to her," said Beverly. "Not to—"

"You matter," Mama repeated. "Not because of whose son you are. Because of who *you* are. You're as important as every other human being that ever was or ever will be. Everyone matters. What that girl thinks of you, how she treats you, can't change the fine person that you are.

"I don't want you walking around thinking of Miss Martha's girls as family. It won't help you. They aren't going to treat you like family. There's nothing we can do about that.

"But you matter. Harriet matters, Maddy matters. Uncle John matters. There's not a soul on this mountain that doesn't matter."

Mama turned suddenly to Harriet. "But you, now, you listen to me," she said. "These few weeks while we've got Miss Martha's girls around, you need to start paying attention to them. How they act. How they dress, how they talk, how they carry themselves. They're being raised as little ladies, and someday, Miss Harriet, you're going to be a lady too. You're going to need to know how to behave just the way they do."

Harriet's face lit into a cheerful gap-toothed grin. She was six now, still a tree-climbing wild child. "I'm going to be a lady?" she asked.

"You're going to be a lovely lady," Mama said. "You're going to grow up so beautiful, folks are just going to love to look at you. You'll need beautiful manners to match."

"If she acts prissy," said Beverly, "I'll punch her."

Harriet bounced off the edge of the bed and twirled Maddy around until they fell down. She looked up at Mama from the floor. "When, Mama?"

"When you're older," Mama said. "When you're grown."

"Can I have a white dress, like Miss Ellen's?" asked Harriet. "And pink shoes with bows?" She looked delighted. "Can I have hair ribbons?"

Ellen, thought Beverly. That was the name of the garden-bed girl.

Mama laughed. "Yes," she said. "You can have any color dress you want, and any kind of shoes, and wear ribbons every single day."

"Good!" said Harriet. "And then I can be rude to Beverly." She laughed. "Like Miss Ellen."

Beverly scowled at her. Harriet, still laughing, stuck out her tongue. She rolled over to grab Beverly's ankles, but missed.

"No, no," Mama said, swooping Beverly into her arms. "You must never be rude to Beverly." Mama leaned forward, but instead of kissing Beverly as he expected, stuck out her own tongue and waggled it. Despite himself, Beverly laughed.

But something stuck in his mind. There was something wrong about Harriet's becoming a lady, something worrisome, but he couldn't figure it out.

No matter. He'd keep his ears open, and his mouth shut, and it would come to him in time.

Chapter Nine

The Lines on the Hearth

Three important things happened in the second half of that year.

The first was that William Stewart, the white blacksmith, finally got so soaked with drink he could barely stagger out of bed. He couldn't be trusted to swing a hammer, much less work near hot coals, and the day he set Joe Fossett's pants on fire, even the white overseer had enough.

The overseer had brought one of the work horses up the mountain to be shod. When Beverly walked into the shop, Joe Fossett had just put the iron bars for the new shoes into the coals to heat.

"Don't just stand there," Joe told him. "Blow the fire up."

Beverly worked the big bellows, and blew the fire up. The smoldering coals glowed. Joe went to the horse, picked up its foot, and started to trim it for the shoe.

Mr. Stewart, slumped in his usual chair, gave a thundering snore. Then, without warning, he jumped to his feet. "Lemme do that!" he sputtered at Joe. He seized the tongs and snatched an iron bar from the fire. It was already red-hot like the coals. Mr. Stewart swung it in a wide arc over the anvil. "Stupid n—"

He missed the anvil and tripped. Stumbling forward, he stabbed the hot bar into the back of Joe Fossett's pants. The pants burst into flames. Joe yelled and shoved his seat into the dowsing bucket. The horse spooked. Beverly screamed.

Everyone went still. The overseer grabbed the horse and steadied it. Mr. Stewart stood swaying, his mouth open, a thread of drool dangling from his lip. The iron bar fell from the tongs. It lay in the dirt, a thin trail of smoke curling up from it.

Beverly barely breathed. He wanted to ask Joe if he was okay, but the silence was so thick he didn't dare make a sound. He took his hand off the bellows, then winced as they creaked open. Joe stood. Water dripped down his legs. His brown skin showed through the charred hole in his pants.

The white overseer kicked at the dirt beside the still-smoking shoe. "That," he said, "is positively the last gol-durn straw. If you kill Joe here, Stewart, who will do your work?"

"'M a fine blacksmith—" Mr. Stewart began.

"You used to be a fine blacksmith," the overseer corrected. "Now you're a common drunk. Get back to your house and start packing."

Mr. Stewart stared at the overseer. The overseer stared back. Finally Mr. Stewart turned and spat over his left shoulder. The gob of spit narrowly missed Beverly. "Crummy job here anyway," Stewart said. "Been six months since I've been paid."

He walked off. Joe Fossett picked the iron bar off the ground with the tongs and put it back into the fire. "Blow the fire up," he said to Beverly, and Beverly did.

Mr. Stewart left the mountain. The overseer wrote to Master Jefferson. Master Jefferson sent back a letter full of good news. He named Joe Fossett head blacksmith, in charge of the whole shop by himself. If Joe took on extra work for people outside Monticello, he would get a cut of the proceeds—sixteen cents out of every dollar they paid. Best of all, Miss Edith had had another baby, a girl. Joe and Miss Edith named her Maria.

Joe shone with joy. He advertised his services all over Charlottesville. He fired the forge early and worked late into the night. He was earning for his family now.

That was the first important thing. The second one Beverly learned right after Master Jefferson came home for Christmas. Mama gathered him and Harriet and even Maddy close around her in their cabin. She had something to tell them, she said, but she'd waited so she could tell Master Jefferson first. Mama put her hand on her belly and smiled. "I'm going to have a baby," she said. "Sometime late spring. A brother or sister for the three of you."

Harriet laid her head against Mama's belly. Maddy scowled. "*I'm* the baby!" he said.

"No, you're not," Beverly told him. "If there's going to be a new baby, that means you're a big boy."

Maddy's scowl vanished. "I'm a big boy!" he said.

"Yes," Mama said, kissing him. "You're a big, beautiful boy."

Master Jefferson was happy about the baby, or so Mama said, but Miss Martha wasn't. When Beverly carried firewood through the hallway of the great house on Christmas Eve, he caught the horrified look Miss Martha gave Mama's swelling belly. "Surely, Sally," Miss Martha said, "surely you're not increasing *again*?"

Mama replied softly, in French. Then she added, her voice soothing and calm, "And so are you?"

Miss Martha pressed her lips together. Tears sprang to her eyes. She looked away angrily. "Again," she said. She didn't seem happy at all. Beverly guessed it was because Miss Martha's husband was so mean. Or maybe having seven living children was enough. He felt a pang of sympathy for Miss Martha.

Miss Martha turned and saw him. "You, boy," she snapped. "Don't stand there. The third floor needs wood." She made a shooing motion with her hands. "Git!"

Beverly got. So much for sympathy, he thought. Miss Martha was a shrew.

The third thing was the most important. It was something he finally figured out. One of Miss Martha's daughters, Miss

Virginia, was just about Harriet's age, and two others, Miss Cornelia and Miss Mary, were not far off on either side. After Mama told Harriet she was going to grow up to be a lady, Harriet started to pay attention to Miss Cornelia and Miss Virginia and the rest. At Christmastime Beverly caught her eavesdropping when Miss Martha spoke to her girls. He could see how Harriet copied them, sitting with her back not touching the back of her chair, folding her legs at the ankles, and brushing her skirts down smooth. It was only a game to her, but Harriet was prettier than Miss Martha's girls, and more graceful, and Beverly watched her with a kind of pride. Harriet would make a good lady someday.

Then it hit him, square in the pit of his stomach.

To be a lady, Harriet would have to be white.

He went to Mama.

She was bent over, stoking the fire in the hearth of their cabin. She had a new shawl wrapped around her shoulders, and for a moment Beverly wanted to bury his face in it, and have her rock him the way she did when he was a little boy, but he knew he was too old. Instead he sat on the edge of the bed and pushed his cold feet closer to the fire.

"Beverly." Mama sat beside him and pulled him toward her. "What's the matter?"

He turned so his face was just a little bit against her shawl, and told Mama what he'd figured out.

"The things you think about," Mama said. "I swear you

were born with an old soul. You're not even ten years old, Beverly. You don't have to worry about this yet."

"But you want her to be white, don't you?" he said. "That's what you mean by being a lady."

"She is white," Mama said.

"She's not. 'Course she's not."

"What does she look like?" Mama said. "If you saw her down in Charlottesville, dressed like one of Miss Martha's girls, wouldn't you think she was white?"

It was like the time Mama had taken off Maddy's clothes, and asked them if he looked like a slave. Harriet's skin was not quite as light as Miss Martha's, but it was much lighter than everyone else's on Mulberry Row, except Beverly's. Harriet's hair was like Mama's, soft and straight, not tightly curled like most slaves' hair.

"You've got to be black to be a slave," Beverly said at last.

"Well," Mama said. She looked at him for a moment. "The law says, if your mama is a slave, then you are too. The law also says white people can't be slaves, so you're right, if you're a slave, then you are legally black. That's the law. But let me show you something." She reached forward and grabbed the poker. "Here's Harriet." She drew a line with the poker in the cool ashes on the edge of the hearth. "Here's me, Harriet's mama, and here's Master Jefferson, her father." Mama drew two more lines, sprouting off the first one. "Above me, we put my mama and daddy, that's Grandma Elizabeth and Master John Wayles, a white man. Okay?"

Beverly nodded. His grandma was dead now, but he remembered her.

"Above your papa we put lines for his mama and daddy, both white. Now, above Grandma Betty we put two lines for her mama and daddy, that's Parthenia and the sea captain, Captain Hemings. One black, one white. You with me?"

Beverly didn't completely follow her, but he nodded again anyway. "Lines for Master Wayles's mama and daddy," said Mama, "and for your papa's four grandparents. Got that? Eight lines, for you and Harriet and Maddy's eight great-grandparents."

"Okay." Beverly said. He did understand that much.

"How many of those eight were black, and how many were white?"

"Well, Grandma Betty—"

"No, no," Mama said patiently. "Just look at that last line of eight. How many white, how many black?"

Beverly counted. "Seven white," he said. "One black."

Mama nodded. "The law says that any slave's children are always slaves, but it also says that any person who has seven out of eight white great-grandparents is legally white. So you and Harriet and Maddy are white people. You're slaves, but you're white."

"Nobody acts like I'm white," Beverly said.

"No. They won't, because you're a slave. But think on it, Beverly. Someday you won't be a slave. You'll be a free white man."

Beverly thought of the white people he knew. They got to

be the bosses, mostly, and they lived in nicer houses than the black people he knew. Still. "I don't want to be white," he said. "White people are mean."

"Not all of them," Mama said. "And the ones that are mean to black people aren't always mean to other white people." She looked at him steadily. "It's easier to be white," she said. "It's safer."

Beverly guessed that was true. Harriet did look like a white person. Maybe he did too. "So when I change into a free man, I just change into a white man?" he asked Mama. "I just tell everybody, look at these seven-eighths? I want to be called a white man now?"

Mama laughed and cuddled him closer. "It doesn't work like that," she said. "If you go down to Charlottesville, where people know you and know your family, and you tell them you used to be black but now you're white, what do you think they'll say?"

Beverly thought. "They'll tell me to get out of town," he said. "They won't listen. They won't change how they think about me."

"That's right," Mama said. "I'm sorry for it, but you know it's true."

"So, Mama, what's the use?"

Mama laughed again. "You won't stay in Charlottesville," she said. "You'll go where nobody knows you. And they'll see you, and say to themselves, 'That looks like a white man.' And you won't tell them any different—why should you? You are white, by law. You'll just go about your business, and Harriet will too. What you don't tell people, they'll never know."

"But I'm black by law too," Beverly said. "Because you said slaves have to be black. I can't be black by law and white by law, both."

"You can," Mama said. "The law says both things." She paused, and put her hands around his face. "You're kind of caught in the middle of the law. It doesn't matter, though. You'll be free and you'll look white, so you'll be a free white man."

"I'm going to have free papers?"

"Of course not," Mama said. "Papers are for black people. You'll be white." Mama took Beverly's hands. "Listen. Neither part of you is better, not the black part nor the white part. They're both what you are. But right now the white people make the laws in this country. They make the rules. It's easier to live like a white person here."

"I'm never leaving Monticello," Beverly said, "so I don't care."

"Don't worry about that," Mama said. "It's a long time from now."

"Harriet can go," Beverly said. "I'll stay. I want to be with you."

Mama didn't say anything. She took the hearth broom and brushed away the lines. Seven white great-grandparents, one black.

"I don't like secrets, Mama," Beverly said.

"Might as well make friends with them," Mama said. "They're here to stay."

Chapter Ten

A Carpenter's Apprentice

Beverly's baby brother, Thomas Eston Hemings, was born May 21, 1808. Papa—*Master Jefferson*—named him, after one of his friends, a white man, Thomas Eston. Mama called the baby Eston from the start. She said it wouldn't do to call him Thomas. The only Thomas at Monticello was Master Jefferson.

"But our first baby was named Thomas," Beverly protested. "My big brother. You said so."

Mama stroked baby Eston's cheek. "He died so soon," she said. "He hardly breathed before he was gone. We never gave him a real name. I call him Thomas, but just to you all and in my heart."

Beverly frowned. "Do you still miss him, Mama?"

"I do," she said softly. "Of course I do."

Master Jefferson wasn't home to see the baby; he'd come and gone for his spring trip, and now he was in Washington until July. He and Mama had discussed baby names before he left. "One more year," Mama said now. "Next summer he'll come home to stay."

"Really?" said Beverly. This was the first he'd heard such a thing—or maybe he'd heard it but not paid attention. "He's going to quit being president?"

Mama laughed. "He can't be president forever," she said. "He'll have finished two terms—eight years, that's plenty. He's earned his retirement."

"Is he going to go to France again, or anywhere like that?"

"No," said Mama. "He's going to just stay here. He won't work anymore. He might visit to his farm near Bedford sometimes, but that'll be all."

Beverly bit his lip to hold back his smile. He imagined life at Monticello with Master Jefferson always there. They wouldn't have nearly as many visitors—no Miss Martha, at least not most of the time. The mountaintop would be quiet the way it was now. Master Jefferson would ride his horse, write his letters, and eat dinner every day at three o'clock. But he'd also have time to be with them, his other family.

"Maybe he'll teach me," Beverly said, thinking of his violin. "He won't want to keep paying Jesse Scott, not when he's here and doesn't have anything better to do."

"I wouldn't count on that," said Mama.

"He liked my playing," Beverly continued. Master Jefferson had listened to him one day in April. "He said—he said he was proud."

"I know he's proud," Mama said, "But, Beverly—"

"Of course I'll be busy too," he said. "I'll be working. But we'll have time, if he's here always. Won't be any kind of rush."

It was a sore spot with him, that he'd turned ten and still not been given a real job. He was old enough to be a nail boy, but Joe Fossett didn't have room for him at the anvils. If Joe kicked an almost-grown boy out to make room for Beverly, the boy would have to go to the ground, which meant he would be sent to work in the fields. Fieldwork was hard, hard, and once you started there, you never did anything else. Joe hoped he could persuade Master Jefferson to let some of the current nail boys continue working on the mountaintop, so he had told Beverly to be patient and wait his turn.

A year, Beverly thought now. One year until Master Jefferson would be home to stay. It felt like forever. He would be patient, because he had no choice.

"I know you need a job," Mama was saying. "More than that, you need a trade. A way to earn a respectable living, once you're free and on your own. It's time we started thinking about it. What do you like to do? I never saw you for a blacksmith."

Beverly blinked. He'd never thought about what he wanted to do. He'd never thought beyond being a nail boy. Mama was right—he didn't really want to be a blacksmith.

"What do you like?" Mama persisted. "What feels good under your hands? Horses? Plants? Wood?"

Beverly thought she meant firewood, and shook his head. "And not dishes either," he said.

Mama sighed. "Who do you like working with, besides Joe Fossett?"

Beverly thought. He liked helping Burwell when Burwell was in a good mood, but not when Burwell was cranky. He liked Wormley—but he didn't like weeding the garden, and plants didn't make him happy.

"Uncle John," Beverly said. Uncle John always seemed patient and calm. His hands were wide and strong. Beverly loved to watch John carve curves and angles into golden pieces of wood. He loved smooth boards, and the smell of fresh shavings.

Mama nodded. "When Master Jefferson comes this summer, I'll speak to him," she said. "For now go help Uncle Peter. And don't you give me that look."

Little baby Eston learned to smile before Master Jefferson's summer visit. He smiled *at* Master Jefferson—Mama snuck them all into Master Jefferson's room early one morning, so they could help her show Master Jefferson the baby—and Master Jefferson laughed. Beverly felt a bolt of jealousy. It was silly to be jealous of his baby brother, but he felt jealous all the same.

But then Master Jefferson turned to Beverly. "So," he said, "I hear it's time we put you to work. Time you learned a trade, your mama says."

Beverly stood tall. "Yes, sir," he said.

"She tells me you have an aptitude for woodworking," Master Jefferson said.

Beverly didn't know what *aptitude* meant, but it sounded good. "Yes, sir," he said.

Master Jefferson smiled. His smile looked so much like baby Eston's that Beverly smiled back without even thinking.

"Good," Master Jefferson said. "Carpentry's a fine craft, a respectable occupation for any man. We'll put you with John, shall we? He'll be working on his own now, head carpenter. Dismore's going back to Ireland."

Beverly felt a small thrill. His father wanted him to have a respectable occupation. His father cared. "I'll work hard," he promised. He wanted to add, *I'll make you proud,* but, before he could, Mama had taken his arm, and hustled them all away.

At first being a carpenter's apprentice felt exactly like being an errand boy. All he did was sweep wood shavings and fetch and carry for Uncle John. It was true that working with Uncle John had a steady pleasantness to it. Unlike Uncle Peter, Uncle John never lost his temper and snapped angry words. He whistled sometimes, especially when he was particularly pleased with his work, but even on days he didn't whistle he seemed content. Every morning, his eyes lit up a little bit when Beverly came into the shop, and Beverly started to treasure that look, that small glow of happiness. It was nice to know Uncle John liked having him there.

Still, he wanted to do useful work, cutting and sawing and fitting together. When he said so, Uncle John smiled. "Sweeping up the shavings is about as useful as it gets," he said. "Awful mess, those shavings make. They blow into all the carpets and bedrooms, Miss Martha like to has a fit."

They were working on something called cornices, which were a kind of fancy wood trim around the top of the walls, doorways, and windows. Master Jefferson and Uncle John together had designed them.

"I don't know why Miss Martha cares," Beverly said. "It's not her business. It's not her house—"

"I'm mighty glad she comes here," Uncle John said with a soft smile.

Beverly looked at him in wonderment. Who on earth was glad to see Miss Martha? All her fuss—then Beverly understood. Uncle John's wife, Aunt Priscilla, belonged to Miss Martha. She took care of all Miss Martha's children. When Miss Martha was gone from Monticello, Aunt Priscilla was gone too. "Well, sure," Beverly said. "I didn't mean—"

"Oh, I know you didn't," Uncle John said. "But it's like they say, no great loss without some gain. I do the gaining, when Miss Martha's here."

Miss Edith and Joe Fossett's son, James, had grown to be a great big boy, as much of a handful as Maddy. Maddy and James spent the whole month of July digging in dirt piles and terrorizing chickens. Maddy sobbed when James went back to Washington. Harriet wasn't very happy, either. It had become her job to take care of Maddy whenever Mama was busy, which, with the new baby, was much of the time, and Maddy was easier to manage when he had James.

One day in early fall Beverly was sweeping the parlor floor for the third time that day when Maddy bolted into the room. "Bev'ly!" he shouted. "Bev'ly!"

"Maddy!" Beverly grabbed him. Maddy's little feet were still tender, and Beverly didn't want him catching a splinter. "What are you doing here? Where's Harriet?"

"No Here-yet," Maddy said. He couldn't say *Harriet*.

"No here yet?" Beverly teased him. "Harriet's not here?"

Maddy laughed, even though he didn't really understand. Beverly swung him around, and Maddy laughed again.

"More!" he shouted. "More, Bev'ly! Swing me again!"

Beverly swung him around and around. When he stopped the walls kept going. He sat down, Maddy on his lap, laughing and breathing hard.

"Maddy, come here." Harriet marched into the room looking cross. "Mama wants you. Naptime." Now that Miss Martha and her children were gone, Harriet had dropped her ladylike ways and reverted to looking wild, her hair escaping in curling locks out of her two braids, her bare feet and arms smudged with dirt.

"No," Maddy said.

"Yes." Harriet held out her arms.

"No, no, NO!" Maddy shouted. He threw himself against Beverly.

"Yes!" said Harriet. "I told you, Mama said!"

"Nooo!" Maddy wailed, clinging to Beverly.

"Here, now." Uncle John set down his chisel and came up behind them. "Come to Uncle John, Maddy boy."

Maddy let go of Beverly's shirt and launched himself at Uncle John. He buried his head against Uncle John's chest. "No nap," he said.

"No, no," Uncle John said, soothing. "I'll just take you on home now, to your mama, and maybe we'll lay down for a spell. Give Beverly a kiss." Maddy kissed Beverly wet on the mouth. Harriet laughed. "Come with me, Miss Harriet," Uncle John said. "Beverly, you can finish that floor. Come, Maddy, my sweet boy." Uncle John's voice dropped to a whisper. "Come, we'll walk, we'll lay down." He went out with Maddy cradled in his arms.

Uncle John and Aunt Priscilla didn't have any children of their own. It was, Mama said, the world's greatest shame.

Beverly looked at Harriet. "Go on," he said. "Go with them. Uncle John said."

Harriet tossed her braids. "I'm tired of watching Maddy," she said. "He's being awful today. He will not behave."

"I'll watch him," Beverly said. "You can stay here and do my work instead. It's harder than playing with Maddy, that's for sure."

She stuck her tongue out at him. "Oh, hard work," she said.

"I'll tell Mama you said sweeping the floor was hard."

"It is," Beverly said. "You try it and see."

"It is not. You want to switch places? I will."

"No. Watching babies is girl's work. Carpentry is for men."

"See!" she said. "You know my job's harder. That's why you won't switch!"

"Is not!"

"Is so!"

Harriet wouldn't let up. By the time Uncle John returned they were shouting at each other nose to nose. Beverly had never hit Harriet—Mama would skin him alive—but he'd never come closer.

"Children!" Uncle John shouted, in a voice of outrage.

Beverly jumped. So did Harriet. They hadn't known Uncle John could sound like that.

Uncle John marched over and grabbed them both by the shoulders. "You must never, ever, yell at each other like that," he said. "You are *family*. Don't you know what that means?"

"Yeah," muttered Harriet. "Means I'm stuck with him."

Uncle John shook her shoulder. "Means you are *privileged* to have each other," he said. "Means you are *lucky,* to live together on this farm. Means you love and take care of each other *always*."

Beverly didn't know what had gotten into Uncle John. "Some privilege," he said.

Uncle John acted like he didn't hear. "Right now you have each other," he continued. "You don't know how long that's going to last. You've got to love each other all you can. You never know what might happen."

"What's going to happen?" Beverly asked. "Nothing's going to happen."

"I wish something would happen," Harriet said. "To *him*."

Uncle John grew sterner still. "You, Harriet, don't you ever wish evil on anybody else. And Beverly, what? You think you're God? You know when folks'll live and when they'll die? Your mama's buried three babies, don't you forget that."

Of course Beverly hadn't forgotten that, but it wasn't what he meant. And Harriet wasn't a baby.

"And you're enslaved," Uncle John said. "You're special, both of you, and your brothers too, on account of who your daddy is. If you don't know that yet, you will soon. I don't reckon anybody's going to sell you. But you're still born into slavery, so you never know. Do you hear me? You never know. Anything could happen—Master Jefferson could die all of a sudden. You'd belong to Miss Martha then, and heaven knows what she would do.

"You think I like having my wife working at Miss Martha's beck and call? You think I don't wish we had a home of our own? But I can't do anything about that. All I can do is let my wife know how much I love her, every minute that I'm with her. All I can do is never let a drop of bitterness or anger toward her touch my heart. Wherever my wife goes, she knows I love her. She carries my love as a sure thing.

"You can't sell love. You can't steal it. It can't run away. You two, you'd better learn this. I don't want to hear anything between you except love. Not *ever*. You got that?"

Beverly got that he'd never heard Uncle John say so many words at one time in his life.

"I'm waiting," Uncle John said. He gave their shoulders another hard shake.

"Yes, sir," Beverly said. "We got it."

"Yes, sir," echoed Harriet.

"Kiss and make up, and then go get something to eat. Peter's just pulled bread out of the oven."

Beverly kissed Harriet because he had to, but he didn't like it. He stalked out of the room. He hated being yelled at.

"Beverly? Beverly, wait!"

It was Harriet. Beverly stopped in his tracks, heaved his shoulders, and sighed. He didn't turn around. But when she slipped her hand into his, he grabbed it, and held it all the way to the kitchen.

Later Mama said it was hogwash. They had nothing to fear. Master Jefferson wouldn't die, and if he did, Mama would handle Miss Martha. "Which is not to say you shouldn't be loving toward each other," Mama said. "Uncle John was right about that."

Beverly said, "I'd like to see you handle Miss Martha."

He expected Mama to laugh, but she didn't. She was quiet a moment before she replied. "I'll only do it if I have to," she said. "She'd never forgive me. But if I have to, to save you children, I will."

Days went by one after another until the year had passed. Eston could walk, Maddy was old enough to run simple errands, and finally, finally Papa was coming home to stay.

Chapter Eleven
Home to Stay

Beverly woke up happy. The summer air smelled like happiness. At breakfast the kitchen talk sounded like happiness. Uncle Peter passed out muffins by way of celebration.

Master Jefferson was coming home. Miss Edith was coming home. James and baby Maria were coming home. Fanny Hern was coming home. All of them were coming home to stay.

After breakfast Beverly didn't know what to do. He and Uncle John had tidied the woodshop the day before, and cleaned away all traces of their work in the great house. "He'll have new projects for us," Uncle John said, "but the first day or two will likely be a mess."

Uncle John didn't care whether Beverly stayed in the shop, so Beverly went out. He walked partway down the mountain road, listening for the sounds of Davy's wagon and Master

Jefferson's carriage. They were all coming home together, Master Jefferson's letter had said.

The overseers were bringing the field hands up the road to the mountaintop. The hands had talked the overseers into giving them the day off work, on account of them loving Master Jefferson so. The overseers, pleased by the slaves' sweet affection, had loaded a wagon with barrels of cider and some good hams for the celebration. "Going to be a party on the mountaintop!" one of the workers shouted to Beverly as they went by. Beverly grinned. The field hands were nobody's fools.

He couldn't see far down the curving road with its canopy of green-leafed trees. After a while he sat in the shade, waiting, listening. They should arrive by dinnertime, unless they were delayed.

He stretched out on the green grass, his stomach buzzing like the bees in the mulberry tree above him. *Papa.* He tried not to think that word. He understood now that it might cause trouble. But still, in his heart—*Papa.* Beverly wished he'd brought his violin.

At last he heard the sound of hooves, the rumbling of a heavy wagon. He hesitated for a moment—did he go down, or up?—before running up the mountaintop as hard and fast as he could. "They're coming!" he yelled. "They're here!"

Davy Hern pulled up first. Fanny sat next to him, her arm tucked through his. Miss Edith sat on his other side, her bright red scarf wrapped around her head, her eyes shining.

She cradled Maria in one arm, and held tight to a wriggling James with the other.

Joe Fossett shouted to Miss Edith. Everyone surged forward in a rush.

Someone grabbed Beverly's leg, nearly knocking him down. It was Maddy, his eyes wide and scared. "It's all right," Beverly told him. "It's happy noise."

Maddy shook his head. Beverly hoisted him up so he could see the wagon. Maddy's face changed in an instant; he gave a shout of joy. "James!" he yelled. "*James!*"

"Maddy!" cried James. He vaulted over the edge of the wagon and ran smack into Maddy, who was running toward him. Both of them fell down. Beverly laughed and went to help them up.

"I got a new ball to play with," Maddy said to James, ignoring Beverly completely.

"I got a new house," James said. "Mama said. I gotta see my new house."

Maddy said, "It's next to *mine!*"

They grabbed hands and disappeared around the corner of the great house. Beverly looked to see if Miss Edith or Mama minded. Miss Edith had her arms around Joe Fossett's neck, and was kissing him while Joe twirled her in the air, but Beverly couldn't find Mama anywhere. Master Jefferson's carriage arrived, and now more people were jumping and shouting and carrying on. They surrounded the carriage and clapped their hands.

Beverly searched the crowd. Mama wasn't among the mountaintop folks around Davy's wagon, and she wasn't in the crowd of field workers around the carriage. Finally Beverly saw her standing on the side of the great house porch, half hidden by one of the pillars. She looked calmly expectant, like she was waiting for something but wasn't in a hurry.

People opened the carriage door and helped Master Jefferson down. He laughed and clasped their hands and spoke to them. A bunch of townspeople had ridden up from Charlottesville, and Master Jefferson shook their hands too, and shook hands with the overseers. After a moment, though, he lifted his head and looked around with a deep breath, like he was drinking in the scenery. His head stopped. Beverly looked to see what he saw.

Master Jefferson had found Mama. Mama looked at him. She didn't smile, but her chin went up and her eyes softened. Master Jefferson held her gaze for a moment, then looked away. Then smiled.

Joy bubbled up inside Beverly like a gurgling mountain stream. Papa was home forever. Beverly never felt so glad.

Chapter Twelve
The End of Tranquility

Beverly had known the first few days of Master Jefferson's homecoming would be busy, but he hadn't expected chaos. Master Jefferson had brought home twice the usual amount of luggage, and all of it had to be unpacked and sorted and put away. Before Uncle John and Beverly were halfway through heaving crates into the great house, another freight wagon stacked with boxes pulled up to the door. A dark-haired white man hopped down from the seat beside the driver. "Please, where is Miss Edith?" he said, with a small bow to Uncle John. "I am Monsieur Julien."

Uncle John acted as though white men bowed to him all the time. He nodded, slowly and politely, and said, "Sir. Come this way."

Beverly trailed them to the new kitchen. It was twice the size of the old one, but it was still empty except for the long table Uncle Peter had brought in from the old kitchen, and a few benches and shelves. Miss Edith and Miss Fanny turned toward the door when Uncle John walked in. They saw the white man, and their faces lit up.

"Monsieur!" cried Miss Edith. She went to him and held out her hands. Beverly watched, horror-struck, as the white man kissed Miss Edith, first on one cheek, then on the other. What would Joe Fossett say?

Now the man was kissing Miss Fanny's cheeks. Beverly gulped. He'd never seen such a thing. The three of them started talking so fast Beverly got lost right after "How was your journey?" Uncle John looked as confused as Beverly felt.

Finally Miss Edith seemed to notice them. "That whole wagon needs to be unpacked," she said. "I want all the crates brought in here. As soon as you've done that, I'll need you to get Joe, to measure for grates for the stew stoves. John, who's the best man for mortar? And do we have bricks on hand, or do we need to have them made?"

Uncle John blinked. "We'll get the wagon," he said. "I'll check on the bricks. How many you need?"

Miss Edith said something to the white man, so quick and incomprehensible Beverly thought it might be a foreign language, like Mama's French. She listened to the man's answer, then turned back to Uncle John. "Two walls, say twelve foot long by three foot high, and some dividing walls—say another twelve foot's worth, maybe a little more. How many bricks is that?"

"I'll get back to you." Uncle John pulled Beverly outside with him. He shook his head. "Phew."

"She's different," Beverly said. When Miss Edith came home on vacation she didn't boss folks around.

"Woman's learned to be a chef," Uncle John said. "Good Lord above."

"We gonna tell Joe and Davy about the kissing?"

"Nah," Uncle John said. "I think that's some kind of French thing."

Beverly looked back over his shoulder. "That man's French?" He wondered if the man would know Mama.

"Sure," said Uncle John. "That 'Monsieur,' that's French for *mister*."

Monsieur Julien had trained Miss Edith for eight years in Washington. The man driving the wagon turned out to be his assistant, and the wagon was packed with all the fancy pots and equipment Miss Edith would need now that she was head French chef for Monticello.

Uncle Peter was going to be the brewer. He would make beer and cider, and take care of the wine Master Jefferson imported from France. He said he didn't mind the change. "That fancy cooking, it's not for me," he said. "Never wanted to work in a kitchen like that."

French cooks didn't settle for regular fireplace cooking. They used something called a stew stove, which was like a long row of small fireplaces built out in the open, against the wall beneath the windows. The stew stove was why Miss Edith needed bricks.

"How's this going to work?" Beverly muttered as he mixed

mortar for Uncle John. "Kitchen'll be full of smoke."

Fanny Hern overheard him. "It won't if it's properly ventilated," she said.

"Oh, *ventilated*." Uncle John waggled his eyebrows at the fancy word. Beverly laughed.

French cooks had spits that both rotated and moved up and down, powered by weights like giant clockworks. They cooked in copper pots, not cast iron. They used so much wine, spices, and other expensive ingredients that Miss Edith tried to make Burwell give her a set of keys to the locked storerooms.

"No, ma'am," Burwell said. "I've got to keep close inventory on that stuff. A couple of hams walk away from the smokehouse, that's one thing. A keg of French brandy walks away, I'll have some fast explaining to do."

"I'll write down whatever I take out," Miss Edith said. "You can trust me."

Beverly was surprised Miss Edith had learned to write, but Burwell didn't seem to be. "I know I can trust you," Burwell said, "but I can't trust everybody, and I don't want trouble."

Beverly didn't want trouble either. The biggest source of trouble right then, he thought, was Monsieur Julien. Beverly'd never met anyone like him at all.

Monsieur Julien directed the layout of the kitchen, the height of the spits, the number and sizes of the stew stoves. He advised Miss Edith on menus and on stocking the pantries. But he also told stories. He made jokes. He listened to the stories Miss Edith told him. He laughed with her. If she said something sad, he sympathized.

Beverly had never known a white man like that.

He tried to talk about it to Mama. "It's like they're *friends,*" he said.

Mama looked at him sharp. "I suppose that's possible," she said at last.

"You and Papa—" Beverly said.

"That's different." Mama waved her hand. She didn't seem to notice that Beverly had said *Papa.* "That's a secret, it's different. And a man and woman thing, that happens all the time."

"I didn't mean that," Beverly said.

"No, no," Mama said. "I know what you mean. I understand the difference." She thought for a moment. "I suppose it's because he's French. France never allowed slavery. In France, people with dark skin aren't automatically seen as inferior to people with light skin."

Beverly thought about that. "What did that feel like?" he asked. "When you were there."

"Different," Mama said. "Good. If I went to a shop, I got waited on right away, even if a white person came in on my heels. The other servants in our house there, besides my brother, who was the cook, were white, and we all got along, better than I expected. When I visited Miss Martha and Miss Maria at their school, their friends liked me. Really liked me;

I got to know some of them pretty well. I forget now, but I had friends who were white, in France."

Mama sighed. "You don't really realize how much color matters in this country, until you go someplace where it matters so much less," she said. "But France wasn't perfect either. I was a servant, part of the servant class, and that meant I was looked down on by anybody who thought they ranked higher. Class matters in France, much more than it does here. If you're born white and poor here, you can work hard and die rich and well-respected. There you can be any color, but if you start out lower class you'll never be able to rise. You couldn't end up a gentleman."

Beverly thought about this. "What would happen to Miss Edith, if she went to France?"

Mama sighed. "Chefs are servants, yes, but they're well-respected upper servants," she said. "With her training, Miss Edith could work in a fancy establishment for very good pay."

Beverly scowled. "And here she isn't paid at all."

"No," Mama said. "She isn't paid, she can't ever leave, and she has to do whatever she's told. If she doesn't, she could be out in the fields tomorrow."

"If she ran away—" Beverly said. He imagined Miss Edith on the deck of a ship sailing for France. Only she'd have to take James and Maria with her—and Joe Fossett—it would be so hard to do, Beverly could see.

"She would endanger her children," Mama said.

Beverly remembered that when Joe Fossett ran away,

Mama had smiled to think of him and Miss Edith fleeing to freedom. Beverly hadn't understood it then, but now he did, at least a little.

Beverly longed to see Master Jefferson, but a surprisingly steady stream of visitors kept Master Jefferson fully occupied. Beverly knew not to expect a smile or a word from him when white strangers filled the dining room and parlor and slept in all the rooms upstairs. No matter, Beverly thought. It would calm down soon.

Meanwhile, one day, when he was helping with the stew stove, Miss Edith and Miss Fanny left the kitchen, and Beverly found himself alone with Monsieur Julien.

Monsieur Julien was mincing roast chicken for a dish for the great house. He smiled at Beverly and handed him a drumstick.

"Thank you," Beverly said, surprised. It wasn't often he ate chicken, let alone a whole leg of it. He took a bite. Before he lost his nerve he said, through his mouthful, "My mama's been to France."

Monsieur Julien nodded. "I thought you looked like one of Miss Sally's children."

"Yes, sir. I've got a sister, and two brothers."

"I spoke with your mother yesterday," Monsieur Julien said. "In French. She still speaks French well despite all the years."

Beverly said, "She and Miss Martha use it when they don't want us to understand them." He studied Monsieur Julien, wondering how much he could trust him. "If my mama went back to France—" Beverly stopped. He wasn't sure exactly what he wanted to say.

Monsieur Julien chopped thoughtfully. "The revolution seems to be over," he said after a while. "I think it would be safe now. Why? Do you want to go? Is that what you're thinking? I asked your mother whether she had considered it."

Beverly shook his head. Not without Papa, he thought.

"She said she believes you children will have better lives in this country," Monsieur Julien said. "I can't say I disagree. This is an astonishing place. A person can become anything."

"White," Beverly said, without thinking.

Monsieur Julien inclined his head. "Certainly," he said. "To have any social standing here, you must appear white. Fortunately, for you and your sister, I think it will not be hard. The baby, perhaps. And the other little boy—his skin may lighten over time."

Beverly blinked. He wondered how Monsieur Julien knew about Eston and Maddy. He wondered what he meant by saying that Maddy's skin might lighten. But Miss Edith swept into the room. Beverly hurried back to his bricks, palming the chicken leg so Miss Edith wouldn't see it. She didn't. "*Ça va?*" she asked Monsieur Julien.

"*Ça va bien,*" he replied.

It must be French, thought Beverly. He felt a wave of sadness, for Mama and Miss Edith, for what they might have had if they were free.

He waited and waited for the fuss to die down. The kitchen was finished. Monsieur Julien went away. Mama moved them into their new room, just one door down from the room beside the kitchen that belonged to Miss Edith and Joe. The workmen who had built the dependencies began to tear the old cabins down.

But at the great house the stream of visitors continued unabated. It was temporary, Beverly felt sure. People wanted to welcome Master Jefferson home. As soon as they had done that, they'd go away, and leave the mountaintop in peace.

Miss Martha's absence felt like sunshine, something Beverly could soak in and enjoy. Without the excuse of Christmas or of being hostess for the president, she'd returned to her husband Mr. Randolph's farm, three miles away. Beverly loved knowing he could walk into the great house anytime without seeing her tight-mouthed glare, or hearing her snap, "You! Boy!"

He and John resumed their finishing work in the great house. Beverly listened for Master Jefferson's voice in the hall, for his step and laugh. Every morning one of the stable boys brought Master Jefferson's horse to the back porch. Master Jefferson would smile at Beverly as he crossed through the parlor on his way out to ride. Beverly tried to always be ready to return that smile.

The horse was waiting, the boy holding it, one day not even a month after Master Jefferson's return. From the front of the house came horses' hoof beats, the rattle of a wagon, and a bustle of noise. Angry steps thumped up the porch stairs, followed by shouts and a pattering of lighter footsteps. Someone knocked once against the doorframe, hard. Burwell hurried into the hall, but before he could reach the door it swept open, and in came Miss Martha, her face flushed, her breath coming in spurts.

"I can't stand it!" she cried. "I won't be treated like—and besides, I know my duty! I know where I'm needed!"

Burwell stared, then carefully made his face look bland. Master Jefferson came out to the hall. He wore the bemused look that usually meant he'd been concentrating on something he was writing. He smiled vaguely at Miss Martha.

The front door had swung shut, but it opened again, and Mister Jeff, the eldest grandson, came through it. He looked at Master Jefferson and bowed uncertainly, his cheeks flushed like his mother's. Behind him trooped his brothers and sisters, baby Ben in Beverly's aunt Priscilla's arms.

"Father," Miss Martha said dramatically, "I've come home!"

Beverly gaped. Surely she didn't mean it? Surely she had to stay with her husband? Behind him, Uncle John made a soft warning noise, and nudged him.

Beverly shut his mouth. He dropped his eyes to the hammer in his hands. He bent forward, as though concentrating on his work. But he kept his ears open, as wide open as ever he could.

"You need me, Father!" Miss Martha said. "I can't bear to

think of you rattling in this enormous house alone! We will be your comfort. I'll manage everything. You can leave the household to me." She took a deep breath. "Mr. Randolph may fend for himself!"

They'd managed just fine without her, Beverly thought. Dinner got served, the house cleaned, everything ran fine without her. Please say no, he begged Master Jefferson in his head. Please tell her she can visit, but she can't stay.

Please don't let her ruin everything.

Beverly didn't dare look up. His emotions would show too plainly on his face. If Miss Martha noticed, she would resent him forever, more than she already did.

Please don't let her stay.

"My dear," Master Jefferson said, and from the first soft syllable Beverly's hopes fell to ashes, "this is always your home. You and the children are most welcome. You may stay here forever if you prefer."

Beverly laid his head against his hands. He was too old, he knew, to cry.

Chapter Thirteen

Nothing

Beverly had always known that Miss Martha disliked him. When she moved back to Monticello her dislike seemed to harden. Her eyes glittered whenever she saw Beverly. She told Uncle John she didn't want Beverly working in the great house. She wanted Beverly to stay in the shop.

"It's because you look like him," Mama said. It was a month after Miss Martha had moved back in. "She worries one of these visitors will guess the truth. She thinks her father's reputation will be ruined."

"He's my father too," Beverly said.

Mama sighed. "You can't keep saying that," she said. "Especially now."

"Why especially now?" Beverly felt furious. "Are *you* worried about his reputation? About what strangers will think?"

"I'm worried about *your* reputation," Mama said. "Your future. The last thing on this earth I want is for the world to know that you are his son. That you, Harriet, Maddy, and Eston belong to him as well as to me."

Beverly scowled. So now Mama was ashamed? He kicked the hearth stool over.

Mama grabbed his arm. "Stop that. Listen. It's already been in newspapers once, years ago, about me and your father, but he lived it down and it's mostly been forgotten. Somebody decides to publish the truth about you and your siblings, and guess what? You'd be famous. Thomas Jefferson's half-white son." Mama's eyes blazed. "A famous *slave*, Beverly. You'd never get away from it. You'd never really be free."

"If he freed me, I'd be free," Beverly said. "He hands me free papers, no newspaper could change it."

"You'd be a freed former slave," Mama said. "A black person. You'd never be able to live as a white person. Your children would grow up black, not white. They'd be in danger their whole lives. Free black people can *disappear* in this country. They get kidnapped, Beverly, they end up down South, enslaved, working in the cotton fields and dying in the heat. That will not happen to my children, nor my grandchildren, nor their children after that."

Beverly waved his hands. "But I don't want to be a white person," he said. "I don't like white people! Mama. You're black. I want to be like you."

Mama said, "You are like me. We're both mixes, black and white. I'm not ashamed of either side, and I hope I'm raising you not to be either. But if you pass for white you'll be safer, and if you're known to be my son by Thomas Jefferson you will never be allowed to pass."

Beverly said, "I don't want to pass. I want my family." Mama didn't say anything. Beverly said, "It's not just Miss Martha. He's acting different too, now that she's here. He used to act like he cared about me."

Mama put her arms around him. She held him tight even when he tried to pull away. "He still cares about you. I promise. He loves you, and me, and Harriet, and Maddy, and Eston. He can't show it, but he does.

"Listen," she said. "People are never all good or all bad. I wish your father would find a way to be closer to you, but he won't, especially not if things keep going the way they are now. He wants you to have a good life, and he'll help you on your way, but he will never treat you like his son. Don't expect it."

She seemed to be waiting for Beverly to reply. "Yes, Mama," he finally said.

"It really is better this way," Mama said. "It doesn't seem like it now, but it is."

Beverly didn't believe it. "At least none of those grandchildren play the violin," he said. If Master Jefferson ever gave Mister Jeff lessons on the Italian violin, Beverly thought, he would chuck his kit violin into the river.

His music was the one thing Master Jefferson sometimes did notice. Beverly still took weekly lessons from Jesse Scott. As the year passed Master Jefferson dropped by Jesse's house every month or two, always while Beverly was there. Master Jefferson always pretended to be surprised to see Beverly, but he always stayed until the lesson was done. Once he even put his hand on Beverly's shoulder.

Meanwhile he spent hours gardening with Miss Anne. He commissioned a portrait of Mister Jeff. He taught Miss Virginia to ride. He timed the younger children every night when they ran races on the lawn. He hugged them and kissed them and carried them in his arms.

Beverly quit looking to find Master Jefferson alone. He quit expecting what he couldn't have. He tried to quit hoping, even though that was difficult.

It wasn't any easier for Harriet. One day she came back from the great house with an especially bitter look in her eyes. She scowled at Beverly. "At least you have that violin."

Beverly felt a twist to his stomach. "What happened?" he asked.

"Nothing," Harriet said. "Nothing, nothing. Same as always. There is *nothing* in that house for me."

Chapter Fourteen

Maddy Learns

Beverly heard a knock on the front door. He looked up, across the parlor he was standing in through the big entrance hall and the glass panes of the door. Yet another stranger was waiting on the porch.

Beverly had his hands full of the broken pieces of glass he was prying out of a window frame. James Madison—Miss Martha's boy, the one that stole Maddy's name—had thrown a ball through the window the night before. Beverly could hear Miss Martha reading to some of her children in the room to the left of the front hall that she used as a classroom. He waited for her to answer the door.

The man knocked again, harder. Beverly sighed. Where was Burwell, anyhow?

It was three years since Master Jefferson had left Washington for good. There had never once been a period of tranquility. White people, complete strangers most of them, had turned the road up the mountain into a kind of highway. No matter what, Master Jefferson asked them to dinner and to stay.

Miss Martha complained that some of them didn't even care about meeting the former president. They just wanted a free meal and a place to sleep on the road. Beverly thought she was right, though he hated to agree with Miss Martha on anything.

Another knock. Beverly sighed. He set the pieces of glass on the floor.

A small, slim figure darted down the hallway toward the door. Maddy. Beverly smiled. Maddy was seven now. He haunted the great house the way Beverly had when he was younger. Only Maddy wasn't looking for Master Jefferson. Maddy was looking for Miss Ellen, Miss Martha's second-oldest girl.

Miss Ellen was teaching Maddy to read.

"Maddy," Beverly called, "let me get that."

It was too late. Maddy had already let the stranger in. It was a white man, of course—a black man would never come to the front door. He was neatly dressed in old-fashioned breeches and a well-made coat. As he stepped inside, the man looked around in amazement—visitors were always amazed by the display in the front hall—and then he looked down at Maddy and smiled.

"Good morning, son," he said. "What's your name?"

Maddy rubbed one bare foot over the other. He looked at the ground. "James Madison," he said.

"Sir," Beverly cut in, "may I help you?"

The man smiled at Beverly. "I'm speaking to this young fellow. Young James Madison here." The man held out his hand. "How do you do, James Madison?"

Beverly knew the man was making a bad mistake, and when he found out he'd made it, he would not be happy. "Maddy," he said, "run along."

Maddy couldn't run along. The white man had picked up Maddy's hand and was showing him how to shake hands properly. Maddy already knew how to shake hands. He also already knew better than to shake hands with a white man.

"Like this, James Madison," the man said. "You want to make your grandpa proud."

Beverly took hold of Maddy's shoulder and pulled him backward. "Sir," he said, flashing the man a bright smile, "can we get you something cold to drink?"

They were almost away, he and Maddy, but at exactly the wrong moment Miss Martha came out to the hall. Her children—the school-age ones, Misses Ellen, Cornelia, Virginia, and Mary, as well as Master James Madison—came out with her.

"Are you here to see my father?" Miss Martha inquired.

The stranger looked her. He looked at the children. He looked at the four girls, with their pretty dresses and beribboned hair. He looked at James Madison Randolph's well-cut breeches, shirt, and waistcoat, and at the loose pants and coarse shirts Beverly and Maddy wore.

He understood. Of course he understood.

The man turned beet red. He waved his hand in the air, as though shaking off Maddy's touch. He bowed to Miss Martha, and he said, with a nervous, angry laugh, "I'll tell you what, I didn't know they grew darkies that white."

Miss Martha cut her eyes at Beverly. Beverly said, "Yes, ma'am," and hustled Maddy away.

"What happened?" Maddy asked. "He was nice at first."

"White people don't like to be fooled," said Beverly.

"I wasn't fooling him," Maddy said. "He asked my name, and I told him."

"Well, don't tell him. Better yet, don't answer the door."

They walked out of the house and down the path. Beverly kept hold of Maddy's hand. "Where we going?" Maddy asked.

"Down to the shop. We'll get Uncle John to fix the window."

"Doesn't that man need us to find Master Jefferson?"

"No," Beverly said. "That man needs us to go away." He shook Maddy's arm a bit. "What were you doing up there, anyway? Bringing a message from Mama?"

Maddy looked at the ground. "No."

"What, then."

Maddy whispered, "Waiting for Miss Ellen."

"Oh, Maddy."

"She told me to!"

Beverly sighed. "You've got to quit hanging around her, Maddy. Miss Martha doesn't like it."

"Miss Ellen likes it. Really she does. She likes teaching me. She wants to be a teacher, she says. That's what she wants to do, instead of getting married. And she likes me 'cause I'm smart and pay attention. I'm a model student, she says."

"Oh, Maddy," Beverly said. "You shouldn't mess with them. It makes trouble."

Maddy stuck out his chin. "Miss Ellen said everybody needs to know how to read. Every-single-body."

"If we needed to know how to read," Beverly said, "our father would have had us taught. And he hasn't, so we don't. You're putting your nose in where it doesn't belong."

"Nobody cares where my nose is," Maddy said.

"I do," Beverly said.

"I'm telling Mama," Maddy said.

"You do that," said Beverly.

Mama listened to the whole story. When Maddy finished, he waited for her to say Beverly was wrong. He knew Beverly was waiting for Mama to say Maddy was wrong, and that made him clench his fists. Beverly thought he knew everything.

Maddy himself knew plenty. For starters, he could name in order all Miss Martha's children: Anne, Jeff, Ellen, Cornelia, Virginia, Mary, James Madison, Ben Franklin, and Meriwether Lewis. Miss Anne didn't live at Monticello anymore; she had married a drunkard who beat her. That worried everyone, even Mama, but nobody would talk about it. Mister Jeff was grown up too, twenty years old. He ran the Monticello farms. Ben was Eston's age, and little Lewis—that was what they called him—was only a baby.

The middle girls could be snippy, like their mother, and Maddy steered clear of them. Beverly claimed Miss Ellen was the same, but Maddy knew better. Miss Ellen was like Master Jefferson in the way she loved to read and write and learn.

Beverly claimed he couldn't tell the middle girls apart. He said all white people looked alike. Harriet snapped at him when he said that, and said he'd better adjust his attitude before he grew up, and also, was he blind?

Sometimes Beverly and Harriet spoke in riddles. Maddy hated it when he couldn't understand them. That was another thing that made him clench his fists.

He understood everything important. He understood that Master Jefferson was their father. He understood that they would be free and white someday, but that for now they were black and slaves, and that until the magic day of freedom came, they were going to have to keep their heads down. Mama said so. Miss Martha was mistress of Monticello, and she did not want to see any part of the truth about Maddy's family, and it was their business, Maddy's and Harriet's and Beverly's and even little Eston's, to keep their heads down and out of Miss Martha's way.

"But Miss Ellen doesn't mind teaching me," Maddy said. "She likes it."

"Huh," Harriet said. "She just likes being able to boss somebody, for a change."

"She can boss me," Maddy said, "so long as she teaches me to read."

Maddy already knew the alphabet, all the letters from A to Z. Miss Ellen had started to show him how they made little words, two-letter words from the beginning of the primer, *ba, be, bi, bo, bu, by*. Maddy wished he had a primer, or any sort of book at all. The great house was full of books, but Maddy wasn't allowed to touch them. Nobody on Mulberry Row owned a single one. He'd asked all around. Joe Fossett wrote accounts sometimes, and so did Miss Edith, but the accounts were just lists of words and numbers, not really anything Maddy could sit and read.

James, who was Maddy's best friend, told him he was a fool for asking. "Who ever heard of a book on Mulberry Row?"

"Could happen," Maddy argued. "Somebody might have one shut up in a box somewhere."

"If somebody's hiding a book," James said, "that somebody's going to keep it hidden, not take it out and loan it to you."

There were words in the great house hall. The hall was hung with all sorts of things—a buffalo head, Indian arrows, a beaded shirt made out of leather, paintings and statues of famous men. The words in the hall were written on a piece of paper in a frame, under glass, hung on the right-hand wall. Miss Ellen said they were called the Declaration of Independence, and Master Jefferson—she called him Grandpa—wrote them. They were powerful words that somehow separated America from England, back before even Mama was born. But Maddy couldn't so much as make out the letters to the words of the Declaration of Independence. Miss Ellen said that was because they were written in script, like handwriting, and first you had to learn to read in print, like books. Maddy had to take it one step at a time.

"After I learn to read," Maddy said now, to Mama and Beverly and Harriet, "I'm going to learn to *write*."

Beverly raised his eyebrows. "She's never going to teach you that. She knows better. At least, she ought to." A slave that could read might be useful. A slave that could write was dangerous. A slave that could write could make a pass. Maddy was old enough to understand that.

"She might," Maddy said.

Beverly said, "If Miss Martha catches her, she'll get the strap."

Harriet said, "It's against the law."

"It's *not*," said Maddy. "Miss Ellen wouldn't break the law."

Mama laid her hand on his head to settle him. "It's not," she agreed. "It's against the law for a free black person to teach a slave, or for anyone to be paid to teach a slave. Miss Ellen's white and you're not paying her, so she's not breaking the law."

"See," said Maddy.

"Which doesn't mean it wouldn't get her in trouble,"

Mama said. "Law or no law. Let me think." She sat down in her chair and folded her arms across her chest. Maddy waited. "Learning to read, well, of course that's a wonderful thing," said Mama. "It's a way out. Writing too. If I were better at either I'd have taught you myself." She looked at Beverly, and uncrossed her arms to run her fingers through her hair. "I should have thought about this beforehand—you all catch me off guard, growing up so fast. White people read, don't they?"

"Not the stupid ones," said Harriet.

"You're none of you stupid," Mama said. "There ought to be something we can do. I just don't want to rile up Miss Martha."

Harriet murmured, "Always the same problem."

Mama quelled her with a look. "Let me think on it," she said. "I'll let you know. Maddy—you stay clear of the great house, you hear me?"

Maddy knew it was important not to rile up Miss Martha. Miss Martha didn't like to even catch sight of Maddy or his brothers or sister. Beverly said she was nastier now than she had been when Master Jefferson was president. Back then, the only folks who came to visit were friends, like the Madisons, who were specially invited. Beverly said it had been quiet most of the time.

Maddy didn't remember it quiet on the mountaintop. Not ever. White folks came every day without invitation, without even knowing Master Jefferson at all. Some nights two dozen strangers slept in the great house beds, and all Miss Martha's children had to bunk down in the attic on the floor. Miss Martha ran around looking for pillows and blankets. Miss Edith cooked dinners for fifty. Each week in the stables Wormley fed the visitors' horses what should have been a month's worth of hay.

The visitors drank four or five or even ten bottles of French wine in a single dinner. They ate up the good hams and had second helpings of the fancy treats Miss Edith made, the ice cream and macaroni and vegetables turned out in a mold. They ate like it was Christmas dinner, ate for hours and scraped their plates clean.

After dinner the visitors wandered around the mountaintop. They promenaded on the lawn, inspected the gardens, and even walked up and down Mulberry Row. Unhappy-looking slaves made the visitors nervous, so Maddy always had to smile at them, whether he felt like smiling or not. Otherwise one of them might complain to Miss Martha.

Miss Martha's biggest fear was that a visitor would guess the truth about Maddy's family. Harriet looked like Mama, only lighter. Beverly had some resemblance to Master Jefferson, and told Maddy he did too, but Eston, who was four, was his spitting image. Eston looked like Master Jefferson in miniature. Mama tried especially hard to keep him out of the visitors' way.

Beverly told Maddy that Master Jefferson used to listen to

him play the violin. Sometimes he went to Beverly's lessons with Jesse Scott. Beverly said that Master Jefferson used to speak to him, and once even put his arm around him. Master Jefferson never did anything like that anymore.

Mama always waited until full dark to go to Master Jefferson's room. The mountaintop people ate dinner in the kitchen, at twilight when the work day was done. Then Maddy's family had time together before Mama went away. Mama sat by the window of their room and looked down Mulberry Row. Maddy sat on the floor beside her and put his head in her lap. Behind them, Beverly tuned his violin.

"Play that song," Eston said. Master Jefferson's favorite tune was called "Money Musk." Eston always called it "that song."

Beverly began to play. Harriet picked up her knitting needles. Eston lay on his back on the floor, humming along to the music. Maddy felt Mama's fingers run soft through his hair. This was his favorite time of day.

"You'd better learn to read," Mama said. "Maddy. Learn to read and to write, however you can. All of you had better learn. I'm thinking, when you go out in the world, it's something you'll be expected to know. For sure it's a good thing to know. Nobody can take what you learn away from you. You learn, Maddy, and this winter in the evenings you can teach Harriet and Beverly."

Maddy sighed happily.

Beverly kept playing. He finished "Money Musk" and went on to a quieter nighttime kind of tune.

"Harriet," Eston said, "tell us a story." Harriet told wonderful stories. Maddy's favorite was about Mama's trip across the ocean to France. Harriet could make it sound like she'd been there too.

"Not tonight," Harriet said. "I'm busy thinking."

"About what?" asked Eston.

"Books," said Harriet. "I bet they have stories in them. I bet some books are just stuffed full of stories."

Mama said, "I bet that's true."

Maddy thought of Harriet reading books full of stories. He thought of himself, reading the declaration on the wall. He felt wonderfully glad.

Chapter Fifteen

Miss Sally's Son

Master Jefferson shut the nailery down. Mama said it was because the United States was at war with England again. The war made the price of metal go up until there wasn't any profit in making nails. The nailery closed. The nail boys went to ground.

Mama promised Maddy he didn't need to worry about the war. The battles were all far away. They were safe at Monticello. He didn't need to worry about the nailery either; when he was old enough for work, in a few years, he'd join Beverly and Uncle John. Maddy's friend James was upset, though. He planned to be his father's apprentice, and he'd counted on starting as a nail boy. Joe Fossett said he didn't think it would matter. He thought Master Jefferson would want James to work in the blacksmith shop. James was smart and strong, and even though he had three sisters now, he was Joe Fossett's only son.

Every morning, Beverly went to work. Harriet minded

Eston. Mama took care of Master Jefferson's room and clothes. James's oldest sister, Maria, helped Miss Edith in the kitchen and watched the younger girls. James and Maddy did chores and ran some errands, but much of their time was their own.

They roamed the mountain. They knew the best streams, and the quiet pools full of fish. They brought home trout, and catfish, and wild blackberries. They picked the first ripe peaches in the orchard, and ate them in the woods where no one could see.

Harriet scowled when Maddy came home dirty and ragged. "Mama," she said, "he's running wild."

Maddy laughed. Harriet acted like a lady now, but Beverly said she used to run wild too.

"Leave him be," Mama said.

In late June the wheat ripened. The wheat harvest was the busiest time in all the year. Mulberry Row shut down, and all the grown-ups went to the fields except Mama and Miss Edith. Even Joe Fossett and Uncle John cut wheat. Beverly bound sheaves. He came home so exhausted every night that Maddy was glad to be too young to help.

On the third day of the harvest he and James decided to go fishing. They took a shortcut along the path between some of the wheat fields, near the road that went down the mountain. The sun shone hot. Maddy skipped and then let himself run down the slope, his arms churning. James pelted after him. Miss Edith had said she'd fry up anything they caught; if the fish were good enough for the great house table, they might even earn a penny or two. The thought of being paid money to go fishing made Maddy laugh out loud.

"What'll you do with your money?" James asked. They pulled up, panting, as the path leveled.

"Keep it in a jar," Maddy said. "Save it up. My mama's got some money saved."

"Us too," James said. "Daddy keeps it in a box under the bed." He grinned at Maddy, and whispered, "A hundred and fifty dollars."

Maddy's mouth fell open. He said, "You're making that up." He'd never heard of anyone having that much money. Master Jefferson, maybe, but nobody else.

"Yes, sir, that's the truth," James said. "'Cause my daddy gets paid sixteen cents out of every dollar from the Charlottesville work. And sometimes one of those visitors gives my mama a nickel 'cause her cooking is so good."

Maddy knew how good Miss Edith's cooking was, and how hard Joe Fossett worked. Still. "It takes a lot of sixteen cents to make a hundred and fifty dollars," he said.

"I know," James said. "Daddy says we're saving every penny for when the hard times come."

Maddy laughed. Mama never said anything about hard times. She'd have told them if there were going to be hard times. "What do you mean?" he asked.

"My daddy says, someday there's going to be hard times, even right here at Monticello."

"That's crazy." Maddy looked at the clear blue sky. In the hot air the wheat stalks gave off the smell of baking bread.

"Nope," James said. "That's thinking ahead. That's what the Fossetts do. We're ready for whatever comes."

"Ready to go fishing?"

"Ready for anything."

Maddy laughed again. "Race you to that tree," he said. Before he got the words out, James sprinted ahead.

"Hey!" Maddy yelled, chasing him.

"I was ready!" James shouted back.

"Boys!" It was a man's voice, hard and sharp like the crack of a whip. Maddy and James skidded to a halt. An overseer, high up on a horse, looked at them over the top of the hedge. "Boys!" he said. "You two on somebody's business?"

"Yes, sir," James said promptly, at the same time as Maddy said, "No, sir."

"Well, the one of you that isn't, get on over here. My water boy's claiming sick, and I need somebody to fetch water to the hands."

Maddy and James looked at each other. Maddy didn't want to, but he knew better than to say so. He dropped to the dirt and wriggled through the hedge. James made to follow, but the overseer stopped him. "You go on about that business you've got," he said. "One boy alone works harder than two."

Maddy stood up, brushing the dust off his pants. The overseer looked at him again. His eyes narrowed. "Wait," he said. "You—you're one of Sally's boys."

"Yes, sir," Maddy said.

"I don't want you. You, boy." He tilted his head at James. "You come instead." When James hesitated, the man said, "Now!"

"Why?" Maddy asked. He didn't mean to speak, but the words came out anyway. "I work as hard as he does."

The overseer didn't answer. He pointed the handle of his riding crop at James. James got down on his stomach and wriggled through the hedge. Maddy stood beside him, not sure what to do. "C'mon," the overseer said to James. He rode away. James followed. Maddy stood watching until the overseer looked back and shouted, "Go along home."

Maddy knew he could still go fishing, but he didn't feel right about fishing when James had to work. His stomach hurt. He trudged back up the mountain.

Mama wasn't around. Miss Edith was kneading bread dough in the hot kitchen, looking harassed. "Where's that rascal James?" she asked when Maddy came in. "I'm glad you gave up fishing. Here I am without Fanny or any of the girls, and half a dozen extra people just showed up for dinner. You'd think it wasn't harvest time."

"James is in the fields," Maddy said. "They told him to be a water boy."

Miss Edith frowned. "Weren't you with him?"

Maddy nodded. "I said I'd do it. The overseer didn't want me."

"Why not?"

Maddy swallowed. He didn't want to answer, but Miss Edith waited until he finally did. "He said—he guessed I was one of Miss Sally's children."

She gave him a hard look. "I see."

"I told him I'd do it. I did."

Miss Edith's mouth tightened.

"I could help you, maybe."

Miss Edith sighed, and the hardness went away from her eyes. She said, "It's a busy day, Maddy. I could use you. How about you snap those beans?"

Maddy pulled the bench closer to the worktable, sat down, and started snapping the ends off green beans. He wanted to tell Miss Edith that he could work hard, that he did work, that his whole family worked hard, whether or not they were Miss Sally's children. But he knew Miss Edith knew that. Besides, he didn't get out of work for being Miss Sally's son. He got out of work for being Master Jefferson's son, and that was something neither he nor Miss Edith could say.

Maddy worked for Miss Edith all afternoon. It was full dark before James and Beverly came home. James was so tired he clung to Beverly's hand.

Chapter Sixteen

Miss Ellen

Miss Ellen took Maddy through the pages of the primer. Each time they had a few moments together, she made him read the words from the section they'd studied the time before. If he knew them all they moved on. *Big, dig, fig, gig, pig, wig. Bog, dog, fog, hog, jog, log.* Maddy loved how the words stacked up. *Bed, fed, led, red, wed.*

"It'd be better if you had your own primer," Miss Ellen said one day. "If you could practice, you'd get on fast." She glanced quickly over her shoulder as she spoke. Maddy knew she was checking to be sure Miss Martha wasn't nearby. They were sitting on a bench on the back porch of the great house, because visitors came to the front porch and because Miss Martha didn't want Maddy in any of the rooms inside.

"I'd loan you ours if I could," Miss Ellen said. "My brother's reading out of it now, so Mama'll notice if it goes missing. Once you're farther along I've got other books you can borrow." She studied Maddy. "Could you buy a primer?"

Maddy shook his head. "No."

"Could your mama?"

Maddy shook his head again. "She wouldn't."

"Don't you have any money? Grandpa could—"

"No. We have money." Maddy wondered how to explain. "I don't know how much a primer costs—but it's not that." It would cause talk, if he or Mama or any other enslaved person tried to buy a book in Charlottesville. "Mama hates talk," he said.

Miss Ellen sighed. She tucked her hair behind her ear. She had red hair, like Master Jefferson. "But that's *nonsensical*," she said. "If you have money, there's no reason why anyone should care what you buy. It shouldn't be anyone's business but your own." She glared at Maddy.

Maddy knew what she meant, but he understood his mama's side too. "If I tried to buy a gun," he said.

"Oh, a gun," said Miss Ellen. "A book is not a gun."

"No," Maddy said. "A book is much more dangerous."

Miss Ellen stared at him.

"Somebody could take a gun away from me," Maddy said. "I learn what's in a book, it's mine for keeps."

Miss Ellen still stared. Maddy dropped his head. "I'm sorry," he said. He should know better than to talk straight to a white person, even Miss Ellen. He thought about the word *nonsensical*. That would be one to remember for Beverly. Beverly loved musical words.

Miss Ellen sighed. "Don't be. I guess I should understand. Only, do you ever think what a stupid world this is, with so many useless rules?" She thrust a book at Maddy. It wasn't the primer, it was the book she had been reading when Maddy found her on the porch. "Look," she said. She opened it under Maddy's nose.

Maddy looked. The letters were print, not script, but he still couldn't read them. He couldn't make sense of them at all. Some looked like letters he'd never seen before. He frowned. "What is that?"

"It's Greek," Miss Ellen said. "Aristotle. Know who he is?"

Maddy shook his head.

"Of course you don't," Miss Ellen said. "How could you? You're still sounding out the primer. But *I* know who he is. I can read this, this Greek, and it makes sense to me." She rattled off a few words, and Maddy laughed. It was like Mama's French, and yet not like it at all.

Miss Ellen grinned. "That means: 'All men by nature desire knowledge.'"

Maddy thought for a moment. He asked, "Does it say what women want?"

Miss Ellen ignored him. "It's a classical language," she said. "Greek and Latin are the classical languages, the languages of scholars. My mother doesn't know them. My brother Jeff doesn't know them, and he doesn't want to either. But I made Grandpa teach me, just a little, enough to start with. I got him to buy me some books, and I taught myself and I *worked*, and now I can read Aristotle and Plato and Xenophon, and—isn't it a waste?"

Maddy wasn't sure why it would be a waste, if it was something Miss Ellen wanted to do. He thought about the word *classical*. Classical, nonsensical. "If you wanted to learn," he started to say, "and you did learn—"

"I want to go to *college*," Miss Ellen said. "To really learn, to be like Grandpa, to think big thoughts. But I can't, and it's not because I'm not smart enough, or because I haven't studied enough. It's because I'm a girl. College is for boys. Jeff got to go, the dolt. For all the good it did him—home again within a year."

Maddy said, "I thought he came back because of the money."

Miss Ellen's head snapped up. "What?"

Maddy hesitated.

"Oh, for heaven's sake," she said. "You can trust *me*. What'd you hear?"

Maddy took a deep breath. "My mama said Master Jefferson told your mama that the college fees were too high and he couldn't afford them, and anyhow they needed Jeff to take charge of the farms." Maddy hoped he wasn't speaking out of turn—keep your mouth shut, Mama would say—but Miss Ellen seemed oddly pleased.

"Well," Miss Ellen said. "I didn't know that, but at least it makes sense. I thought he got kicked out for bad grades. It made me so angry, that he'd get a chance and toss it away. *I'd* try hard—but all I'm allowed to do is get married and have a dozen babies. Like I'd want babies, or a husband. It's *stupid*." She glared at Maddy.

"Yes, ma'am," Maddy said.

Miss Ellen whacked his arm. "Don't you 'yes, ma'am' me!" she said. She shook her head. "Money, money. People around here are always talking about money. But they never quit spending it, have you noticed that?"

Maddy nodded. He had heard whispers. No matter how much the farms made, Master Jefferson spent more. Miss Ellen continued, "So. If you can't buy a primer, can you buy a slate?"

Maddy drew his breath. "A what?"

"A slate. A slate, Maddy. For writing."

Maddy thought of what Mama said. Miss Martha would take a strap to Miss Ellen, if Miss Ellen tried to teach Maddy to write. "I don't need a slate. Why would I want a slate?"

Miss Ellen's temper flared. "Don't—don't pretend to be stupid around me. You're too smart for that."

"Your mama—"

"She doesn't matter," Miss Ellen said. "You want to learn, and I'm teaching you. My brains ought to be good for something."

"I can't have a slate," Maddy said. "My mama would kill me."

"You shouldn't be more afraid of your mama than I am of mine."

"I'm not," Maddy said. "I'm not afraid of my mama at

all. But if you do something wrong, you get in trouble. If I do something wrong, my mama gets in trouble. Maybe bad trouble. Worse trouble than there'd be for you."

Miss Ellen looked at him. Maddy could tell she was really seeing him, the way Mama or Harriet saw him. All of a sudden he felt he could trust her, at least a little. "I could write on a roof slate," he said. "There are a couple of broken ones left from when they were repairing the stables. Nobody'd care if I took one. It wouldn't be as smooth as a school slate, but I bet it would work."

Miss Ellen grinned. "That's thinking. Good." She reached into her pocket. "Here." She pushed something into Maddy's hand. "Tragically, I seem to have lost my slate pencil. Mama'll have to buy me another one."

Miss Cornelia came out of the house, calling for Miss Ellen. Miss Ellen jumped up, taking the primer and the Greek book with her. She didn't say good-bye. Maddy knew why. The less Miss Ellen pretended to care about teaching him, the less anybody would try to stop her. He headed down to the stables for a piece of slate, his fingers tight around the slate pencil she had just given him.

Chapter Seventeen

The Mockingbird

Master Jefferson had a tame mockingbird. It perched on his shoulder while he wrote and took bites of food from between his lips. It whistled Master Jefferson's favorite tunes. Mama said Master Jefferson left the door of the bird's cage open, so the bird could fly wherever it wanted inside Master Jefferson's room and among the plants on the greenhouse porch. When it was tired it settled on Master Jefferson's shoulder to sleep.

Mama told Maddy she liked the bird well enough, but she was glad it didn't sit on her shoulder. She said sometimes the bird made a mess.

One morning, when Mama came back from the great house, she told Maddy and Eston that the bird was dead.

"What killed it?" Eston asked.

"Nothing killed it," Mama said. "It looked fine last night, and this morning it was cold on the bottom of the cage. Maybe it was just old."

Eston nodded solemnly. "Its time had come."

Maddy wasn't sad about Master Jefferson's bird—it was just a bird—but he did like mockingbirds. He saw them sometimes in the woods. You never heard them—they mimicked other birds' songs, so they always sounded like something else. He told James about the dead bird, and right away James said, "Let's catch him a new one."

Maddy grinned. James had worked three whole weeks as water boy, and he'd been a little angry about it. Maddy hadn't known how to make things right. He was glad now that James wanted to be friends again. He was happy to hunt for a mockingbird.

Joe Fossett showed them how to make a bird trap out of a wooden box propped up on a stick. James and Maddy searched the woods for a week, off and on, until they finally saw a mockingbird perched high in the branches of a tree. They set up the trap on the ground beneath the tree, and scattered a handful of corn inside the box for bait.

They huddled in the brush to wait. Patches of sunlight flickered through the green leaves. James had tied a string to the stick holding the box up. Now he pulled the string until it was taut on the ground. He bit the tip of his tongue, the way he always did when he was concentrating. He looked exactly like Joe Fossett. Maddy laughed.

"Shh," James warned him, smiling.

The mockingbird hopped to a lower branch and cocked its head toward them.

"Might be a while yet," Maddy whispered.

"No hurry," whispered James.

Maddy agreed. He felt completely happy. The mocking-bird had pretty gray feathers and a flash of white on its wings. Maddy wondered if Master Jefferson's old bird had looked so fine. He wondered too if it had been hard to catch, before it became tame. This new bird did not suspect a trap. Sooner than Maddy expected, it hopped to the ground and began to peck the corn, and then it walked right into the little box. James yanked the string, and the box dropped. They'd caught the mockingbird.

Maddy whooped, and James whooped, and the bird got upset and flapped the box around.

"Shh," said James. He was laughing. "Don't let him hurt himself."

Maddy took his shirt off and laid it out on the ground, and they carefully dragged the box sideways onto it. They flipped the box over, holding Maddy's shirt tight across the open bottom like a lid. The bird fought a bit more, but not much.

They took turns carrying the box on the long walk back to the great house. Maddy couldn't wait to see Master Jefferson's face. He'd smile the way he used to smile at Beverly. Maybe he'd even give them a hug. James was carrying the box when they reached the great house, and Maddy reached for one end.

"Let's give it to him together," he said.

When they got to Master Jefferson's room, Maddy kicked the closed door. Mama came out, a broom in her hand. She gave them the eye. "What are you doing, bothering Master

Jefferson? And bringing some kind of mess into this house?"

"It's a bird," James said, at the same time as Maddy said, "A surprise."

"Let me see." Mama peeked beneath Maddy's shirt. "A mockingbird! Did you catch him yourselves?"

They nodded, proud. Mama hugged James with one arm, and Maddy with the other. "Aren't you clever. Stay here. I'll get him."

She went away and in a moment Master Jefferson came out, holding a pen. He had ink smeared across his chin. He smiled at them. "Sally said you two have brought me a bird," he said. "Bring him back here—bring him to my office."

Master Jefferson's office was the middle part of his big private room. He took the box from James and directed Maddy to clear a space among the piles of books on the floor. He set the box down. "Let's see him," he said. He wrapped Maddy's shirt around the bird's body until he could lift it up, and then he held on to the bird's feet and uncovered its head. The bird looked around with sharp eyes, twisting its head from side to side. Maddy couldn't tell if it was frightened or just mighty surprised.

Master Jefferson whistled to it, the first part of the song "Money Musk." The bird tilted its head, listening. Master Jefferson whistled the notes again. Then he took the bird to the empty birdcage on the side of the room and shut it inside. He threw a blanket over the cage and gave Maddy's shirt back to Maddy.

"We'll let him settle for a bit," he said. "That's a fine bird, boys. You did a good job to catch him. How did you know I wanted a mockingbird?"

"Mama said," Maddy told him.

Master Jefferson fished through the wallet on his desk. "Here's fifty cents," he said. "Fifty cents for each of you. Thank you for bringing me such a fine bird."

Maddy looked at the money. He looked at Master Jefferson. He didn't want money. But James reached for it quick enough, so Maddy had to too, or he would look like he was trying to show up James. Fifty cents was a lot of money. Maddy'd never had fifty cents before.

The coins were cold in his hand. Inside the cage, the bird made a sudden, wild squawk, and beat its wings against the bars.

Maddy swallowed. The most awful feeling came over him, all at once, like water poured out of a bucket onto his head.

That bird had been free, and now it was a slave. From now on it had to live where Master Jefferson wanted it to live, eat what Master Jefferson gave it to eat, even whistle the songs Master Jefferson wanted it to sing. He, Maddy, had sold that bird into slavery.

Master Jefferson was looking at him. A moment before, Maddy had craved his attention. Now he just wanted to get away. If he could, he'd take back the bird—hand Master Jefferson his money, and take back the bird. Set it free in the woods like it was meant to be. But Master Jefferson was talking.

"My, James Madison," he said. "How you've grown." Then he looked at James. "And what's your name?"

"He's James too," Maddy said. "James Fossett."

"My goodness," Master Jefferson said. "Time flies."

"We got to go," Maddy said. He grabbed James's arm and hustled him out to the hall.

"Why are you in such a hurry?" James asked. Maddy kept going, out the house door, dragging James. "That's the first time I've ever been inside that room," James said. "I wanted to ask him about stuff. I bet he'd have told us. He was awful pleased about that bird."

"We shouldn't have caught it," Maddy said. "That bird was *free.*"

James laughed. "Don't be stupid," he said.

"It was free, and we sold it."

"Maddy," James said, "birds aren't people. They're birds. You want to set all our chickens free?"

That wasn't what Maddy meant.

"No more chicken for you? How about coons? You going to quit eating them, starting telling them to go be free? Pigs? You want to set free all the ham?"

"No," said Maddy, scowling. He kicked at the ground. He didn't know what he wanted. "I wish he hadn't paid us. I wanted the bird to be a gift."

James frowned. "Well, I didn't. I wanted to be paid. If you don't like it, hand me your fifty cents. I won't mind. Why would you want to give Master Jefferson a gift? What's he ever done for you?"

Maddy looked around before he spoke. "He's my father," Maddy said.

James sighed. "I know that," he said. "Everybody knows, your mama goes up there every night. It's why I had to carry water all day in the hot sun, and you didn't. But just because he's your father doesn't mean you've got to like him. Why would you want to give him anything? What's he given you?"

Anger blazed up in Maddy. James was with his father all the time. Maddy said, "Maybe not much yet, but someday he's going to make me free. He can do that anytime he wants to. *Your* father can't."

He caught his breath. He wished he could take that back. James looked furious. "I didn't mean it," Maddy said. He thrust his two quarters at James. "Here. Take them. Your father's saving up, I know. Put this with the money under your bed."

James smacked Maddy's hand. The coins flew through the air. "I don't need your money!" James said. "My father is too going to get us free. That's what he's saving for. He makes good money. We don't need help from you."

James turned and ran toward Mulberry Row. After a moment, Maddy picked the quarters out of the dirt, put them in his pocket, and followed.

Chapter Eighteen

They All Play the Violin

When Mama came home that afternoon, she told Maddy Master Jefferson said it was time he started learning to play the violin.

Mama sat on the edge of the bed and stroked his hair. "What's the matter?" she asked. "Aren't you glad?"

Maddy shrugged. "I guess."

"I thought you wanted lessons. You said so before."

"Yeah," Maddy said. "I mean, yes, ma'am. I do. I'm glad. Thank you."

Mama looked at him. "What's wrong?"

Maddy looked away. "I sold him that bird. I wish I hadn't. I wish I had the bird back." Mostly, though, he wished he had his words back—the words he'd said to James.

Mama looked puzzled. "What would you do with a mockingbird?"

"Set him free," said Maddy.

"Oh, baby." Mama wrapped her arms around him, and

rocked him back and forth. "Don't you worry about that. Don't you worry. You're going to be free, I promise. You and Beverly and Harriet and Eston—"

"How about James?"

Mama's smile faded. She quit rocking Maddy, but she held him tight. "I can't save other women's children, Maddy, darling. I can only save my own."

"He's mad at me," Maddy said. "James."

Mama nodded like she understood, even though she couldn't really, since Maddy hadn't told her the whole story.

"When I came back from France," Mama said, "I came home to family I hadn't seen for nearly three years. Everyone could tell I was going to have a baby, and it didn't take them too long to realize who the father of the baby was. Some folks thought I was a fool. Others were jealous, both then and now. We've got advantages because of Master Jefferson, but there are disadvantages too. I'm sorry James feels bad. You've got to keep on loving him, Maddy. No matter what. You can't help all the other stuff, but you can love him no matter what, and when he knows you do he'll come around. Can you understand that? I know you love James."

"I wish Joe Fossett was my daddy," Maddy said.

"Well, I don't," Mama said. "It doesn't matter anyhow. We can't change your daddy. Aren't you pleased about violin lessons? You like listening to Beverly play."

"I won't sound like Beverly. He's good." Maddy had messed around with Beverly's violin, but it never sounded right.

"Jesse will fix you up," Mama said. "You go down with Beverly this week. Work hard. Make your father proud."

Maddy rolled his eyes. He couldn't imagine making his father proud. On the other hand, the next time James asked him what his father had given him, he'd be able to say, "Violin lessons." James would think it was stupid, but at least Maddy would have something to say.

Two days later, when Maddy and Beverly set out for Jesse Scott's, Eston followed them down the row, whining. "Can I come?" he said. "Please? I want to come!" Eston was four years old.

"You can't come," Maddy said. "We're walking all the way down the mountain, and then we have to walk all the way back up again. It's miles and miles. You're too small."

Eston's face puckered up, ready to cry. "Oh, hush," Beverly told Maddy. "You can come, Eston. Run tell Mama."

"He'll be nothing but trouble," Maddy said.

"He'll be fine." Beverly handed Maddy the violin. When Eston dashed back, all smiles, Beverly lifted Eston onto his shoulders.

Maddy said, "You don't ever carry me."

Beverly slipped an arm around Maddy's shoulder. "I don't have to, you're so big and strong. Tell me the story about catching that bird."

"I don't want to talk about it," said Maddy.

"A bird's not a person," Beverly said, as if he could read

Maddy's thoughts. "People and animals are not the same. We eat birds, and rabbits, and coons, and possums. All sorts of wild things from the woods. That mockingbird, he'd be glad not to be eaten, if he knew the difference. He'd be happy to sing."

"Maybe," said Maddy.

"Absolutely," said Beverly. "He'll get tame, like the old bird. He'll ride on Papa's shoulder and take food from Papa's mouth."

Maddy's eyes widened. Eston, from his perch on Beverly's shoulders, laughed aloud. "You said *Papa*!" Eston said.

Beverly smiled. "I can when it's just us together. But don't tell Mama."

"I don't think of him as Papa," Maddy said. "That word never comes to my head."

"I know," Beverly said. "I'm sorry."

At Jesse Scott's, when Beverly opened the violin case, Eston grabbed the violin. His arms were too short to hold it properly, but he stuck the side of it under his chin, and he put the bow right by his face, and he played! He played a lot better than Maddy could. Maddy wanted to be annoyed, but Eston's face was so bright with excitement, and his eyes were so round, and what he was doing sounded so much like actual music that Maddy had to laugh.

Jesse Scott laughed too, and Beverly laughed loudest of all. "Eston," he said, "have you been messing with my violin?"

"N-no," Eston said, stammering with excitement. "N-no, no, I just watch when you play." He turned to Jesse Scott. "I got to learn to play the violin, sir. My daddy wants me to."

"He does, does he?" Jesse Scott raised his eyebrows.

"Yes, sir, he said so."

"When did he say so?" Maddy asked. "Mama just said me!"

"He talks to me when I'm sleeping," Eston said. "My daddy does. He comes in when I'm dreaming and he tells me how I'm supposed to play the violin. And I'm supposed to learn to make it go like this." Eston started to whistle, exactly on tune, the song "Money Musk."

Maddy didn't know what to say. Master Jefferson walked past their room on his way to the blacksmith shop or the garden, but Maddy'd never known him to step inside. He didn't visit Eston in the night. Maddy felt sorry for Eston, that he would make up a story like that.

Jesse Scott said, "Eston, if I had a violin small enough, I'd teach you to play right now. But I don't, so you'll just have to wait until your arms grow."

Eston looked up, very solemn. "I *can't* wait," he said.

Jesse Scott looked solemn too. "You come down with Beverly and Madison, every week. You pay attention, and see what you can learn. All right? Then, when your arms get long enough, I'll teach you."

On the way home Maddy started to teach his brothers the alphabet. "*B*, that sounds like *buh*," he said. "Like baby. Like biscuit."

"Baby," said Eston. "Biscuit. Board. Biolin!"

"Not biolin," Maddy said. "It's *violin*. It starts with a *V*. *Vuh*, violin."

"Can you spell the whole word violin?" Beverly asked.

"Not yet," Maddy said. "But I know it doesn't start with a *B*."

"Yes, it does," Eston said. "*B* starts *biolin,* and that sounds like *violin*."

Beverly put his arms around Eston and swung him around. "*B* starts *billy* and that sounds like *silly* and that sounds like *Eston*!"

"You're crazy, both of you," Maddy said, laughing.

Eston was plumb crazy about playing the violin. He spent the next day climbing a mulberry tree and hanging from a branch until he fell off, over and over again.

Harriet said, "What are you doing, training to be a monkey?"

"He's trying to stretch his arms," Maddy said.

"Pull on me!" Eston said. "Stretch me out! I can't wait to be big!"

A week after the mockingbird argument, James poked his head inside Maddy's cabin door. Maddy jumped up. He'd been writing on his piece of roof slate. He tried to hide the slate pencil in the palm of his hand.

James looked him up and down. Maddy knew he'd seen the pencil.

Maddy shrugged. He held the slate toward James. "I'm practicing my letters," he said. "Want to try?"

James took the pencil and the slate. Maddy rubbed the slate clean. James said, "I came to see if you wanted to go fishing."

"Sure," Maddy said. "We haven't been all week."

"I guess you've been busy," James said, "going down to Charlottesville and all."

"That was just once," Maddy said. "I'll be going every week, I guess, but only once so far. James—"

"I'm sorry," James cut in. "I shouldn't have talked bad about Master Jefferson to you. I'd be plenty mad if you talked bad about my father."

"I couldn't," Maddy said. "Nobody could say anything bad about your father." He paused. "I'm sorry about what I said too."

James looked at the slate. He carefully wrote a wobbly *J*. He handed the slate back to Maddy. "My daddy can write," he said. "He writes his accounts. He doesn't have much time to teach me, but I asked him and he said he's going to try."

"I know where you can get a roof slate," Maddy said.

James grinned. Maddy loved James's grin. "Later. Right now, let's fish."

Chapter Nineteen

James Hubbard Flogged Again

One of the field hands, a man named James Hubbard, had run away the winter before. Maddy didn't know him, but Beverly said it was the second time James Hubbard had run. The first had been years ago. Maddy hoped James Hubbard got away. As months went by, it seemed that he had. But then someone found him, in Roanoke, caught him, and brought him back to Monticello.

Master Jefferson was angry. He said he was going to have James Hubbard flogged in front of everyone and then sold so far south he'd never see his family again.

Those were his words. "*So far south he'll never see his family again.*" Mama and Burwell both overheard.

Mama said her hands were tied.

Maddy knew Mama meant that she was afraid to stand up to Master Jefferson. She could do it for her children, or maybe for herself, but not for James Hubbard, whom she didn't know at all.

"No one blames you, Mama," Harriet said. "No one else can help him either."

So far south he'll never see his family again. Folks said the Deep South was a terrible place. Field hands died like flies in the heat. If you went south, your days were numbered.

On the day of James Hubbard's flogging the overseers called everyone up the mountain to watch. Maddy argued with Mama.

"I don't want to," he said. "Even if you can't make him stop it, you could make it so I didn't have to watch."

Mama shook her head. "I'd rather you didn't have to," she said. "But you do. It's something you need to understand, and even if I didn't think that, I'd still make you go."

Beverly opened his mouth like he wanted to say something, then shut it and looked away. Mama saw. She said, "What?"

Beverly said, "It's too hard."

"It's very hard," Mama said. "It's hard for everybody. Should I make a display of how my children get to have it easier? Everyone on this mountain would notice if you weren't there."

Maddy didn't understand, but Beverly looked as though he did. He reached for Maddy's hand. Harriet took hold of Eston's. They walked together to where James Hubbard was waiting to be flogged.

James Hubbard slumped over the post, his wrists tied together in front of him. His head hung down. Old scars crisscrossed his bare back, the white and pink lines standing out against his dark skin. His muscles stretched taut beneath the scars. James Hubbard lifted his head and stared across the mountains, like he was searching for something far away.

"Where's his mama?" Maddy asked.

"Poplar Forest," said Harriet. That was Master Jefferson's big farm in Bedford, a few days' ride away. "He came from there. Most of his kin lives there still. His brother's here—his brother used to be a nail boy too."

The overseer came forward with the long, thin oxwhip in his hand. He cracked it once upon the ground, *thwack!* The crowd flinched. He raised the whip again.

Harriet covered Eston's face with the edge of her skirt. Beverly moved in front of Maddy and pushed Maddy back with his hand. "Don't look," Beverly whispered. "It's bad enough to listen."

"They should look," Mama said. "They ought to see it so they understand."

"No," said Beverly, calm and firm. "It's too hard."

Beverly almost never contradicted Mama like that. Mama didn't reply. She put her arm around Beverly's shoulder, and pulled him toward her. Maddy looked up. Beverly was taller than Mama now.

The first lash landed on James Hubbard's back with a smack that sounded wet at the end. James Hubbard moaned. In the crowd, a woman screamed. Maddy turned his head so all he could see was the seam of Beverly's shirt, and the curve of Beverly's arm, but he couldn't stop his ears from hearing.

When it was over, people moved to help James Hubbard, but the overseer barked at them to get away. "You'll never see him again, you understand?" he said. His face had turned bright pink, like a pig's face. "He's going down to the cotton fields. You'll never see him again. That's what happens to runaways. You all understand?" He waved his whip, threatening, and a woman who must have cared about James Hubbard began to sob. Beverly pulled Maddy's hand and grabbed Eston to his hip, and marched them back to their room, and it wasn't until he'd shut the door behind them that he reached under the bed, pulled out the privy pot, and was sick.

Beverly wiped his mouth with a rag. "I vomited the first time too," he said.

"First time what?" asked Eston.

"First time they flogged James Hubbard," Beverly said. "Didn't you see the scars?"

Eston nodded. He was sucking his thumb, something he almost never did anymore.

"He ran off once before," Beverly said. "He was a nail boy then, not a field hand. He got flogged, but not sold. It was a long time ago."

Mama opened the door and came in, Harriet behind her. Beverly turned to Mama. He was angry, Maddy could tell. "If I go away and live as a white man," he said, "it'll be just like I was sold south. You'll never see me again."

Mama surged forward and slapped Beverly hard across the

face. "If you think being a white man is anything like being a slave in the cotton fields, you don't know *anything*," she said. "James Hubbard's mama was *happy* when he ran. She was *happy* to know he was free."

"He wasn't free," Beverly shot back. "He just hadn't been caught."

Chapter Twenty

Maddy on His Own

That winter Maddy truly learned to read. For a long time, when Miss Ellen handed him the primer, he had to sound each word out, one letter at a time. Then, all of a sudden, the sounds blended themselves together. He could pick up a book and read the words as they came.

One day he met Miss Ellen in the front hall. It was bitter cold there, with no fire, and wind rattling the panes of glass in the doors, so unless a visitor showed up they were likely to have a moment to themselves.

Miss Ellen pulled her shawl higher around her head. She looked around, anxious. She opened the primer to the middle, beyond the lists of easy words, to where the sentences began. She pointed to a section, and Maddy read:

No man can say that he has done no ill,
For all men have gone out of the way.

There is none that doth good; no, not one.

If I have done harm, I must do it no more.

"Huh," said Maddy. He was pleased he could read whole sentences, but he didn't like those particular sentences. "Why'd you pick that?"

Miss Ellen shrugged. "It's all like that," she said. "Little sermons on how to be good."

"That's not how to be good," Maddy argued. "That's saying everybody's bad."

"I think it's supposed to be a warning," Miss Ellen said. "That we shouldn't think too highly of ourselves, no matter who we are." She closed the primer and tucked it behind her shawl. "I bought you something," she said. "Grandpa gave me money for Christmas, and I went shopping in Charlottesville. I spent some of it on hair ribbons, so nobody'd suspect, but I got something for you too. This."

She pushed a paper-wrapped parcel into Maddy's hands. Maddy opened it. It was a blue primer, just like Miss Ellen's, only brand-new.

"You're going to have to study on your own now," Miss Ellen said. "You can do it. You'll have this to help you."

"But—" Maddy stared at the book. His own book. His own. Yet what was Miss Ellen saying? "I still want you to teach me," Maddy said. "Thank you for the primer—thank you very much—but I haven't gotten to any of the big words yet. I still need teaching. You like teaching, you said so. And my brother Eston—"

Miss Ellen shook her head. "I'm trying to tell you. I can't teach you anymore. Mama wants me to take more responsibility around the house, so I can manage my own household someday. She wants me to learn to supervise the cooking and the laundry."

Maddy stared. Miss Martha went down to the kitchen every morning to tell Miss Edith what to cook, and on Mondays she sorted the piles of clothes that needed to be washed. She didn't do any of the actual cooking or washing or ironing. What Miss Martha did wasn't exactly work. Miss Ellen could do it and still spend a few minutes once a week teaching Maddy.

Miss Ellen wouldn't meet his eyes. "I need to spend more time on my sewing too," she said. "And practicing my music."

"You don't want to help me," Maddy said.

Miss Ellen bit her lip. "I can't. Not anymore. I'm seventeen and I've got to act like a lady. Mama said so. She's watching me. I can still read Greek, if I'm careful, if I don't do anything else that upsets her." She paused. "I'll still help you once in a while. Okay? Just for a few minutes, if you get stuck. When I can. Okay? But not very often."

"Your mama found out you were teaching me. And if she catches you doing it again, she's going to take away your Greek," said Maddy. He wanted the truth plain between them.

Miss Ellen nodded. "I'm sorry."

Maddy thought about it. Miss Martha meant what she said, Maddy knew. If Miss Ellen crossed her, that would be the end of Latin and Greek. Even if he and Miss Ellen tried to meet in secret, Miss Martha would be bound to find out. There were too many people at Monticello who could spy for her. Not much got by Miss Martha when she didn't want it to.

Maddy tucked the new primer carefully inside the waistband of his pants. He pulled his shirt out to hide it. "Thank you," he said. "Thank you very much for the book, and for teaching me."

"Oh, Maddy. I wish—"

A gust of wind shook the doors in their frames. Miss Ellen shuddered. Maddy went over to the Declaration of Independence, those fancy handwritten words on the wall. He'd see if he could read it now. "*When*," he read triumphantly. "*When in the—*" He paused. The next word was harder.

"*Course*," said Miss Ellen. She came over to stand beside him. "*When in the course of human events, it becomes necessary for one—*"

"What's that mean?" Maddy asked. "*The course of human—* what did you say?"

"*The course of human events*," Miss Ellen repeated. She said, "It means, when in history."

"Why doesn't it just say that?"

"I don't know," Miss Ellen said. "Do you want me to keep going?" A hall door opened. Miss Ellen flinched.

"No," Maddy said. "It's okay."

He stood in front of the declaration for a few minutes after she left, before he grew too cold. Someday he was going to read those words, every last one of them, and understand them too. He felt the primer firm against his belly. In a way he felt sorry for Miss Ellen, but then again he didn't. She'd chosen Latin and Greek over teaching him, but if he had to choose, he might do the same thing, pick having his own primer over learning from her.

One night, after dark, James came by to see if Maddy wanted to hunt coons with him and his daddy. Harriet let James in. Maddy was sitting beside Eston in the firelight, helping Eston practice his ABCs.

"Coming?" James said.

Maddy thought about it. He liked coon hunting, but it was cold outside, and warm in the cabin.

James frowned. "Don't bother if you've got better things to do."

Maddy got up. "No, I'll come. It sounds fun." He put on his coat and they went outside.

"So, now you're teaching Eston," said James.

James sounded annoyed. Maddy didn't understand. "Somebody has to," Maddy said.

James snorted. "I don't see why. My sisters can't read or write. They're every bit as smart as your brother."

"I never said they weren't."

"And you're not any smarter than me, even if you do waste a bunch of your time on these things."

They were almost to the blacksmith shop. Maddy looked

at James. "I never said I was smarter than you," he said. "I like reading. I don't think I'm wasting my time."

"I understand learning to read," James said. "I don't understand why you care about it so much. Like it makes you some kind of special. What good's it going to do?"

"I don't think that," Maddy said. "I'm not showing off." He hated the expression on James's face. When James was upset he looked just like Joe Fossett, hard and stern. Maddy tried to explain. "Mama thinks we need to be real good at reading. For when we're white and all."

James stopped dead in the path. "Say that again," he said.

Maddy knew this was trouble, but he didn't know how to fix it. "For when we're white," he said. "And all."

James shook his head. "That's what I thought you said." He looked Maddy up and down. "That's crazy, Maddy. When you're *white*? You're not white. You might be free someday. I might be too. But I'm not white and neither are you. Who told you that? Your mama?"

"I am too white," Maddy said. "I'm seven-eighths white. That's white by law. Mama *did* tell me that. She says someday we're going to be free, me and Beverly and Harriet and Eston, and we're going to be white folks, free white folks out doing whatever we want in the world."

They had reached the blacksmith shop door. James stopped with his hand against the door frame. Maddy knew he shouldn't have said all that. It sounded like bragging. James would be even angrier and Mama would wallop him if she heard. Still Maddy went on, "You better not call my mama a liar."

But the look on James's face faded to something like sympathy. "Maddy," he said, "you ain't white."

"I'm a slave," Maddy said. "Slaves are black. But I'm white too."

James shook his head. "Beverly and Harriet, maybe. Dress them up, get them out of Charlottesville, and they'd pass. But not you. Forget what the law says. You're close, I guess. Not close enough."

Maddy held up his hand. It shone pale in the moonlight. He said, "I'm lighter than you."

"That doesn't make you white," James said. After a pause he added, "I already know I'm not white." He paused again. "Neither are you."

Maddy didn't go coon hunting. He left James at the blacksmith shop and slowly trudged back to the warm room where his family waited. His heart fluttered in his chest. Mama sometimes talked to Harriet and Beverly about how they should act in the white world. When they met another white person, they were to shake hands and look that person in the eye. They were not to look down. Beverly wouldn't touch his hat or his forehead, and Harriet wouldn't bob her head, they way they did now. Mama talked about how they'd dress, and where they might live. She reminded them to watch the way white folks ate at the dinner table, with napkins on their laps and all those forks and spoons.

Mama promised Maddy he'd be free when he was grown. He'd always thought he'd be with Harriet and Beverly. He thought they would all be the same.

Mama, Beverly, and Harriet looked up when he came into the room. Eston had climbed into bed.

"Catch a coon already?" asked Beverly.

Mama was studying him. "What is it?" she asked.

"James says I'm not white. Says I don't look white enough to pass."

Maddy clenched his fists. He waited for them to tell him that James was wrong. Instead Beverly bit his lip and turned toward the fire. Mama took a deep breath. "I don't know yet," she said slowly. "I hope you will, when you're grown. I just don't know."

"But you said white," Maddy said. "Because of Master Jefferson and seven-out-of-eight. I know you said it. I heard you."

Mama reached for his hand. "I said it, and it's true. If you're seven-eighths white, you're white by law. But if you look black, people will still call you black. They'll still treat you like you're black."

"If I tell them I'm white—if I explain—"

"That won't do any good, Maddy. If you have to explain, you've got to tell them your mama was a slave. That'll be all they need to know. You can't be white if your mama isn't free."

"But you said—"

"We'll have to pretend we were never slaves," Beverly said. "Harriet and me. When we're living with white people. We'll have to pretend our mama was someone else. We'll have to pretend we're someone else too. We'll have to spend our entire lives living one great big lie."

Maddy had never understood before why Beverly got angry whenever Mama talked about him being free, but now he did, a little. But still. If Beverly was living a lie, Maddy wanted to live that lie too. He licked his lips, which had suddenly gone dry. "Mama. When will you know about me?"

"Not 'til you're all the way grown. People can change when they get older."

"But Beverly and Harriet—you already know about them?"

"I'm sorry, Maddy," Beverly said.

"Nobody's sorry," Mama said. "Come here, Maddy. Come sit by the fire."

"I think I'll just go to sleep," he said. He crawled into the bed beside Eston. He snugged up next to Eston's warm body—Eston's warm *white* body—and watched the firelight dance on the walls. His thoughts whirled. He was still wide awake when Mama wrapped her shawl around her shoulders and went to be with Master Jefferson.

Chapter Twenty-one

A Landau, Septimia, and a Funny Sort of Sweet Potato

Mama said not to borrow trouble. She said nobody could tell the future. Maddy's skin was only a little bit darker than Beverly's, and maybe it would lighten when he got older. His hair was enough like white people's hair, curly but not kinky. Mama was kind and soothing. She tried to make Maddy forget he was different.

Maddy remembered. It wasn't the sort of thing you forgot.

"I don't know, Maddy," Beverly said. "I'm not sure I want to be white. I'm not sure I can be. It's really hard to think of myself that way. You, you'll always know who you are."

"I'm the only one that's different," Maddy said. "The only one. You'll all go away and I'll be alone."

"You'll be able to stay with Mama," Beverly said. "We'll never see her again."

Eston came up behind Maddy and hugged him hard. "I'll stay with you," he said. "We'll let them go off. I'll stay with you."

Maddy didn't know what to say, so he just kissed the top of Eston's head.

James was gentle too. "Here's what we'll do," James said, "we'll both get free, and we'll travel together. We'll go out west like Lewis and Clark. We'll go see the Indians."

Maddy liked the sound of that. "How much money do you think it will take," he asked, "for your daddy to get you all free?"

James shrugged. "A bunch, I reckon. That's okay. We've got time."

Summer returned. Master Jefferson designed a new landau. That was a type of carriage that could seat four people, front and back, and had a top that opened up and folded down. Master Jefferson drew pictures of exactly what he wanted, and Uncle John and Joe Fossett built it. All through the summer and fall, Uncle John shaped the landau's body out of wood, and Joe Fossett made the metal parts, springs and hinges and iron-bound wheels. Beverly helped Uncle John, and James helped Joe Fossett. Maddy wanted to help someone, but Mama said he was still too young.

Maddy was almost nine years old. He was tired of being too young.

In November Burwell painted the landau with six coats of paint until it was as shiny as a new coin. The first day Burwell started painting, Eston, Maddy, James, James's sisters, and Burwell's children all wanted to help. Burwell wouldn't let them. He said he didn't need a bunch of paint-covered children putting fingerprints on the new landau, and did they all need something to do? James and Maddy laughed as they ran away.

By the start of December, the landau was ready for its first trip, to Poplar Forest, Master Jefferson's other big farm. Master Jefferson went there whenever he was tired of visitors, because nobody ever visited him there. Davy Hern harnessed the carriage horses to the landau and drove up to the great house. Maddy watched them get ready to leave.

Miss Ellen and Miss Cornelia, who were accompanying Master Jefferson, came out with carpetbags and workbags. Miss Ellen struggled under a big box of books. Maddy grinned. He bet Miss Ellen would read the entire time she was gone. Burwell handed Davy Hern a cheese, and what looked like a wrapped ham, and Davy tucked them beneath the driver's seat. Gill and Israel, two of Fanny Hern's brothers, climbed bareback onto the horses that pulled the landau. They looked excited, but Maddy thought it would be tiring to ride those horses for three full days. Wormley handed Burwell the reins to Master Jefferson's saddle horse, which Burwell would ride.

Miss Martha stood on the house steps, watching, while Master Jefferson settled the girls and piled fur lap robes over them. The wind whipped her shawl around her great big belly. She was expecting another baby soon. She didn't live with her husband, but he visited often. "Papa, you bring them back before Christmas, do you hear me?" she called, into the wind. "I want them home for Christmas!"

Mama came up behind Maddy, and put her arm around him. "Will they be back by Christmas?" he asked.

"They will," she said.

The landau pulled away. A sort of emptiness settled over the mountain. Miss Martha sighed and went into the house. Mama followed her quietly, and Maddy followed Mama.

"Sally," Miss Martha said, "should any visitors knock in the next two weeks, you tell them Mr. Jefferson is gone away, and you shut the door. We aren't feeding them, we aren't housing them, and we aren't even showing them the farm."

"Yes, ma'am," Mama said.

"And bring a cup of tea to my room. I'm going to go lie down."

Master Jefferson came back two days before Christmas. On the third of January, 1814, Miss Martha had another baby girl. A few days later Mama gave Maddy the job of keeping up the fire in Miss Martha's bedroom, on the second floor. "She's feeling poorly and the house is cold," Mama said. "You make sure that one room stays warm."

When Maddy went into the room, Miss Martha didn't

speak. She lay motionless in the alcove bed, which was a bed built into a little cave in the wall. Master Jefferson loved alcove beds. He put them in every bedroom in Monticello. It was a gray day, so the alcove lay in shadow. A mound of blankets covered the bed. Maddy couldn't tell whether Miss Martha was awake or asleep.

He set his armful of wood on the hearth as gently as he could. He took the poker and began to make up the fire. A log crackled as it fell apart.

"Who's that?" Miss Martha asked. Her voice was soft, hoarse, worn-out like the rest of her.

"Ma'am?" Maddy asked.

"Oh. It's you."

"Are you warm enough? Mama told me to ask." Miss Martha's bedroom was a lot colder than Maddy's family's room in the dependency row. The wind rattled the windows.

"I'm fine."

"You need some water or anything? Something to eat?" Much as he disliked Miss Martha, Maddy couldn't help feeling sorry for her. She looked old and tired and awfully alone.

"No. I don't need anything."

The baby gave a sudden cry. Maddy jumped. He'd almost forgotten about the baby. She settled into wailing, and Miss Martha sighed. "Hand her to me, will you? She'll be hungry."

Maddy looked at the cradle near the bed. He could hardly see the new baby beneath the blankets she was wrapped in and the wool bonnet she was wearing.

"Careful," Miss Martha said. "Put a hand under her head."

Maddy put one hand under the baby's head and one under the wad of blankets. He heaved up, the way he would if he were picking up Eston, or James Fossett's baby sister Elizabeth Ann, but this baby was so much lighter than both of them that he nearly flung her into the air. He pulled her back, and sort of hugged her for a moment, in case he'd frightened her, and then he handed her to Miss Martha. The baby wailed nonstop. Her face was bright red and bumpy, and her nose and mouth and eyes were all scrunched together. She was the ugliest baby Maddy ever saw.

Miss Martha didn't say another word, just messed with the front of her gown and put the baby to nurse. The wailing stopped short. One of the baby's hands came out of the blankets and waved in the air, tiny fingers opening and closing like a chicken claw.

Miss Martha said, "Get me a glass of water."

Maddy looked, but there wasn't any water in the pitcher in her room, nor any glass. He took the empty pitcher and went down two sets of stairs to the basement, then over to the side where the well was. He hauled up a bucket of water, filled the pitcher, and set it by the stairs. Then he went across to the kitchen. "Miss Martha needs a drinking glass," he said. "She maybe ought to have something to eat too. She looks poorly."

Miss Edith made up a plate of food, and put it and a glass into a basket so he could carry them easily. Maddy took the basket and the pitcher up to Miss Martha's room. He poured her a glass of water. He took the glass from her when she'd finished drinking, and put the plate where she could reach it. "Miss Edith says, she hopes you're feeling better," he said.

"Go find Priscilla," Miss Martha said. "Septimia needs her clout changed."

"Septimia?" Maddy said before he could stop himself.

Miss Martha narrowed her eyes. "That's her name. Septimia."

Maddy felt sorry for the baby, a scrunched face and a name like Septimia. Sounded like something you could die from. *I got a bad case of septimia,* Maddy thought, *I think I'm going to be sick.* He never expected Miss Martha to thank him for anything, but it might have been nice, he thought, if she'd noticed that he had brought her something to eat without being asked.

Maddy went to find Priscilla, Uncle John's wife, who cared for all Miss Martha's children. She was up on the third floor with the little boys, Benjamin and Lewis. She came right away when Maddy beckoned. "I was listening," she said. "I didn't hear the baby cry."

"I picked her up quick," Maddy said. "Aunt 'Cilla, what's the matter with that baby?"

Priscilla looked worried. "Nothing I know of. Why?"

"Her face is all mashed. Something's wrong with her face."

She laughed. "Babies all look like that when they're first born. She'll be pretty in a few weeks, you'll see."

"And why's she got such a stupid name?"

Priscilla waved him away. "Can't help you there. Bring

some wood up for the nursery, will you? We can't get the house warm today."

Maddy puzzled over that name. *I've got a patch of septimia on my skin.* Finally he asked Miss Ellen. He had been looking for an excuse to speak to her.

Miss Ellen made a face. "It means 'seventh,'" she explained. "Because she's Mama's seventh girl."

Maddy counted quick in his head, but by his reckoning the baby made six, after Misses Anne, Ellen, Cornelia, Virginia, and Mary, plus the four boys, Jeff, James, Ben, and Lewis, which if you added them together made ten.

"There were two of us named Ellen," Miss Ellen explained. "I'm the second. The first one died."

Maddy nodded. "We had two Harriets."

"I'm not calling her Septimia," Miss Ellen said. "I'm going to call her Tim."

Maddy nodded again. After a pause he said, "My reading's coming right along."

Miss Ellen didn't look at him. "That's good."

"Lots of fine words in the back of that primer," he said. "*Glorification, academician, supposition.* 'Course, we don't know what all of them mean, but they're fine words. Beverly likes them."

"That's good," Miss Ellen said again.

"If we had another book—something you all were finished with, maybe—"

Miss Ellen shook her head, the tiniest bit.

"If someone was to drop a book in the kitchen," Maddy persisted, "maybe someone who comes to help supervise the work, if a book just sort of fell out of that person's hands, I reckon it would get to me. Any old book."

Miss Ellen still didn't look at Maddy, but the edge of her mouth lifted slightly. Maddy took that to be a smile.

"And not any Greek books," he said. "Only plain old English, none of that fancy educated stuff, no sir."

This time he was sure he saw her smile.

The next evening, when Maddy went to the kitchen for dinner, Miss Edith gave him the eye. "Go fetch me that bushel of sweet potatoes," she said. When Maddy brought it over, Miss Edith put her hand down into it. "Why, look here! This is a funny sort of sweet potato. Where do you suppose it grew?" She pulled a book from the basket and handed it to Maddy. "Better not be more of these funny potatoes," she warned him. "We don't need trouble, no, we don't. Not in my kitchen."

It was a book of stories, written by a man named Aesop. They were all about foxes, and crows, and greedy boys and trickery. Maddy loved them. Harriet loved them even more. She read them until she knew them by heart, and then she told them to all the children up and down Mulberry Row.

Chapter Twenty-two

Money Musk

For years people around the mountain heard rumors that Master Jefferson was running out of money, but no one ever knew whether or not they were true. Now suddenly the rumors intensified.

Times were hard all over, after the war. The price of Virginia farmland had dropped to almost nothing, though Beverly said that didn't matter because Master Jefferson would never sell any of his land. Miss Martha's grown son, Jeff, who ran the farms, looked tight and worried all the time, and Joe Fossett heard one of the white overseers complain that he hadn't been paid. But the very next week a wagon drove up the mountain loaded with wooden casks full of French wine. The grapes had been grown in France, made into wine, put into oak casks, and shipped first in a ship across the ocean and then in a wagon to Monticello, and all that cost a bundle, you'd better believe. Burwell shook his head and said the wine wouldn't last three months, the way the visitors drank like they were parched and dying.

Master Jefferson wrote letters in the mornings with his mockingbird on his shoulder. He whistled while he rode his horse around the farm. At night, in the crowded dining room, he laughed and talked and poured wine with a generous hand. Miss Martha seemed anxious, but Master Jefferson never did. Nobody knew what to think.

"Will it matter, Mama?" Maddy asked. "If the money runs out?"

Mama shook her head. "I don't know," she said. "You're safe, Maddy, I have his promise on that."

Maddy knew what she meant: the big promise, the freedom promise.

Mama continued, "I think, while he's alive, it won't matter. He was a president, and a great patriot, and nobody's going to fuss at him if he can't pay all he owes. When he dies it might be a problem, if there are still debts to pay. Miss Martha would have to pay them, or Mister Jeff."

Maddy hadn't known you could inherit debts. "Oh, yes," Mama assured him. "Master Jefferson took on a whole bunch of debt after his wife's father—my father too—Master Wayles—died. He inherited everything, land and people and debt."

"How long will Master Jefferson live, Mama?" Eston asked.

"A long time," Mama said. "He's a very healthy man."

"A very *old* healthy man," Harriet said. "He could die to-morrow."

"He could," Mama said. "I don't think he will."

In May Harriet turned thirteen. She wasn't quite a woman yet, but she was getting close. She was tall and light-stepping, and even prettier than Mama, and when she was dressed up, which wasn't often, people thought she was one of Miss Martha's girls.

Harriet never put on airs; she was smarter than that. Miss Cornelia and Miss Virginia were just a year on each side of her in age. They'd never liked Harriet. Mama told her to keep her head down around them, and Harriet did, and when she worked in the great house Mama made her wear a scarf over her head to hide her hair, her straight, flowing, white-person's hair.

Next year Maddy would be apprenticed to Uncle John, like Beverly, but for now he was still an errand boy, fetching wood and water and whatever else Mama, Burwell, or Miss Martha needed. He was passing through the front hallway one morning when he heard Miss Cornelia ask Miss Martha if Harriet could be her personal maid.

Maddy stopped short. Miss Cornelia and Miss Martha were in the schoolroom, and the schoolroom door was open wide. Maddy could hear them plain as anything.

Miss Martha said, "Cornelia, what would you do with a maid? You're not old enough."

"Please, Mama," Miss Cornelia said. "My cousins have maids, and they're younger than me."

"Their circumstances are different from ours. You know that. You're not out in society, you don't need a chaperone."

"You mean they have more money."

"I mean they live differently," Miss Martha said.

"I'll be out soon. And you already let me eat dinner with you and Grandpa. I need someone to help me dress and do my hair. Priscilla's always busy."

Maddy thought how unpleasant Cornelia's voice was, like the drone of a mosquito.

"Priscilla doesn't have time for me, not with the new baby," Miss Cornelia went on. "My clothes are always a mess—"

Maddy clenched his fists. Couldn't Miss Cornelia get dressed on her own?

"And that girl that helps her, she's no use at all. It's not like it would cost anything for me to get Harriet. I'm not asking Grandpa to *buy* me a maid. We already own her."

Maddy held his breath. Miss Martha said, "We'll see about a maid. But not Harriet."

Maddy relaxed. Miss Cornelia went on. "But Mama! I *want* Harriet. She's my age, she'd be the best."

Harriet would hate being Miss Cornelia's maid. Miss Cornelia would treat her like dirt, and Harriet would have to take it.

"It won't do. Perhaps Mary Brown, she'd do."

"But I want *Harriet*. Please, Mama. Please!"

If Maddy whined to Mama like that, Mama would set him

straight with a slap. But Miss Martha only said, "It's out of the question. Surely you see why."

Miss Cornelia's voice took on an edge Maddy couldn't quite identify. "No, Mama. I don't see. Why wouldn't Harriet be a good maid for me?"

Because she's your aunt, Maddy thought. Not that Miss Martha would say it. Suddenly a cold feeling came over Maddy. He understood, though he wished he didn't. Miss Cornelia knew exactly who Harriet was—that was why she wanted her.

"I've said no," Miss Martha said. "That's enough."

Miss Cornelia sniffed loudly. Maddy could imagine the toss of her head. "I'm going to ask Grandpa!" she said. She stormed out of the classroom. Maddy had just enough time to put his head down and pull a stupid look over his face before she rushed past him, but Miss Cornelia didn't even glance his way. She turned down the hall and ran up the stairs.

Maddy took a deep breath, and went to find Mama.

"Well," Mama said, "that would start some talk, for sure. And Harriet doesn't need to be involved with Miss Martha's girls. I'll speak to your father."

Three days later Harriet started work in the mountaintop textile factory.

Master Jefferson was proud of his little factory. He had two spinning jennies that spun thread faster than eight women working with regular wheels, and two big looms with fly shuttles that made cloth faster than regular looms. With only four female workers, the factory produced over two thousand yards of cloth a year from raw wool and flax—almost the entire allotment for nearly two hundred slaves. Harriet didn't mind working there; she said it wasn't hard, and she liked it better than keeping her head down in the great house. At least in the shop she wasn't afraid to talk or laugh, and she didn't have to worry about working for Miss Cornelia.

Mama was also pleased. "Spinning is a useful occupation," she said. "Even proper white ladies often know how to spin. You'll be able to provide for yourself, Harriet, if something happens to Beverly and you're out in the world alone."

Mama had a plan for Beverly and Harriet. Beverly would leave when he was twenty-one, because that was the earliest Master Jefferson would set him free. He would travel, and find a job and a place to live, and make a nice life for himself, and then when Harriet was twenty-one she would join him. White women weren't supposed to live alone; they were supposed to have protection.

Whenever Mama talked about her plan Beverly scowled, but Harriet nodded as though the thought of leaving the rest of them didn't bother her at all. Maddy couldn't understand it.

No one spoke of Maddy going to join them when he was older. He only had to look down at himself to know why. He was darker than the rest of them—nearly as dark as Mama. Beverly's and Harriet's skin was white, and as for Eston, he was the spit image of Master Jefferson. Maddy was the odd one out. It was like he had none of their father in him at all.

He tried to tell himself it didn't matter. Jesse Scott was a free black man, and he had a house, a wife, and children. He made good money with his violin. He was happy.

But once Harriet and Beverly went to live as white people, Maddy would never see them again. They didn't say so, not in words, but Maddy knew it. They would be gone as far from him as if they were already dead.

Some nights after work, Beverly would ask Maddy to take a walk with him. Beverly's legs grew tired, standing in the shop all day, and he needed to move around. He had long legs and he walked fast, but never so fast that Maddy couldn't stay with him. They'd head down to the orchard, where the ripening fruits swung on the trees.

"Maddy, look here." Beverly stopped and pointed at a patch of smooth dirt near the fence. Right in the middle was a hoof print from a deer. "Think the deer came to eat peaches?"

Twilight was falling fast, and a hum of insect noise rose from the grass. Bats flitted across the sky. Even in the dim light, Maddy could see Beverly's smile. "Let's take some peaches to Mama," Beverly said.

Whenever Maddy thought about life without Beverly, he wanted to lie down in the grass and howl.

Then one day a different awful thought struck him. "Mama," he said, "what if Beverly gets caught like James Hubbard, when he's out free? What if *Harriet* gets caught? Would they whip Harriet? Or Beverly—or me?"

"No, no," Mama said soothingly. "Nobody will ever whip you. Nobody will ever catch you. When you're free, you'll be just that—free. Not escaped. Free."

"Why won't anybody catch us? The white man that caught James Hubbard, he wasn't from around here. He got paid too, for catching him."

"Nobody will be looking for you," Mama said. "You have to be reported as missing for slave catchers to know to look for you. And you won't be. Your father will let you go. He'll stay quiet. No one will capture you."

"We're supposed to trust Master Jefferson?" Maddy said. Mama nodded. Maddy thought of James Hubbard. He said, "What if Master Jefferson changes his mind?"

"He won't," Mama said. She looked at Maddy for a while and then she said, "You don't have to trust him. All you have to do is trust me."

Maddy nodded. That, he could do.

Maddy and James took over a patch of dirt behind the black-smith shop. They hoed it, mixed in some rotted horse manure from the stables, and planted it with melon seeds. All summer long they tended the patch. They watered it with buckets from the well. They pulled weeds, and trained the vines to grow up sticks pushed into the ground. They picked off slugs. The little green melons they grew were so sweet and good that eating them was like eating sugar candy.

By the time frost came they had grown thirty-five melons. They sold twenty-nine to Miss Edith for the great house table, and ate three apiece on their own.

Mama kept her money in an old cracked jar that had come from France and had French words written on it. Mama said it once held fancy lotion for softening her hands. She laughed and said, "I'm back to goose grease now."

Maddy had put his fifty cents from the mockingbird into the French jar, and it was there still. Now that he had melon money he wanted to keep his money separate from Mama's, so he got an old bottle from Burwell that was chipped on top, and put all his money into that. He also had a penny Mama had given him for his birthday; altogether it added up to one dollar and thirty-eight cents.

"What are you going to do with all that money?" Beverly asked him.

"Don't know," he said. "Save it until I need it, I guess." He thought of James, who still claimed hard times were coming.

"I'm going to buy a violin," said Eston. Maddy rolled his eyes. Eston didn't have any money, he was just making things up.

Eston took real violin lessons now. He played awfully well. They all three went down to Charlottesville for lessons once a week. But now they had trouble finding time for all of them to practice, with only one violin. Eston could practice anytime—and he did—but Beverly worked from sunup to sundown, same as a grown person, and nowadays Maddy stayed plenty busy too.

"You can't buy a violin," Maddy said. "You'll never have enough money for that."

"Will too," said Eston.

"Will not."

"People are going to *pay* to hear me play the violin," Eston insisted.

"Nobody's going to pay you," Maddy said.

"Sure they will," said Beverly. "Why not? I'd pay a penny to hear you play right now." He pulled a penny from the French lotion jar. It was Beverly's penny; he still kept all his money there.

Eston's eyes grew wide. He dove beneath the bed for the violin. "What do you want to hear?" he asked.

"'Money Musk,'" said Beverly.

"I am sick of 'Money Musk,'" said Maddy. Nobody paid attention. Eston set to playing, lickety-split, a big grin stretched across his face. He made mistakes, but he kept going. Maddy watched him and kicked his feet in anger and frustration. There was Eston with his happy face, his happy white face. There was Beverly, with his. And both of them nuts for the violin, and both of them looking more like their father than Maddy did. There was not one thing Maddy could do about it.

Beverly would leave, and Harriet would leave, and then even Eston would leave. Maddy would be left alone.

Chapter Twenty-three

Field-Hand Socks

That fall Maddy was almost ten, and he got his first pair of real shoes at give-out time. Always before, he'd worn leather moccasins that Mama made for him, or gone barefoot when it wasn't cold.

Give-out time happened twice a year, spring and fall. It was when all the enslaved people were given their clothes or the cloth to make them. The kind of clothes or cloth they received depended on the job they did. Burwell's elegant coat, waistcoat, and breeches were tailor-made for him in Charlottesville, and his wife got fine linen to sew into his shirts and cravats. Mama and Miss Edith got fine linen too, for their underthings, and wool flannel for winter, and in the summer pretty lengths of callimanco printed with bright flowers. Mama got enough cloth to make two dresses each season for herself, and enough to make good clothes for Beverly and Harriet and Eston and Maddy.

In the summer the field workers got osnaburg, a scratchy, dirty-looking fabric made from linen and hemp. In the winter they got undyed coarse woven wool. Field workers got enough for just one dress apiece per season, or one shirt and one pair of pants.

The women got a needle apiece and plenty of thread. The men didn't; they had to talk women into sewing for them. Nobody got scissors. Scissors, Mama said, you had to buy on your own, from money you made by working on Sundays or selling vegetables to Miss Martha. Shoes were given out once a year, in the fall, and blankets every three years, or sooner if you could convince the overseers that you wore your blanket out.

Maddy never paid much attention to give-out time. He didn't care what he wore.

But this time the Monticello overseer called him over. He held up a pair of leather shoes. "Here, boy," he said. "Try these on."

Maddy shoved his foot into the first shoe. It hurt. The overseer felt for Maddy's toes, and shook his head. He reached for a larger pair. "Try these."

Mama came up behind them. "He ought to put them on over stockings," she said. "Be sure he has room enough to grow."

The overseer grunted agreement. He looked around in the wagonload of clothes and pulled a pair of child's stockings out of a box.

Maddy stared at them. They were nothing like the stockings he usually wore, knit out of good woolen yarn. These were tubes of coarse woven fabric, with thick seams running up the long sides.

The overseer waved them impatiently.

"No," Mama said. "Not those. We get the other kind."

The overseer looked at the stockings, and then at Mama. "Ah," he said. He threw the ugly stockings back into the wagon bed and brought out a pair like Maddy usually wore.

Mama and the overseer approved the way the second pair of shoes fit, so Maddy wore them home. As soon as he could he took off the stockings, because they made his feet hot, but he kept the shoes on, even though they scraped his heels. He was proud to have shoes.

"Mama," he said, "what were those ugly stockings?"

"For the field workers," Mama said. "We work at the great house, so we get knit ones."

"They didn't even look like stockings. They looked like shirtsleeves." Heavy, ugly shirtsleeves.

"I know," Mama said. "They can't be comfortable. I almost never see people wearing them."

"So why not give real stockings to everybody?"

"It's cheaper to weave fabric than to knit it," Mama said. "Woven stockings cost less."

"How much less?"

"I don't know," Mama said. "It's not my business."

"How many stockings is it?" Maddy persisted. "For how many people?"

Mama pursed her lips. "About thirty up here on the mountaintop," she said. "Maybe a bit more. Say one hundred and sixty working on the farms. That would count the children."

"And everybody gets three pairs of stockings, twice a year—"

"Well, no," Mama said. "Field hands get one pair, twice a year."

"That's not enough," Maddy said. "They'd wear out."

"Not if nobody can stand to wear them," said Mama. "I can't stay here talking with you, Maddy. I've got work to do."

"But Mama—" Maddy said.

Mama turned in the doorway. "Yes?"

"The field hands do the important work. They grow the crops that make the money."

"I know," Mama said.

"So why don't they get the good clothes and we get the ugly ones?"

Mama sighed. "You know the answer to that. Don't ask questions when you already know the answer."

Maddy thought for a moment. He said, "But I don't like the answer I know."

A week later Master Jefferson bought Miss Cornelia her first grown-up silk dress. She squealed when she saw it, threw her arms around Master Jefferson, and kissed him hard. She put the dress on and paraded up and down the parlor.

Maddy couldn't help but stare. He wanted to ask what a

dress like that cost. He wanted to say, "How much is that in field-hand socks?"

Harriet took a different view. "When I grow up I'm going to have a silk dress," she said, back in their room that evening. "I'm going to have one even prettier."

Beverly looked as cross as Maddy felt. "Mama doesn't wear silk," he said. "I don't see why you should."

But Mama sided with Harriet. "I want you in silk dresses," she said to her. "Beautiful clothing and fine buckled shoes. You, and all your little girls." Harriet and Mama smiled at each other.

Maddy thought of Harriet having little girls. Little white girls, with a white daddy, if Harriet could pull it off. "You going to tell them about me?" he asked Harriet. "You going to tell your little girls about your darky little brother?"

Harriet reached toward Maddy, but he ducked away. "I will never forget you," she told him. "I'll always love you and I'll never forget you."

"You going to tell them about me?" Maddy asked. "You going to wear a silk dress when you bring them to visit me?"

Harriet's eyes filled with tears. "Don't," she said. "I can't help that you're—I can't help it, that's all."

Beverly got up. "Let's go for a walk," he said to Maddy.

Maddy ignored him. "You could stay," Maddy said to Harriet. "You and Beverly. You could stay."

"Would you?" Harriet asked. She was angry now; her eyes flashed the way Mama's did. "Would you stay if you had a choice? You think this is easy! Would you stay?"

"It's not easy," said Maddy. "But maybe I would."

"Liar," said Harriet.

"*Maddy.*" Beverly had him by the arm now. He hustled Maddy out the door, calling, "We'll be back, Mama, don't worry," over his shoulder.

"I'll be back," Maddy muttered. "I don't have a choice."

Beverly gripped his arm until they were almost to the orchards, to where a pile of big rocks stood by a half-built stone wall. "Here," said Beverly. He picked up a rock with both hands. "Heave it. Far as you can."

Maddy took the rock. He threw it over his head as hard as he could. The rock crashed against the base of the wall.

"Good," said Beverly. "Here's another."

Maddy threw it. He threw rocks until his arm muscles trembled, until a film of sweat covered his body and his breath came ragged.

"Better?" asked Beverly.

Maddy nodded.

"Good," said Beverly. "Let's get back before Mama leaves, so she knows you're all right."

"Okay," said Maddy. His voice sounded hoarse.

"You need to throw rocks, you throw actual rocks, okay? Don't throw words at Harriet. It's not her fault." He looked at Maddy. "I hope you've got enough sense that in her shoes or mine you'd do the same. We've got to think of the children we might have. We've got to do what's best for them. You hear me?"

"I guess," said Maddy.

"If Harriet died tomorrow, you'd be sorry your last words to her were angry."

Maddy shrugged.

Beverly sighed. "We won't forget you, Maddy. How could we? We never will." After a pause he added, "We'll be able to write to each other, since you taught us all to read."

"Will you write to me?"

Beverly reached for Maddy's hand. "I will. I promise."

Maddy went through and through the primer. It had so many words, easy and hard, so many he could read out loud but didn't understand. *Embellish, transcendent, luminary, apocalypse.* "Embellish," Mama said. "That means to make fancy. You might embellish your shirt with some lace."

"I might not," Maddy said.

"Transcendent," Beverly said. "Sounds like *transcend,* right? So you got to figure it means something that rises."

"Huh," Maddy said.

"*Luminary* means full of light," Miss Ellen said, when Maddy caught up with her as she was walking to the kitchen. She gave him a sideways glance. "You don't really need to know the big words. Most people use little ones most of the time."

"I like big words," Maddy said. "I like to teach them to Beverly."

Apocalypse. "I know that one," Uncle John said, to Maddy's surprise. "That's in the Bible, it means the end of world."

"You've got a Bible?" Maddy asked. He knew Uncle John could read, and write too: Uncle John sometimes wrote to Master Jefferson when Master Jefferson was away.

Uncle John shook his head. "I go down to Charlottesville sometimes on a Sunday, listen to a preacher there. He reads passages out of the Bible. There's a part called the Apocalypse."

Maddy nodded. He knew some about the Bible, but not much. Preachers didn't come to the top of the mountain. "Apocalypse," he said. "So, when's that going to be?"

"No one knows," Uncle John said cheerfully. "No one knows the day nor yet the hour. Got to stay ready. That's what they say."

"That's what James says," Maddy said. "That's what he says his daddy says."

Uncle John nodded. "No flies on Joe Fossett," he said.

"Does *apocalypse* mean what it's going to be like when Master Jefferson dies?" asked Maddy.

Uncle John gave him a sidelong look. "What makes you think that?"

"Money, I guess," Maddy said. "Everybody talks about money. But worry too."

Uncle John took a deep breath. "Most people wouldn't say so," he said. "But I don't know, you could be right."

Chapter Twenty-four

Peter Fossett

The money problems finally got so bad that Master Jefferson sold all his books to the government. The Library of Congress had been destroyed during the war with the British. Master Jefferson offered the government his own books as its replacement.

He had thousands, filling shelves all over the great house. Mama said he loved books like most folks loved children. People in Charlottesville said that giving up his books proved Master Jefferson was a great man.

"He might be a great man," Burwell said, down in the kitchen, "but he's not doing it for nothing." Burwell said the government was paying more than twenty thousand dollars for the books—more than all the Monticello farms together could earn in five good years.

With money on hand, Miss Martha laughed more often.

Master Jefferson bought another wagonload of wine. He drew up improvements for his house at Poplar Forest, and spoke of buying new carriage horses.

"How long will this book money last?" asked Maddy.

Mama glared at him. "That's not our business," she said. Then she sighed, and added, "You'd think it'd last forever, money like that. But I doubt it will."

Maddy wanted to ask if twenty thousand dollars was enough to buy the field hands decent socks, but the look on Mama's face kept him silent.

Miss Edith was pregnant; as summer came on her belly grew round and firm like a watermelon. One morning when Maddy came into the kitchen, he found James with his ear pressed against his mother's side. "I'm listening to the baby," James said, grinning at Maddy. "I've been telling him, he's got to grow big and strong, so we can take on all the girls in this family. He's saying, 'Yes, sir! Yes, sir, I'm a big boy, and I'm ready!' "

Miss Edith laughed. "Not quite ready," she said. "But soon."

"You can tell it's a boy," James said. "The midwife said so, 'cause Mama's carrying him high."

Maria, James's oldest sister, gave him a cross look. "High means a girl," she said. "It's low for a boy."

"That's not what she said," argued James.

"It is," said Miss Edith.

"Well, then, you must be carrying him low," said James, "because I know that's a boy."

Maria laughed. "What do you think, Maddy?"

"Of course it's a boy," Maddy said. "Anybody can see that."

Later James said, "You're lucky, Maddy. Two brothers and only one girl." They had tried to get away fishing, but Wormley had seen them and put them to work weeding the vegetable garden.

"Harriet's all right," Maddy said. He dug into the soil to pull out a thistle by its roots. "Just bossy sometimes. She tells good stories."

"All girls are bossy." James sighed. "You'd think mine would have to listen to me, since I'm oldest, but they don't."

"Eston doesn't listen to me either," Maddy said. "He's probably the bossiest of us all." He looked around. "I wonder where he's run off to. He could weed."

"Probably playing his fiddle."

"If I hear that fiddle," Maddy said, "I'm going to go track him down. He can work." Maddy looked around. The garden was enormous; they could weed all day and not be done.

"Anyway," James said, "you're lucky."

Maddy carried a bushel of weeds to the dump pile and came back. "They'll all be white, and leave me," he said. "You were right. I can't pass."

James looked like he wanted to say something, but didn't know what. After a while he blew out his breath. "You get to be free," he said.

"So Mama says," Maddy said. "Harriet and Beverly, they believe her."

"You don't?"

"Anything could happen," Maddy said. Wormley walked by, and Maddy and James bent to their work. When he was gone Maddy said, "I worry that it's always going to be different for me."

Two weeks later Maddy woke in the dark to the noise of someone pounding on their door. He sat up, quick. Pale streaks of dawn showed around the edges of the shutters. Beverly opened the door, since Mama was still at the great house.

Joe Fossett stood with his arms around his little girls and James beside him. "Edith's time has come," Joe Fossett said. "Davy's gone for the midwife."

"Out of bed, Maddy," Harriet said, kicking him. "Eston, you too." She called to the girls, Maria, Patsy, and Betsy-Ann, to come under the covers with her. "We can go back to sleep," Harriet said.

"We aren't *sleepy*," protested Patsy.

Maddy got out of bed. He grinned at James. James grinned back. Beverly poked the dead ashes in the fireplace. "You want something to eat?" he asked Joe Fossett.

"I do," Maria called, from the bed.

Maddy watched Beverly look around. Of course they didn't have anything to eat. Mama didn't let them keep food in the room: It attracted mice. "How about something to drink?" Beverly said. "I got water."

Joe laughed. "Just keep them out of trouble, Beverly," he said. "Fanny'll get the fire going in the kitchen and you all can get something to eat in a bit. I'm going to sit with Edith 'til the midwife comes."

"We got to keep you out of trouble," Maddy said to James, when Joe had gone.

"Going to be hard to do," James said. "You might have to tie me down." He paced the length of the room twice, then sat on the chair and twiddled his fingers.

"We might," Beverly said. "Don't be nervous. Your mama's used to babies."

"I don't want another girl," James said, glancing sideways at his sisters.

"We do," said Maria, and Patsy said, "So there."

At dawn Harriet and Beverly went off to work like always. "What are we supposed to do?" Maddy asked before they left.

"What do you usually do?" Harriet said. "Use your head, Maddy. You're not the one having the baby, you don't have to do anything special."

Maddy felt like he did. Maria was a big girl, eight years old, and usually she watched Patsy and Betsy-Ann, but usually Miss Edith was in the kitchen making breakfast, and it felt strange to know she was having a baby instead. "Do we go eat?" he asked James.

"Might as well," James said.

Eston grabbed Maddy's hand. "I'm hungry."

The door to the Fossetts' room stood propped open, and as they walked past it Maddy could hear the midwife talking to Miss Edith inside. He carefully looked the other way. So did James and Eston. None of them wanted to see a baby half-born. The girls stopped and waved, and tried to go in and talk to their mother, but James pushed them into the kitchen.

Fanny had hot corn cakes ready, and milk to drink. "You all ought to go somewhere else," she said. "You're already fidgety. Babies take a long time."

James shook his head. "Not this one." He wiped the milk off his upper lip with the back of his hand.

Fanny laughed at him. "How would you know?"

"I've got a feeling." James grinned. "My brother's in a hurry, he's coming fast."

At that exact second the baby screamed. It was a long, loud, angry wail, as though the baby had not wanted to be born. Maddy and Eston and James and Maria all threw down their plates and jumped up, quick, but Fanny moved faster. She barred the door with her wooden spoon. "You are not going anywhere," she said. "You will sit on that bench until I say so. Your mother does not want an audience yet."

They sat. Maddy's mama came in, and kissed and hugged them all around. "The baby just yelled," Maddy said. "It's born."

Mama's eyes were sparkling. "I know," she said. "I took a

little look at it. The midwife's got to clean it up, and then clean up Miss Edith."

"I told them to sit until I said so," Fanny said.

"Good," said Mama.

"Boy or girl?" asked James.

Mama's eyes sparkled more. "I'll let your mama tell you," she said.

Time went by at a crawl even though Fanny gave them jobs to do. Maddy didn't know what Fanny was listening for or how she knew what was happening on the other side of the kitchen wall, but finally she nodded and said, "James. Go get your father from the shop. Then you can all go in together."

The girls got up and ran out with James. Maddy and Eston waited until they had gotten Joe Fossett and come back. After a few minutes they followed them into the Fossetts' room.

Miss Edith lay flat on the bed, covered with a sheet, looking sweaty but happy. Joe Fossett sat beside her, cradling a tiny baby wrapped tight in a blanket. Joe Fossett's hands were almost as big as the baby.

"We've named him Peter," Miss Edith said.

Maddy came closer. The baby stared at him with wide black eyes. "Hello, Peter Fossett," Maddy said.

James put his arm around his father's shoulder and touched the baby with his finger. "See, Maddy," he said. "We've both got little brothers now."

Chapter Twenty-five

The Declaration

James was just nuts for baby Peter. At night he sat in the doorway of their room with Peter on his lap, and made faces at the baby and waggled his fingers in front of his nose. The first morning Peter smiled, James woke Maddy up to tell him the news. Whenever Maddy or Beverly or Eston practiced the violin, James popped his head into their room and said, "Come on over, and play that for my brother. He likes it." Sometimes, when Peter was fussy, James asked Maddy to play for him special.

"Was I that excited when Eston was born?" Maddy asked Mama.

Mama laughed. "You liked Eston fine, but you weren't as wound up as James. I've never seen anybody make as much fuss over a baby as James."

· · ·

That summer Maddy finally began working for Uncle John. He swept shavings and carried tools, just like Beverly did when he began. Uncle John taught him the names of the tools and how they were used, and the different kinds of wood and what each was good for. Maddy took a piece of charcoal and labeled the wood in the shop, alder, pine, hickory, chestnut.

"That's helpful, isn't it?"

"It would be," Beverly said, "if we couldn't already tell what kind of wood it was just by looking."

"Now, Beverly," Uncle John chided him. "Words are fine things."

"Beverly knows that," Maddy said. "He collects them."

"Loquacious," Uncle John said, with a glint in his eye. "Commotion, bedlam, infliction."

"What's that mean?" Maddy asked.

"Means we talk too much," Beverly said. "How about we try for tranquility."

Maddy swept awhile in silent tranquility. Then he said to Uncle John, "Say that first word again."

"Loquacious," Uncle John said. He went to one of the woodshop cabinets and pulled out a heavy green-bound book. It was much bigger than Maddy's blue primer or the little book of stories Miss Ellen had given him. "Look it up," Uncle John said. "Loquacious. *L-o-q—*"

Maddy stared at the green book. "Look it up?"

"This is a dictionary," Uncle John said. "A man named Mr. Webster wrote it. You can look up any word there is, any word at all, and this book will tell you what it means." He showed Maddy how to go through the pages, finding first *l*, then *lo*, then *loq*, and then, right beneath *lopping, loquacious*.

"*Talkative*," Maddy read. "*Given to continual talking*." He grinned. "Eston is a loquacious fool. Where'd you get this book?"

"Miss Cornelia gave it to me," Uncle John said. "She said it would help me with the letters I write."

"Not Miss Ellen?" Maddy asked.

Uncle John shook his head. "Miss Cornelia. Mighty handsome gift, wouldn't you say?"

"Can I look up—can I look up all my words?" Maddy meant all the words in the primer, the ones he could read but didn't understand.

"In time," Uncle John said. "We've got to get our work done. You bring your primer tomorrow, you can look up a couple of words a day."

Maddy looked at the big, beautiful book. He looked at Beverly. "How come you didn't tell me?"

"I didn't know," Beverly said.

Uncle John closed the book and put it back in the cabinet. "Which I only got last week," he said. "Nobody's holding out on you boys. But you'll not talk too much about it, I hope."

"Don't worry," Beverly said. "We won't tell Miss Martha."

Bedlam: a place appropriated for lunatics. Commotion: agitation, perturbation. Well, that was no help. Maddy looked those up too. Agitation: disturbance of tranquility. Ah. Beverly's favorite word. Maddy smiled. And perturbation: disturbance, disorder.

There were so many words in that dictionary. Maddy worked his way through it, day after day, in the short spurts of time Uncle John would allow. All the words in the primer that confused him—and then he had a great burst of thought. "That declaration," he said.

"What declaration?" Uncle John said. "I didn't hear anybody declaring."

"It's lunchtime," Beverly said. "I declare."

Maddy brushed them aside. "The one in the hallway."

Uncle John pursed his lips like he disapproved, but after a bit he said, "Have at it, young'un. Just don't be in the great house when you shouldn't be. You're too old for that now."

It turned out that it wasn't the individual words of the declaration that were hard to understand: It was the way the words, each simple enough by itself, were arranged into complicated sentences. Maddy had to read a bit, and then wait, and think, and read a bit more, and think a bit more. When he finally understood the long first paragraph he felt sad.

"Is slavery a form of government?" he asked Uncle John.

"The government allows slavery," Uncle John replied.

"*Governments rule by consent of the people,*" Beverly cut in. "Haven't you gotten to that part yet?" So Beverly had read the declaration too; Maddy had wondered. "For sure, nobody's giving their consent to be a slave. It's not a government."

"If it was," Maddy said, "we could get rid of it."

"I suppose," said Uncle John. "You best leave all that, Maddy. Thinking about it won't make it better. Come hold this chair rail for me while I heat up some glue."

"Let's both save our money," Maddy said to James. "When I'm twenty-one, Master Jefferson will set me free. Then we'll put our money together and buy you your freedom. And we'll go out west together, just like we said."

James raised an eyebrow. "What, you'd buy me? I'd belong to you?"

"'Course not. I'll give you what money I've got, and you can buy yourself."

James grinned. "All right. Only now we've got to save up extra, so we can buy Peter's freedom too. I'm not leaving him behind."

They wouldn't be twenty-one for more than ten years. Maddy hated to think of how long that was. Once, when he and James saw Master Jefferson on his horse a long way off, Maddy was struck by how frail Master Jefferson looked. James must have thought the same thing, because he turned to Maddy and asked, "What happens if he dies before you're twenty-one? Do you still get to be free?"

"I don't know," Maddy said. "Hope he don't die."

Later Mama said, "I trust him, Maddy. He'll get it fixed in time."

"If he just keeled over dead tomorrow—"

"I trust him," Mama said.

Maddy knew he didn't need to trust Master Jefferson. He only needed to trust Mama. But sometimes even that was hard to do. Maddy saved his money. He had over two dollars now.

Joe Fossett asked Master Jefferson if James could apprentice in the blacksmith shop, and Master Jefferson agreed. So now, in the early summer mornings, Maddy and James both went off to work like men. In Maddy's family's room only Eston was left in the big bed, waiting for Mama to come home, and even though he was a big boy, seven years old, he didn't like that at all. "Go see Miss Fanny," Harriet said, stroking his head when he complained. "She'll be glad to see you. You can help her." Miss Fanny was still running the kitchen for Miss Edith until Miss Edith got over having a baby.

"I don't want to help Miss Fanny," Eston said, opening his eyes wide at Harriet. "I'm a little boy. I'm too little to help her." He stuck out his lower lip and tried to look pitiful. "I need somebody to help me."

Harriet laughed and hugged him. "You're a good little boy," she said. Harriet snuck a skein of woolen yarn out of the textile shop and traded it with Miss Fanny for a pair of laying hens. She gave the hens to Eston. Every morning Eston had to let his hens out of the coop Beverly built for them, and throw them some grain, and get them water. Then he collected their eggs—always one, more often two—and took them to Miss Fanny. He'd sell them to her, and sometimes she'd turn right around and cook him one for breakfast. She wasn't supposed to do that—eggs were too expensive for slaves to eat—and it made Eston giggle. He said, "You paid me to eat that egg."

"You could pay me to eat three of them," Maddy offered. Miss Fanny laughed and whapped him with her spoon.

Later Eston came into the workshop. He handed Maddy half a leftover fried egg sandwiched between two pieces of bread. "It came off the breakfast table," he said. "Miss Martha didn't finish it." Mmm, Maddy loved fried egg.

When the weather grew cold again and work slowed in the carpentry shop, Burwell sent for Beverly and Maddy to wait table at the great house. Master Jefferson still had every kind of visitor, from strangers who dropped by and ended up staying four days, to all Miss Martha's folks, to Mr. and Mrs. Madison, who visited so often that one of the bedrooms was named after them. If fewer than a dozen people sat down to dinner, Burwell and Beverly handled it just the two of them, but if there was more than that they started having Maddy work the table too.

Master Jefferson liked a tranquil dining room. He didn't want servants standing behind every chair, or constantly walking in and out of the room. He'd invented things to make serving dinner easier.

On one side of the dining room was an alcove with a special swinging door. Instead of having hinges down one side like a regular door, it swung around on an axle in its center. The door had shelves on both sides. When the food was ready, one of the girls working for Miss Edith carried it down the basement hallway to the dumbwaiter there. A dumbwaiter was a box on a pulley system that could be hauled up and down between floors. The girl stacked the food on the shelves in the dumbwaiter. Then another girl on the main floor hauled the dumbwaiter up, took out the dishes, and put them on the shelves of the swinging door. Beverly swung it around, and all the food came into the dining room at once without the girls having to carry it in and out. When the dishes were empty Beverly sent them out of the room the same way.

One side of the dining room fireplace opened up like a little cabinet, and held a smaller dumbwaiter just for bottles of wine. Whenever Burwell emptied a bottle, he handed it to Maddy. Maddy stuck it into the fireplace dumbwaiter and hauled on a little rope, and the bottle went down to the basement. In the cellar Uncle Peter replaced the empty bottle with a full one, and Maddy hauled that bottle up and handed it to Burwell.

Folks always carried on about Master Jefferson's fine French wine. It did look pretty, shining ruby-red in the fancy long-stemmed glasses—it looked like juice from raspberries, which Maddy loved. He could imagine how sweet that wine must taste, and he kept hoping for a sip, but the blamed guests kept drinking the bottles dry. Finally, one evening when he was clearing the table, he saw that one bottle wasn't quite empty. Before Burwell could catch him he drank the wine.

"PPffhht!" Maddy spat his mouthful across the table. It was awful—like drinking vinegar straight from the jar.

Burwell whirled around at the noise. He looked at Maddy and laughed.

"Better hope you didn't stain the tablecloth," Beverly said. He was laughing too.

"No matter if he did," Burwell said, "we'll tell Miss Martha it was one of those hick farmers from Ohio."

"Why do they like it so much?" Maddy asked. He looked around the table for something to eat, to clear the taste of the wine from his mouth. Not much left. He grabbed a piece of bread.

"It grows on you," Burwell said, still grinning.

"Not on me it won't," said Maddy.

Burwell poured the wine and laid the food on the table, and passed plates, and took away any dish that was empty. Beverly and Maddy made sure the diners had whatever they needed—water in their glasses, or salt or butter, or fresh napkins. When they weren't fetching things they stood still as statues, Maddy by the fireplace, Beverly by the swinging door. They never, ever spoke, but of course they always listened.

Master Jefferson loved to tell stories, and he would do that if the guests at the table enjoyed listening. But sometimes, especially when he had law students living in the pavilion at the end of the dependency row, his guests were more argumentative, and then conversation grew lively. Maddy enjoyed the debates even when he only understood half of what was said.

"But sir," one of the students might say, holding his wineglass up like he was about to make a toast, "have you considered Socrates?"

"Socrates?" Master Jefferson replied. "Socrates!" His eyes blazed. He leaned forward and said something in a different language, which made absolutely no sense to Maddy, though he guessed it was probably Miss Ellen's Greek. The student fired back with something else Maddy didn't understand. Master Jefferson replied—Maddy wished they'd switch back to English—and half the room applauded. Not Mister Jeff, who, like Maddy, only knew one language, nor Miss Martha—but the people that understood what was going on. Sometimes Miss Ellen forgot herself, and said something in Greek too. When that happened Miss Martha's lips pressed together. If Ellen looked up Miss Martha shook her head.

But if Master Jefferson looked around, and saw that half the dinner guests seemed confused, he would lean back in his chair and smile. "That reminds me," he would say, and start to tell a story about his life in France, or when he was president, or anything at all but at least in English, and all around the table people would nod their heads in relief, and smile.

Maddy moved over to Beverly on the excuse of bringing him a bottle. "What's a Socrates?" he murmured.

"Some kind of promise?" Beverly guessed. Burwell thumped Maddy's head and hissed at him to be quiet. After dinner Burwell said Socrates was a dead man, who said a whole bunch of smart stuff back when.

"Kind of like Master Jefferson," Beverly joked.

"Only a lot more dead," said Maddy.

Burwell told them to hush, but his lips twitched, so Maddy knew he thought it was funny.

When Maddy listened to Master Jefferson speak at the dinner table, and saw how all the other people, including Miss Martha and her husband, listened to him, and how highly they regarded him, Maddy was proud. This was his father, a great and intelligent man. Generous too, at least at the table. He seemed delighted by how much his guests ate and drank.

Yet sometimes when Maddy set another empty wine bottle into the dumbwaiter, he'd wonder what the wine cost, in terms of field-hand socks. He'd place dishes of ice cream around the table, and think of the work it took to pull the ice out of the river, and how the people who cut the ice never tasted the ice cream. Work in the fields was far more laborious than work in the great house, but witnessing the injustice of Master Jefferson's daily extravagances was hard in a different way.

One evening when Maddy was standing in his place minding his business he noticed one of the dinner guests staring at him. Maddy looked quickly at the man's plate and glass, but both were full. The salt and butter were within the man's reach. Maddy didn't know what the man wanted, and when the man saw Maddy looking at him, he dropped his eyes. Next thing, though, the man started staring at Beverly. He looked at Beverly, then at Master Jefferson, then back at Beverly. Then, a moment later, back at Maddy. The man seemed astonished and concerned.

Maddy tried to think what might be wrong. He'd washed his hands and face before he came inside, and he could see that Beverly looked clean too. Maddy studied Beverly and then looked at Master Jefferson the way the guest had.

Then he understood.

Beverly looked like Master Jefferson.

Beverly's hair was darker, not red, and his eyes were darker, but the shape of his face and eyes matched Master Jefferson's. When Beverly was thinking he put his lips together just the way Master Jefferson did.

The visitor seemed unnerved. He spent the whole dinner sneaking glances at Beverly and Maddy. Maddy was glad when the meal was done.

He hadn't spent much time looking in mirrors. With his darker skin he always figured he didn't look like Master Jefferson at all.

"You do," Beverly said, later that night when Maddy asked him. "Especially around the eyes. Not as much as Eston does, but you still do."

"Have people stared at you like that before?"

Beverly shrugged. "Sure. Not so much the Southerners—

they'd rather not look. Some of the Yankees, their eyes about bug out of their heads."

"Do they say anything?" Maddy asked.

"Not to me," Beverly said. "Once I heard Miss Martha say our 'strong Jefferson family resemblance' was because Master Jefferson's nephews came here and fooled around with Mama."

"That's not true!" Everyone who knew Mama knew she was faithful. "Miss Martha knows better."

Beverly shrugged again. "What's she supposed to say?"

"What are you going to tell people, when you're white and they want to know who your daddy is?"

"I'm not going to tell them anything," Beverly said. "I can't tell them about my mama or my father, either one."

"I know that," Maddy said. "But folks'll ask. What are you going to say?"

Beverly looked worried. "I don't know. I guess I'll just tell them it's none of their business. I never was any good at telling lies."

Christmastime came, and with it celebration. Joe Fossett let the forge go cold. The weaving shop shut down, and Uncle John padlocked his workroom. Mulberry Row felt like one long party. Of course Miss Edith and Miss Fanny had to cook like the devil was after them to feed all the guests in the great house, but lots of people helped them. Some folks got passes, to visit relatives on other plantations, and some folks from other plantations came to Monticello. When Mama was around she was always singing. Beverly played his violin, and folks danced, and a couple of times he even went up to the great house and played so the white folks could dance too.

Maddy felt so happy. He remembered that later.

On the first day of January, Master Jefferson sold James.

Chapter Twenty-six

Master Jefferson Sells James

It wasn't even Master Jefferson who told them. It was the white overseer Mr. Bacon.

Maddy was in the kitchen eating breakfast before work, along with James and Beverly and the usual crowd of people. When Mr. Bacon walked in all conversation stopped. People stepped out of his way until he had a clear space around him.

Mr. Bacon scanned the room. He cleared his throat. "Edy," he said, "your boy's going to Edgehill."

The first boy Maddy thought of was baby Peter, but that didn't make sense. Then his heart froze. *James.*

Miss Edith nodded slowly. "He's going to do some work over there? For how long?" Edgehill was Miss Martha's husband's plantation, three miles away.

"He's going there," Mr. Bacon said. "For good. Get his things."

"I don't know what you mean." Miss Edith spoke slowly and politely. "James is apprenticed to the blacksmith shop. He hasn't got business at Edgehill."

Maddy felt a strange buzzing sensation in his head. He looked at James. James was staring at his mother.

Mr. Bacon sounded annoyed. "Don't be stupid, Edy. Mr. Randolph said he needed a boy. Mr. Jefferson sold him yours. Your James. It's not your place to say what anyone's business is. Get his things, or he'll go there without."

The silence in the room was deafening. Maddy felt his mouth go dry. He looked at the floor, afraid to lift his eyes. In the corner, in Maria's arms, baby Peter started to cry.

Miss Edith tried again. "You don't mean my James? *My* James?"

"He ain't your James," Mr. Bacon said. "He was Mr. Jefferson's James, and now he's Mr. Randolph's James."

"But he's just eleven," she said.

Mr. Bacon took a deep breath. "I don't know about that."

"He's only just eleven," Miss Edith repeated. "Master Jefferson always says he would never sell a child before they turned twelve. I know that's what he says. Besides, James is going to be a blacksmith. He's apprenticed to his father. We need another blacksmith. It's income for the farm."

Behind James, his sister Betsy-Ann began to cry too.

"I've got nothing to do with it," Mr. Bacon said. "All I know is what I've been told. Mr. Randolph wanted a boy, Master Jefferson sold him this one. I'm supposed to take him to Edgehill. Get your things together, boy. The wagon's waiting."

"No," Miss Edith said.

Mr. Bacon took a step toward her, his face darkening. Miss Edith held her ground. "He's my boy," she said. Her hand clenched the spoon she was holding. *He is my son.*"

"Not anymore he isn't," Mr. Bacon said. "You ought to feel lucky. He's not going far. You'll see him on Sundays."

Miss Edith moved slowly around the big table in front of the hearth. People stepped silently out of her way. She went to James and wrapped her arms around him, and whispered something into his ear. James's round eyes filled with tears. His hands, when he put them around his mother, were shaking.

Maddy pushed his way out of the kitchen. He ran for the great house and pounded on Master Jefferson's bedroom door. "Mama!" Maddy shouted. "Mama!"

Burwell came running and tried to pull him away. Maddy screeched and held on to the doorknob until he felt it turn in his grasp. Mama opened the door.

"What?" she said. "Who's hurt?"

"He's sold James," Maddy gasped. "He's sold James."

Mama came all the way through the door and shut it hard behind her. She grabbed Maddy's arm and pulled him down the hall, and gave Burwell a look that made him back away. "Tell me," she said.

Maddy told her quick. "You've got to do something, Mama. Stop him. He can't sell James."

She shut her eyes and said, "I didn't know. I'm sorry."

"Do something!" Maddy said. "*Mama!* Stop him! Tell our father! He can't sell James! It's James, Mama! James!"

"Be quiet!" Mama said. "You'll wake the house!" Maddy didn't care who he woke. He'd scream all day long if he had to. Mama grabbed his arm and shook it. "You be still!"

"Help him! Why won't you help him?"

"I can't do that," Mama said in a fierce whisper. "It's not possible. It's not my business."

"But it's *James.*"

"Unless it's you, or Beverly, or Harriet, or Eston, I can't do anything. It's no use. I'll only make trouble if I try."

"But Mama—"

"Come," Mama said, still holding his arm. "We'll go say good-bye."

Maddy would not have thought it possible that he could walk back to the kitchen, that he could stand beside the overseer's wagon and watch James climb into the wagon and be driven away. He would not have thought it possible that Joe Fossett could look so hard and cold, or that Miss Edith could keep from screaming, or that James could kiss baby Peter good-bye without bursting into sobs.

Maddy didn't go to work that day. He lay on the bed with his face to the wall, and he wasn't sure who he hated more, his mother or Master Jefferson.

. . .

The next day Beverly kicked him out of bed. "You wanted to be grown enough for a real job," he said. "You've got to do that job. Get up."

Maddy balked in front of the kitchen door. "I can't go in there," he said. "What'll Miss Edith say?"

"What's she going to say?" Beverly asked. "She cooked dinner last night, didn't she?" Maddy didn't know if she had or not. "Twenty people," Beverly said. "I waited table. It was a handful. We could have used you, but I thought I'd give you the one day."

In the kitchen breakfast was laid out like usual. Miss Edith had bacon for the great house frying on the hearth, and was mixing the batter for her famous breakfast muffins. She handed Maddy a bowl of grits without saying a word. Maddy studied her. Miss Edith looked haggard, like she hadn't slept for a week, but the kitchen itself was pristine.

Eston slid behind the table and put his arms around Miss Edith. He buried his face in her apron, and she buried her face in his hair.

"Where's Mama?" Maddy whispered to Beverly.

Beverly shook his head, the tiniest bit, so Maddy knew: Mama was at the great house. Maddy's stomach clenched. He put down the bowl of grits and walked out. Beverly followed.

"How can they?" Maddy asked as they walked to the woodshop. "How can Miss Edith make breakfast? How can Mama go up there?"

"What're they supposed to do?" Beverly asked. "You want Miss Edith to burn the kitchen down? Tell everyone she doesn't want to be cook no more? You want Mama to scorn Master Jefferson? That'd help us get free, sure enough."

"Maybe," Maddy said. He thought Miss Edith could at least not make muffins. She could serve the great house scorched porridge for a few days. And Mama—

"It won't bring James back," Beverly said. "He's gone. Miss Edith's got four other children, and Mama's got us. Last thing Miss Edith needs is to be sent to work in the fields, instead of somewhere she can sit down and keep warm in winter and feed her family good food."

"Mama should have done something," Maddy said.

"I don't think she could," said Beverly. "If she knew it was coming, if she heard about it ahead of time, maybe she could have talked him out of it. But once James was sold—Master Jefferson wouldn't go back on his word to Mr. Randolph. You know that. Anyhow, as far as I know Mama's never stopped a slave from being sold before."

They'd never had a slave sold from Monticello before, except James Hubbard. When Maddy said so, Beverly shook his head. "Master Jefferson sells people all the time. He sells field hands, you just don't know them. He sold Joe Fossett's mama and brother and sisters. Mama's sister Thenia, he sold her to James Monroe."

Maddy didn't know his aunt Thenia, though he'd heard her name. She died before he was born. "I thought Master

Jefferson liked James," he said. "I thought he liked Miss Edith and Joe Fossett. I thought he'd be fair to people he liked."

Beverly took his hand and squeezed it. "I thought so too."

There wasn't much work in the woodshop that day, and if there had been, none of them would have had the heart to do it. Uncle John was silent, closed down from sorrow. "Fine boy like James," he muttered, halfway through the morning. He shook his head and sighed. Maddy didn't say a word. He scraped at a rough piece of wood with a bit of broken glass, scraped and scraped it, until the wood was as smooth as the glass, but the wood wasn't meant for anything, it was just something for his hands to do. He thought of Uncle John's dictionary. What were the words for this? He didn't know them.

A few hours later Uncle John got up. "Lock the door when you leave, Beverly," he said. "I'm going to go find me a drink." He walked out the door, carefully shutting it behind him.

Beverly got up to put another log on the woodshop fire. "I hope he doesn't steal the good brandy," Beverly said. "They'll sell him next."

Maddy looked up from his scraping. "*Papa* will sell him," he said. "You say '*they'll* sell him,' but what you mean is, '*Papa* will sell him.' *Our father* will sell him."

Beverly nodded.

Maddy said, "Nobody around here speaks the truth."

"Why, no, of course not," Beverly said with a bitter smile.

"That would not be gentlemanlike. It would be the end of all tranquility."

Maddy got up. "*Would* Uncle John steal the brandy?" he asked. "'Cause if he would, I'm going to go steal it for him." He'd like to see Master Jefferson try to sell him or whip him, either one.

Beverly waved his hand. "No, no, he's got a jar of hooch in his cabin. Some kind of corn liquor Uncle Peter makes on Sundays."

"Then I'm leaving," Maddy said.

He went down to the blacksmith shop. Joe Fossett had the forge hot, and he was making nails the way the nail boys used to. *Pound, pound, pound, pound!* and then a flip of the newly made nail into a bucket, and then, *pound, pound, pound, pound!* over and over again. It looked to Maddy like Joe Fossett's version of throwing rocks. He sat down on a keg to watch.

Joe Fossett made twelve more nails. "We're going to miss him, Maddy," he said at last.

Maddy nodded.

"It's true he's not far. That's some comfort. I tell myself, that's some comfort. Right?"

Maddy snorted. He said, "Beverly says he sold your mama."

Joe nodded. He put down the hammer and wiped his hands on his pants legs. "That was a little different, maybe," he said. Joe Fossett pulled out another keg, and sat down on it beside Maddy.

"When Master Jefferson went away to France," Joe Fossett said, "my mama got hired out to a white man named Thomas Bell. They fell in love, I guess, and Mama had Robert and Sally—you know Sally, she's Jesse Scott's wife. We all lived down there in Charlottesville with Thomas Bell. He was a real good man, even if he was white. He told everybody flat out that Robert and Sally were his children, and later on when he died, he left his house and all his goods to Mama and to them.

"Anyhow, when Master Jefferson came back from France, Mama asked him if he would sell her to Thomas Bell—she and all her children. Well, the ones of us that were left. Thomas Bell was willing to buy all of us, not just the ones that were his blood. He was going to set us all free. He did free Mama and Robert and Sally."

"Why not you?" asked Maddy.

Joe Fossett held up his hand. "Master Jefferson sold Mama and the little ones. But he wouldn't sell me or my sister Betsey. He made us come back to Monticello instead. I was eleven. Betsey was nine." Joe hesitated. "It was hard for us, here without Mama."

Maddy thought for a moment. "You could have been free."

Joe shrugged. "I reckon. It didn't work out like that."

Maddy wanted to ask if Joe Fossett ever thought about that, about the difference between his brother Robert and himself. But Maddy guessed he knew the answer. Instead he said, "What did you mean, saying all your mama's children, well, the ones of you that were left? Did you have family that died?" Maddy knew Sally Bell, and he'd heard of Robert, but he'd never known any of Joe Fossett's other kin, not a sister named Betsey nor anybody else.

Joe shrugged. "I had a brother, Daniel, he was eight years older than me, and he got sold when I was about three. He's far away and I don't hear about him. And then my sister Molly, she was just three years older than me. She was sold when she was thirteen—that was when we lived with Mr. Bell. She went to Mr. Randolph's, like James. She's dead now too."

Joe wiped his hands down his pants legs again. He stood and picked up his hammer. "It's hard," he said. "You think you'd get used to it, but you don't."

"Who was your daddy?" Maddy asked. It was a terrible question; none of his business, he knew. Mama would be angry if she found out he asked it.

Joe Fossett didn't seem to mind. "His last name was Fossett—that figures, doesn't it—and Mama says he was a good man. That's all she says. I figure, if she doesn't want to say more, I ought not to ask."

Maddy nodded. Some stories were too sad to tell. "What happened to your sister Betsey?"

"Master Jefferson gave her to his daughter Maria, the one that died. For a wedding present. Miss Maria's husband still has her. They live on a farm called Millbrook, out in Buckingham County. I get word of her once in a while. Haven't seen her in twenty years. We named Betsy-Ann for her."

Maddy thought Joe Fossett's face was the saddest thing in the world.

"I knew it could happen," Joe Fossett said. "James. I just didn't think it would happen yet. I thought, maybe, me being a good blacksmith and Edith a good cook, we might have some protection—and making James my apprentice—" Joe stopped and swallowed hard. After another pause he said, "I tried to keep us all together. James was born in the President's House. In Washington, D.C. Did you know that?"

Maddy nodded.

"Hard to believe, isn't it." It wasn't a question, so Maddy didn't answer.

"I got two dollars," Maddy said. "How much—"

Joe Fossett shook his head. "I already been to Mr. Randolph's," he said. "Went there yesterday with all my money in my hand. He won't sell. I don't know why he wants James, but he won't sell."

When Maddy waited tables that night, and the next, he kept his eyes down. He didn't even glance at Master Jefferson. He tried not to hear what he was saying. Maddy didn't understand how everyone could go on with their work, how Miss Edith could keep cooking, same as always, without burning the meat or poisoning the soup or spitting into the food. How Joe Fossett could shoe Master Jefferson's riding horse without driving the nails too deep.

How Mama could go to Master Jefferson's room at night.

After a few days Harriet took Maddy aside. She walked him past the garden and sat him down on an old log on the hill. "What," she said, "do you think slavery *is*?"

Maddy glared at her. Harriet took no notice.

"I'll tell you," she said. "It's not having any say. Any choice. Not about you, not about your family, not about anything. Forget having to work for someone. Forget not being paid. It's the say. The not having any say."

"I know that," Maddy said.

"You act like you don't. You act like you're just now discovering what everyone else understood all along."

Maddy searched for the words to explain. "I thought Master Jefferson cared about Miss Edith and Joe," he said. "He liked James for bringing him that bird. I thought he wouldn't sell people he liked, not if they worked hard."

Harriet shook her head. "You thought wrong."

Maddy plucked some of the dead grass on the hillside and threw it into the air. He watched the wind carry it away. "So that's why you're so glad to go," he said. "To leave us."

Harriet nodded. "If I'm not free, it will be terrible when I grow up." She tucked the edge of her skirt around her ankles and shivered at a gust of wind. She pulled Maddy's arm until he leaned against her. She rubbed his forehead with her hand. "I'm pretty, I know I am," she said. "I'm not saying it to be vain. And if I'm not free, or even just not white, and some white man decides he fancies me—I might not be able to tell him no. Mama's lucky, she had more choice than most."

Maddy flinched. He understood what Harriet meant. Harriet looked down at him. "Okay?" she said.

"Okay," said Maddy. "I get it. But Beverly, he acts like he doesn't want to leave. You act like you do."

"He doesn't want to leave Mama. He sure wants to be free." When Maddy didn't reply, Harriet added, "You ask him." A moment later she said, "Ask Mama to tell you about her brothers. James, that was the cook in France. And Robert. Ask her."

Uncle John and Uncle Peter were Mama's brothers. Maddy had heard of James the cook, but he didn't know anything about an uncle Robert. Mama had had eleven brothers and sisters; some were dead, and it was hard to keep track of them all.

"You ask her," Harriet said. She sat him up and stood and brushed grass from her skirt. "Meanwhile, stop being mad at Miss Edith. Stop being mad at everybody if you can, but especially Miss Edith. She's got trouble enough."

When Maddy asked Mama about her brothers, she sighed. Her face softened, but Maddy couldn't tell whether she was happy or sad. "Robert was always Master Jefferson's favorite," Mama said. "Right from when my family first came to Monticello." She smiled. "Have I never told you this story?" When Maddy shook his head, Mama called Eston over. "You ought to hear this too." She sat them down by the fire, picked up her knitting, and began.

"Master Jefferson's wife was named Martha Wayles. Her father, Mr. Wayles, was my father too. He was the father of half my brothers and sisters, from Robert straight down to me. A few years after Martha Wayles and Master Jefferson married, Mr. Wayles died. Master Jefferson inherited everything Mr. Wayles owned."

"People, land, debts," Maddy said, remembering.

Mama nodded. "He got everything."

"Counting you?" asked Eston.

Mama nodded. "My mother, the sea captain's child, and all her children—ten of us, at the time—we all came to Monticello."

"You stayed together," Maddy said.

Mama nodded. "I was two years old. Robert would have been about thirteen. He was a lovely boy, and Master Jefferson favored him. Robert was Master Jefferson's personal servant at the Continental Congress in Philadelphia. He stayed with him throughout the war and returned to Monticello afterward. James, you know, went to France and trained to be a chef.

"Master Jefferson thought so highly of Robert and James that when he returned from France he set them both free."

Mama stopped for a moment. She stared hard at her knitting, as if she had dropped a stitch. "What happened?" Maddy prompted.

Mama looked up. "They left. They went away from Monticello to live their own lives. James found trouble; he's dead now. But I think Robert is still alive. He was in Richmond with a wife and children. I don't hear from him. He doesn't come back here."

"But that's okay, isn't it?" Eston said. "If he's free, he's allowed to live in Richmond."

"Yes," Mama said. "He can live wherever he wants. That's what freedom means. The problem was, Master Jefferson set James and Robert free because he thought they were his friends. He thought that when Robert and James were free they'd keep on at Monticello forever, that nothing would change except that he'd pay them. He didn't understand that freedom was bigger than that to them. They did like Master Jefferson—sure they did. But they loved being free.

"It upset Master Jefferson when they left. It hurt his feelings."

"They weren't trying to upset him," Eston said.

"They weren't," Mama said. "Master Jefferson didn't understand what it's like to live under somebody else's control. He still doesn't; he never will. That was the last time he ever set anyone free."

Maddy said, "Is that why he won't make you free?" It was a bold question, but Maddy had to ask it. "You always say we'll be free, but never you. If he cares about you—"

"He does," Mama said quickly. "He does care about me. I know that. But he'll never set me free." She dropped her knitting into her lap and leaned forward. "If he did, it would have to be recorded at the courthouse. The records are filed where anyone can read them. Newspapers would find out, and there'd be talk. There's already talk, but it would be worse. Free papers would be proof, in some people's minds."

"So?" Maddy asked. Mr. Wayles was Mama's daddy. Captain Hemings had been Grandma's daddy. There were white daddies everywhere.

"It would stain his reputation," Mama said. "We've been over this before. A president, a leader of the revolution, an important man in history—he's not supposed to have children with a woman he owns."

"But it is okay that he owns people?" Maddy said. "That he sells little boys?"

"You wouldn't think so," Mama said. "I can't explain it. I don't think it's okay, but some people do."

Maddy thought of the story Harriet was always telling them, about Great-grandma being kidnapped in Africa. "What's the difference," he asked, "between the men that kidnapped Great-grandma, and Master Jefferson? They took her away from her family. Master Jefferson took James away from his."

Mama thought for a moment, and then spoke slowly, as though choosing her words with care. "Master Jefferson would think it impossible that he could be in any way compared to a slave trader. He would say that he's a gentleman, an educated man. He would say that he works for the good of his country, and therefore for the good of all Americans. He'd say he's a farmer, a landowner. He wouldn't understand how you could possibly ask such a question."

"What would you say, Mama?" Eston asked.

Mama thought for a while again. "I'd say Master Jefferson avoids causing pain to anyone where he can see it," she said. "But if he can't see it, or won't see it, he doesn't think the pain he causes is real."

Mama continued, "I would say that slave catchers—the ones who kidnapped Great-grandma—are the lowest of the low. The ships, the whips—I don't know what that's like, thank mercy. Never in my life have I been hit, or physically harmed."

Mama sighed, and picked her knitting up again before she went on. "I've had a comfortable life," she said. "I don't work very hard and I'm never hungry or cold. I have four healthy children and I am treated well.

"But it's not freedom. Sometimes it looks pretty close to freedom. Sometimes it feels okay. Then something happens like with James, and I'm reminded all over again that we live in a prison on this mountain. It's a prison no matter how comfortable it may appear. You children will be free. That's the joy of my life, the one thing I hold to. You will be free."

Mama sat quiet. Eston huddled closer to Maddy. Maddy thought for a moment of Harriet, of the bright little sons and daughters she said she wanted to have. Free.

"Your father acts the same with money," Mama said. "If his debts aren't right in front of him, it's as though they don't exist, as though it doesn't matter how much he spends every day. He knows Miss Martha or Mister Jeff will have to pay whatever he owes once he's gone—but that doesn't change how he behaves. He orders his life the way he wants it, no matter what it costs other people, even other people he believes he loves.

"All of the good things about him," Mama said, "president, patriot, gentleman. Educated and intelligent man—those are all true too. He's done many great things. I hope you can be proud of that part of him."

Maddy snorted. After James, he would never be proud of his father again.

Jesse Scott gave Maddy a long, difficult piece to learn on the violin. It sounded like grief, like the wind sobbing, and he played it over and over except when little Peter Fossett couldn't sleep. Then he played dance tunes to make the baby laugh.

When it was Eston's turn with the violin he played "Money Musk." Maddy told him to stop. "I hate that song. I don't ever want to hear it again."

"You can't tell me what to play," Eston said. "I'm sad too. I want to play happy."

"It's his song," Maddy said. "I don't want to hear it."

"It's *my* song," Eston said. "It used to be his, but now it's mine. And just because you hate him doesn't mean I have to."

"How can you not hate him?" Maddy asked.

Eston shrugged his narrow shoulders. "I don't like hating," he said. "It makes me feel bad."

Chapter Twenty-seven

Moving On

The first Sunday after James was sold, sleet fell in driving sheets the whole day long. James didn't come home. No one expected him to, not with a three-mile walk in such horrible weather, but when Maddy went into the kitchen at noon to get something to eat, Miss Edith swung around from the hearth, hope lighting her eyes.

"I'm sorry," Maddy said. "It's just me."

Miss Edith gave a short laugh. "Oh, I know I raised him smart enough to stay out of the rain," she said. "We'll see him next Sunday, I'm sure."

They did. James was skinnier and dirtier. His shirt was torn. His face looked closed, almost wary. He cuddled Peter on his lap in the kitchen while his sister Maria mended his shirt, and Miss Edith made Sunday dinner for the great house.

"Aren't they feeding you?" Miss Edith asked. She pushed a

plate of chicken toward James. "That's from yesterday. Eat it."

James pushed the plate toward Maddy. Maddy loved chicken, but he shook his head. He hadn't thought James would look hungry.

"They give out plenty of food," James said between mouthfuls. "It's just not good food, not like here. Since Master Randolph rides over here for dinner most nights they don't bother keeping much of a cook. All the hands are on their own. I get my week's allotment, cornmeal and half a pound of fatback and salt. Couple of salt fish. Like the field hands here. They gave me a pot too. I handed it over to one of the women, and she cooks for me in exchange." James snorted. "Which is good, because if I had to cook for myself, I'd probably starve."

Miss Edith pushed another bowl toward James. Mashed turnips, flavored with pieces of bacon. This time, when James offered it to Maddy, Maddy did take a bite.

"What's the forge like there?" Maddy asked.

James didn't raise his eyes. "Master Randolph doesn't have a forge. Doesn't need one, he sends his work here." He looked up. "I got put to ground." James scooped another spoonful of turnips. Miss Edith poured him a glass of milk. "How's the carpentry shop?"

"Pretty good," Maddy said. "We're working on a set of chairs."

"That's nice," said James. He turned and spoke to one of his sisters.

Maddy looked at James's thin shoulders, his grimy shirt. He felt ashamed of becoming a carpenter while James had to work in a field. It wasn't his fault, but he still felt ashamed.

Just before James left Maddy pulled him aside. "I'll take care of Peter for you," he said. "I'll be good to him, and I'll make sure he knows all about you. You'll see him a lot, I know, I just—" He stopped. James's eyes were full of tears.

"Thanks," James said.

"I know you'll be here every week."

"He looked bigger already," James said, his voice shaking a little. "He changed so much, in just those two weeks."

Beverly said they couldn't forget, but they could choose to move on. He said anger was like a heavy rock, hard to carry every day. It was easier to get through life if you could set your anger down.

Maddy said if anger was a rock, then he meant to throw it hard. He might hit somebody with it, did he get the chance. Beverly's eyes grew sad, sad. "Won't do any good," he said.

"Might," Maddy said.

"Oh, Maddy." He pulled Maddy tight against him, like Mama did, and kissed the top of his head before Maddy could squirm away.

In spring Master Jefferson went for a month to Poplar Forest. The bustle of visitors ceased. When Miss Martha was in charge of the house, she didn't invite everyone in the world to dinner, so Maddy didn't have to stand in the dining room while white folks stared. Burwell traveled with Master Jefferson, but Miss Martha said she'd do just fine with one of the women to wait table, thank you. Beverly and Maddy could go back to Mulberry Row.

"Why doesn't Miss Martha ever go home?" Maddy asked Mama.

"She is home," Mama said. "She lives here."

"I mean to Edgehill," Maddy said. "Her husband's farm. Where James is."

Mama shook her head. "She doesn't like her husband," Mama said, "and he's considered a failure. His farm isn't profitable. He can't keep Miss Martha and the children in the style they're accustomed to. Master Jefferson can."

"How?" asked Maddy. "Everyone says Master Jefferson doesn't have any money either."

Mama sighed. "He has some," she said. "The Monticello farms do make money. Mister Jeff manages them well."

"But everyone says that Master Jefferson spends more than he has. That there's no money, but all sorts of debts to pay, and all that French wine—"

"The wine is the least of it, I assure you—"

"I know, but Mama? If Master Jefferson didn't have to keep Miss Martha's children, could he have afforded to keep James? And if Mr. Randolph doesn't have any money, how could he buy James?"

Mama hugged him. "I don't think selling James was about

money. I think Mr. Randolph just wanted another slave."

"But it doesn't make sense," Maddy said. "James was going to be a blacksmith. Now he's just a field hand. If Mr. Randolph wanted a field hand, a grown man would have been more useful to him than James."

"I don't know why he wanted James," Mama said. "I don't understand it either."

In June, Beverly and Uncle John worked the wheat harvest. Mama insisted Maddy was still too young. It was a bad year. When all the wheat had been ground into flour, and enough for everyone to eat during the year put by, there was hardly any left over to sell.

Wheat was the most profitable crop Monticello grew. Now there would be no wheat money that year. Mama said not to worry. She said worry couldn't change a thing.

After a while Maddy did start to feel like his anger was weighing him down. He wanted James back so badly it made his stomach hurt, but sometimes his head throbbed with all the anger inside of it, and more than anything he wanted rest.

Tranquility. Wasn't that what Beverly said?

One evening in late summer, as Maddy walked home from the shop, he saw Master Jefferson on the bottom porch step of the great house, using his pocket watch to time his younger grandchildren running laps of the lush green lawn.

Miss Mary watched, laughing, holding Tim's little hands, while the boys, James, Lewis, and Ben, raced. Lewis lost, of course; he was littlest. But he tried so hard to catch up to his brothers that when he reached the porch he couldn't stop. He cannoned into Master Jefferson and knocked him down.

Without thinking, Maddy ran. Master Jefferson lay on his side, unmoving, his legs tangled up with Lewis's. The other James Madison began to pull his arm. "Don't touch him," Maddy yelled. "Don't touch him 'til we know if he's hurt." He looked at Miss Mary. "Get Burwell!" Mary nodded and ran.

Master Jefferson gasped and wheezed and clutched his belly.

"Grandpa," said the other James Madison, sounding panicked. "Grandpa!"

Maddy remembered when Eston had fallen off a chair and caught the edge of a table on his stomach. "He's knocked the air out of himself," he said. It was frightening but not dangerous. "You've knocked the air out, right, sir?"

Master Jefferson nodded. He looked like he was starting to breathe again. Maddy knelt beside him, relieved. The other James Madison hauled Lewis up. After another minute, Master Jefferson rose shakily to his feet. He waved off Burwell, who had started to run from the house.

"No need to fuss," he said.

"We were worried, sir," the other James Madison said. He glared at Lewis, who started to sob. "You're too old to fall down."

"Too old! Why, I should hope not." He rumpled the other James Madison's hair, and smiled just a bit at Maddy. "You don't think I'm old, do you?" he asked Maddy.

Maddy looked at the wrinkles on Master Jefferson's face, and the age spots on his long hands; he could see how frail and thin Master Jefferson was. "I'm glad you're all right, sir," he said.

"A diplomat." Master Jefferson chuckled. "Very good. Thank you for that answer."

Maddy walked home, more confused than ever. He guessed he'd managed to set some of his anger down after all. He'd just rushed to help the man who sold James.

"You rushed to help your elderly father," Beverly said, later, when Maddy told him about it. "That's a good thing. You can't change him, but you can decide what kind of person you're going to be."

Maddy shook his head. His elderly father. The man who sold James. How could Master Jefferson be both?

What did Master Jefferson see when he looked at Maddy? His son, or his slave?

Chapter Twenty-eight

Poplar Forest

At the start of September, Uncle John came into the wood-shop whistling a happy tune. "I'm taking a trip to Poplar Forest," he told Maddy and Beverly. "Leaving this afternoon. Master Jefferson's got a bunch of work for me there, and he wants me to take the wagon, load it up with wood, and leave today so I can get there ahead of him."

Maddy knew Master Jefferson had been planning to take Miss Virginia and Miss Ellen there. It made sense to send Uncle John early, since the heavy wagon would travel more slowly than the landau.

Beverly said, "What do you want us to do while you're gone?"

Uncle John grinned. "I don't know quite yet. I guess you'll have to wait until I tell you." Beverly looked puzzled. Uncle John started to laugh. "I'm taking my two apprentices with me," he said. "That's what I was told. 'Take your two apprentices, John, there's a lot of work to do.'"

"We're going to Poplar Forest?" Maddy couldn't believe it. He'd never been farther from Monticello than Charlottesville.

"We'll be gone a couple of weeks. Maddy, you'd best go tell your mama."

Mama was glad for them. Eston pouted, but that couldn't be helped. Miss Edith packed them a great big basket of food, and they loaded the wagon with wood and tools and set out just after noontime.

It was the most beautiful day. The sky was like an upside-down bowl, bright blue, covering the whole world as they came down the mountain. As far as Maddy could see there was not one single cloud. The leaves on the top of the mountain had begun to change to gold and brown, but lower down everything was still green, and the sunlight was so clear Maddy had to squint to look at the sky.

Uncle John was in a high mood, and Beverly too. They took turns telling jokes and stories, and they all laughed so hard that once Beverly almost fell out of the wagon. He leaned sideways on the seat, clutching his guts while he laughed, and the wagon bounced into a rut. Beverly fell straight over the edge. Uncle John caught him by the back of his shirt and hauled him back, and then they laughed until they howled.

After a few hours they came to a river spanned by a long bridge. Uncle John halted the horses off the road. "What's wrong?" Maddy asked. "We need some kind of paper to cross that bridge?"

Uncle John shook his head. "What's wrong is my legs are stiff and my seat's gone numb. I need a break, and so do the horses. Get them some water, Maddy. Beverly, oats." Uncle John walked off behind a bush. Maddy dipped river water into a bucket and watered the horses, then took a long drink himself. Beverly put oats into the horses' nosebags and strapped them into place. Then he got out the basket of food and carried it to the clear spot by the river where Uncle John sat. "Mmm," Uncle John said. "Smart boy."

"Can I eat something?" Maddy asked.

"Help yourself."

"What can I have?"

Uncle John pulled out a corn pone and took a bite. "Anything you want."

Maddy sat back like Uncle John and let the sunshine warm his legs. He ate a cookie, then an apple, then a hunk of cheese. "This has to last until we get there?" he asked, looking through the rest of the food. "Three days?" The basket was big, but maybe not that big. He'd better slow down.

"Nah, nah, we'll get hot food where we stop," Uncle John said.

Maddy ate another cookie. On the riverbank, a long-legged bird took flight. Maddy had never seen a bird like it before. "That's a heron," Uncle John said. "They live near water." Uncle John lay back and shut his eyes.

Another wagon was crossing the bridge coming toward them. A white man drove it. Maddy nudged Uncle John. "Uncle John," he said. "Uncle John, there's a white man."

"Maddy," Uncle John said, without opening his eyes, "you've seen white men before."

Maddy whispered, "Don't you have to show him your pass?"

"No, Maddy. I'm not bothering him, he's not going to bother me." After a moment he added, "Do we look like run-aways, with this nice wagon and a load full of wood? Hmm?"

"I thought we always had to show white people a pass."

"Only if they ask for it. Don't fuss. Anybody'd think you'd never been on the road before."

Maddy hadn't ever been on the road before. He opened his mouth to say so, but then saw the corner of Uncle John's mouth twitch, so he knew Uncle John was just making fun.

"Beverly hasn't been anywhere either," Maddy pointed out.

"No, but he's not the one waking me up with his questions."

"I've got questions," Beverly said. "I just like to find out the answers myself."

Uncle John slept. The horses finished their oats, cocked their hips, and dozed. Beverly found a stone and tossed it back and forth to Maddy a few times, and then the two of them went down to the river's edge to try to skip stones, but the river was running too fast. Uncle John called them back, and they went on.

They reached Mr. Nicholas's farm at twilight. Mr. Nicholas was one of Master Jefferson's great friends, a frequent visitor at Monticello. His daughter Jane had just married Mister Jeff. Mr. Nicholas's farm was large and sumptuous, freshly painted, freshly mown, and much finer-looking than Monticello. Uncle John pulled up at the quarters, and the stable man helped them settle the horses, showed them a spare cabin where they could sleep, and took them to the kitchen to eat. Mr. Nicholas's kitchen was not as fancy as the Monticello kitchen, but it was comfortable and the food was very good. Maddy ate two big bowls of beans and ham while Uncle John told all the Monticello news. After that, Mr. Nicholas's people told all the news they knew. It was interesting, but after a while Maddy's eyes grew heavy. He stretched out beneath a bench and fell asleep.

He woke to the sound of logs thudding onto the hearth. He opened his eyes and saw a pair of bare feet. He looked up. The kitchen was flooded with morning light. The cook's assistant, a girl a few years older than Maddy, looked down at him and winked. "Your brother and uncle left you where you lay," she said. "I wondered if you'd get confused in the night."

Maddy crawled out from the bench, his arms and legs stiff and cold. "I didn't even move," he said.

"Yeah, I got a brother your age, he sleeps like the dead. Want coffee?"

"Yes, ma'am."

"Be a minute before I get the water boiling. Want biscuits?"

"Yes, ma'am."

"You're awful polite, ain't you, you and your brother both."

"Thank you, ma'am."

"You 'ma'am' me one more time, I won't give you breakfast. Didn't I tell you I got a brother your age?"

"Yes, m—" Maddy bit back the word *ma'am* and grinned at her. "I got a sister your age," he said.

"Where's she?"

"Home," he said. "Monticello—she works in the weaving factory. On the farm. And Beverly you met, and Eston, he's littler."

The girl nodded. She was an ugly girl, with a big ugly scar across one side of her face, but she was smart, Maddy could tell. "Lucky you, still together," she said. "My brother's on a farm near Appomattox. There's a tavern you might stop at near there, an' if you do, tell one of the yard boys to tell him I say hey. Will you? Tell him I'm fine, tell him the burn's healed up all right." She touched her cheek, where the scar was. "I was leaning over the fire and something popped. Hit me right here. Got infected, so I was sick a long time."

Maddy nodded. "I'll tell Uncle John, and he'll be sure we stop to give the message. He'll know the tavern."

The girl smiled. "Much obliged."

They spent three and a half days and three nights on the road, the second and third nights at taverns. They weren't allowed to sleep inside—the rooms were for white people—but that didn't matter, Uncle John said, because out in public they needed to guard the wagon and its contents anyhow. They rolled up in blankets and slept on the ground beneath the wagon, and they were warm enough, and dry.

"Horses must be white," Maddy said. They got to sleep in the tavern stables.

Uncle John grinned. "Horses have black skin," he said. "Didn't you ever notice? Beneath the hair."

Maddy shook his head. "Don't tell the white folks," Uncle John said. "They find out, they'll make the horses sleep under the wagon with us."

Master Jefferson had given Uncle John money to buy food, so they had plenty to eat, though they had to use the back doors of the tavern kitchens and eat out in the yard. On the first day, not knowing the rules, Beverly started to go through the front door of a tavern. Uncle John called him back, sharp. "Watch yourself," he said. "You're out here with me and you don't want people thinking you're trying to pass."

"Why not?" Maddy asked.

"White people hate when black people try to pass for white," Uncle John said. "It makes them nervous."

Maddy glanced at Beverly. "But when he's free—"

"Yep," Uncle John said. "We best not talk about that. Beverly will be okay on his own. But right now, dressed like he is, and traveling with me in this wagon, he appears to be a black person. He's going to get hurt if he doesn't follow the rules."

Maddy scowled. He didn't like being reminded of the difference between Beverly's skin color and his. Uncle John seemed to understand. "I'm same as your mama, aren't I?" he said. "Same Mama, same Papa. But I could see circumstances where maybe she could pass. Me, not a chance." He showed Beverly the back of his warm brown hand.

"You're just tan," Maddy said. "From working outside."

"Maddy," Uncle John said, "I'm tan where the sun don't shine."

Maddy knew Uncle John meant to be funny, but Maddy couldn't laugh. Neither did Beverly, who seemed uneasy and kept swallowing as though he had something stuck in his throat. When they had traveled down the road a few miles, Beverly asked, very quietly, "What happens if you don't follow the rules?"

Uncle John looked serious. "You mean the rules white people make for black people?" Beverly nodded. "I'll tell you," Uncle John said. "A black man who doesn't follow the rules is a dangerous man in a white person's eyes. A black man who doesn't follow the rules doesn't live very long."

The brightness of the day seemed to fade. Maddy thought about Uncle John's words. He thought about Beverly, who would be breaking the rules every moment of his white life. He looked at Beverly, but couldn't tell what his brother was thinking.

Uncle John cleared his throat. "Beverly," he said, "I don't know what you're planning, and I don't ever need to know.

But I will say this. If you pass for white, you'd better pass in your heart too. You better be white all the way. There will never be a single white person you can trust with the truth about your past. Do you hear me? Never a one. No matter how much you think they might care about you. Love you, even. Don't you ever, ever tell."

Beverly nodded. He held on to the edge of the wagon seat with both hands. He seemed to be studying the hills far away. "I hear you," he said.

They drove through towns and villages, past big farms and little houses. Maddy had never realized there were so many people in the world. He'd never thought about them—nor about the roads, the bridges, and fields of corn and trees and everything else. From the Monticello mountaintop he could see a long way, but nothing like as far as they'd driven. When he thought about all the things he'd seen in only three days, and how Lewis and Clark had walked west for months, and how Mama had sailed for weeks across the ocean, he started to understand how big the world might be.

"Beverly," Maddy said, at the end of the third day, "is this what it's like to be free? Driving along this road? Go wherever you want? Do whatever you want to?"

"We can't go wherever we want," Beverly said. "We're going from Monticello to Poplar Forest. We can't go any-where else."

"Yeah, but nobody's telling us how fast to go. We can stop

and rest whenever we want to. At the taverns we can order whatever we want to eat."

Beverly said, "This is nothing. Freedom will be a whole lot better than this."

The great house at Poplar Forest had the same kind of windows as Monticello, and the same white Chinese railing on the roof, but it was much smaller, and its oddly shaped rooms fit together like pieces of a puzzle. Uncle John called it an octagon. He made Maddy repeat the word *octagon*. "That means eight-sided," he said. "This house has eight outside walls, all exactly the same size."

Maddy thought it was easier to say *eight-sided* than *octagon,* but he didn't say so. Uncle John seemed proud as he showed them through the house. "No Irish carpenters here," he said. "Local people built the brick walls, but all this fine woodwork was done by yours truly. All these good-looking windows and sashes and cornice boards."

In the center of the house the dining room was built as a perfect cube, twenty feet long, twenty feet wide, with a ceiling twenty feet high. It had windows in its roof called skylights. "They're clever," Uncle John said. "Otherwise this room wouldn't have windows. It'd be dark all the time. Of course, if it gets too hot, one of you will have to climb onto the roof to pull the blinds."

Maddy looked, but Uncle John wasn't joking. "You do it," he said to Beverly.

"No way," Beverly said. "That's a job for you."

The only way to reach the dining room from the kitchen was to walk through the bedroom Miss Ellen and Miss Virginia would be sharing. "Burwell will serve dinner," Uncle John said, "but if you get called on to give a hand, be sure you knock before you open their door."

The ground floor was divided into rooms the same size as the main floor. Beneath the big dining room was a deep cellar full of food and wine. "Fine peach brandy they make here," Uncle John said. "We'll take some of that with us when we go home." He showed them the small room where they would all sleep. The way the house looked from the outside, Maddy would have guessed their room was underground, but it wasn't: It had a regular door to the outside, two fine glass windows, a brick floor, a bed with a shuck mattress, and a fireplace.

A short, plump black woman came into the room, wiping her hands on her apron. "Everything all right?" she asked.

Uncle John swept her a deep bow. "Miss Hannah," he said, "allow me to introduce my nephews. Madison and Beverly."

Miss Hannah grinned and shook them both by the hand. "Come eat," she said. "Dinner's ready."

The kitchen was a smaller version of Monticello's, with a set kettle in the corner and a stew stove against the wall. "You must cook like Miss Edith," Maddy said.

"Laws, no." Miss Hannah laughed. "I've heard about that woman's table. I'm just a plain cook. When Master Jefferson ain't here I work in the fields."

"Plain cook nothing," Uncle John said. "Unless you mean plain good."

Hannah laughed again. Maddy liked her.

Before sunset they heard the landau coming up the long sloped drive. They went out to meet it. Beverly took the horse Burwell had been riding while Burwell went to the landau and helped Miss Ellen and Miss Virginia down. Miss Ellen looked around, her eyes bright. "Oh, I do love it here!" she said. She smiled at Maddy, but didn't say hello.

Master Jefferson clutched Burwell's arm as he stepped from the carriage. He looked tired. His hair was coated with dust from the road. He smiled at Uncle John and Maddy. "I see you made it here all right. Madison, what do you think of the place? Handsome, isn't it?"

"Yes, sir," Maddy said.

"I thought you'd like it," Master Jefferson said.

Life at Poplar Forest was different from life at Monticello. Everything was quiet. There weren't any white visitors, except occasional old friends. Master Jefferson followed his usual routine, writing letters, riding, and eating a fine dinner in the afternoons, but he did it without fuss or interruption, with only his granddaughters for company. Miss Ellen spent most of each day reading, her hair tucked behind her ears, her lips silently moving.

"Greek?" Maddy asked as he passed her one day.

She shook her head without looking up. "Latin," she said.

"I will never read the Aeneid in translation again."

Miss Virginia wandered the gardens, sketching flowers. "We need a piano here, Grandpapa," she said.

"Hmm—mm," Master Jefferson said. "Someday."

Uncle John was carving more fancy woodwork, like he'd done at Monticello. Master Jefferson often spent part of a morning watching him, and discussing things Maddy'd never heard of before—cornices, entablatures, classic Greek design. Uncle John seemed to know just as much about those things as Master Jefferson. Maddy was impressed.

Master Jefferson had brought his Italian violin. One day he handed it to Maddy. "Try it," he said. "See what you think. It'll feel quite different from your kit violin."

The Italian violin was bigger, and heavier, and Maddy knew how expensive it must be. He was half-afraid to touch it. Once he started, though, he found himself mesmerized by the instrument's lovely pure sound.

"That was very fine," Master Jefferson said when Maddy had finished. "You have a good ear."

"Beverly's better," Maddy said. "And Eston, he's the best of us all."

"Beverly has had many more years of practice," Master Jefferson said. "You play well. Eston I understand may be a prodigy."

"Yes, sir," Maddy said. He didn't know the word, but the way Master Jefferson said it made him think it was a good thing. "Were you a prodigy?"

Master Jefferson looked thoughtful. He flexed his wrist, the stiff one. "I don't know," he said. "I loved to play, I practiced hard, I played well—but no, I don't think I would have said I was a prodigy. A good amateur, perhaps. Nothing more."

It was so strange, to talk with Master Jefferson like that— to have his full attention, to not need to worry about what Mama or Miss Martha or some white stranger might think. In a way it was wonderful—and yet . . . Master Jefferson had sold James. No matter how kind he was to Maddy, he had still done that to James.

"If you could pick anyone to be our father," he asked Beverly one day, when everyone else was out of hearing, "who would you choose?"

Beverly looked at him for a long moment. "I never think like that," he said. "We don't get to pick, so what's the use of asking?"

"I'd pick Uncle John," Maddy said.

"He'd be good," Beverly agreed.

A few days later Beverly brought the subject back up. "Master Jefferson has done a lot of great things," he said. "Everyone says he was a leader in the war. He wrote that declaration thing. He made us a new country. And then he went to France, and he was president. He reads and writes and thinks all the time."

"Yes," said Maddy. He wasn't sure where Beverly was headed.

"So," Beverly said, "does all that mean he's a great person? White folks seem to think so. If you're great enough in some areas, does it make up for the rest?"

Maddy asked, "Would a great person sell someone else's son?"

Uncle John had walked up behind Maddy. "What was that?" he asked. Maddy repeated the question. "You want to know if great people can own slaves?" Uncle John asked. "Can a person be great and still participate in evil?" He tapped Maddy's shoulder. "That's what you're asking?"

Maddy nodded.

Uncle John seemed to have already thought it out. "You can be great in the eyes of mankind," he said, "but not great in the eyes of God. God calls slavery a sin, an evil, corruptible sin. Do you know the Bible verse? 'And God brought them out of Egypt, that place of slavery.'"

"Mama always says she's bringing us out of Jordan," Maddy said.

"Yes, sir," Uncle John said, nodding. "Yes, sir. Your mama, she is a great woman. You remember that."

The next day Maddy was sawing a piece of wood for Uncle John when the blade slipped and cut deep into his hand. Blood poured down his forearm. Uncle John clapped a rag over the cut and pressed hard. Blood welled up around Uncle John's fingers. It hurt so much Maddy could barely breathe.

Master Jefferson hurried to him. "Let's see," he said, peeling back the bloody rag. "Ah. Get Hannah, Beverly. Tell her to bring clean cloth."

Master Jefferson sent Burwell for a doctor. He led Maddy to the great house porch and bound his hand tightly with the bandage Hannah brought. He made Maddy drink a tot of peach brandy. "Medicinal," he said. He sat with Maddy while they waited for the doctor to arrive.

When the doctor came he pressed on the edges of the cut. They gaped open. Fresh blood flowed. Maddy felt sick. "Mmm," the doctor said. He picked up the bottle of brandy and poured some into the wound.

It felt like Maddy's hand had been thrust into a fire. He screamed, and would have jerked his hand away if Master Jefferson hadn't had such a tight grip on his arm.

"Steady," Master Jefferson said. "That's the worst of it."

Maddy wanted to be brave, but it hurt so much he sobbed.

"It's all right," Master Jefferson said, as soothingly as though he were talking to a tiny child. "It's all right. It'll be over soon."

The doctor sewed the wound shut with a needle and thread. He bandaged Maddy's entire hand. "Keep that clean and dry," he said. "We don't want infection."

"Yes, sir," Maddy said. "Thank you."

"He won't lose the use of it, will he?" Master Jefferson asked.

"Shouldn't," said the doctor. "I didn't see any tendons cut. If we can keep infection out, he ought to be fine. I'll come around to check it tomorrow."

Master Jefferson got up, squeezing Maddy's shoulder. "Go lie down," he said. "Keep quiet the rest of the day."

Maddy went to their room and lay down. He took a book

with him—with so many books around the house no one would notice, plus here he didn't think anyone would mind—but found he couldn't focus. He stared out the open window, lost in thought. Mama would have held him the same way Master Jefferson had. She would have soothed him, but she also would have made him hold still for the brandy and the stitching.

It was the first time he ever felt like he had a father.

Later that night he discussed it with Beverly. "Maybe he does care about us," Maddy said. "Maybe he does think of us as his children."

Beverly said, "We are his children, whether he thinks about us that way or not."

"I know, but—" Maddy struggled to say what he meant. "It's like there's a secret side of him, and here, since it's not Monticello, he can let it show."

Beverly didn't say anything. Maddy's hand throbbed. "He loves Mama," Beverly said, after a while. "I'll give him that."

"How do you know?"

"I just know," Beverly said. Maddy nodded. He knew it too.

Poplar Forest was a better place for them than Monticello. Maddy wished he and his family could live there all the time.

Chapter Twenty-nine

Three Months of Grief

Two years passed. Peter grew into a sturdy little boy the very image of James. Eston started working in the woodshop. He grew skinny and tall; Beverly, broad-shouldered and strong. Beverly was a good carpenter and a lively musician. He played for the dances Miss Martha's girls held. Master Jefferson turned seventy-six years old and was still strong enough to ride every day. He went to Poplar Forest twice a year, and always took Maddy and Beverly along. Sometimes Maddy felt like everything inside him waited for those days.

At Christmastime Mama gave Harriet a long length of fine linen, bleached snow-white. Harriet smiled in delight. "That'll be your underthings," Mama said. "Petticoats and shifts and stays."

"Why's she need those?" Maddy asked. No one wore fancy shifts in the weaving room. He moved closer to the fire. Beverly was tuning the violin. Eston whittled a chunk of wood.

Harriet rolled her eyes at Maddy. "They'll be white," she said.

"I can see that," Maddy said. "I know my colors pretty well by now, thank you."

Eston's head came up. "I'm not so sure—" he joked.

"I don't mean the *cloth* is white," Harriet said. "I mean it's for my white person's clothes—for when I'm living as a white woman."

Harriet would never say when she "became a white woman," or "passed for a white woman." Harriet said she was exactly what she was. Right now she was living as a slave, later she would live as a free white woman. Who or what she *was* wouldn't change one bit.

No matter who or what Maddy was, he wouldn't pass for white. Eston would. Maddy still hated being the one left out. Sometimes he wanted to ask Eston to stay black with him, but Eston was only ten years old, and anyhow the question wasn't fair.

"I don't know why you're worried about clothes now," Maddy said. Harriet wasn't even eighteen. She wouldn't be allowed to leave until she was twenty-one.

"Time enough we get started," Mama said. "The sewing will take a while, especially if we do it right, which we will. We'll take it bit by bit." She smiled at Harriet. "I'm not sending you out into the world in a ragged shift and old leather shoes."

Harriet held out her foot, clad in the rough leather shoes all the slaves wore. "I won't be sorry to be rid of these," she said.

"Get white shoes," Eston said. "Little white shoes like Miss Cornelia."

"Satin shoes," Harriet said dreamily, "for dancing."

"Dancing!" Maddy snorted. What would Harriet do at a white dance? She wouldn't know the figures. She wouldn't have the first clue what to do.

Eston sprang up in the firelight. He stood in front of Harriet and bowed from the waist, like a gentleman. Harriet laughed. Eston took her hand, lifted her from her chair, and swung her around the room. He hummed while they danced.

Eston, Maddy thought, could make himself into anyone. He asked Mama, "Why aren't you worried about Beverly's clothes?"

In answer, Mama held up the shirt she was sewing. Maddy had assumed it was for Master Jefferson. "No," Mama said, guessing what Maddy was thinking, "this is for Beverly. I've got half a dozen shirts put by, and some fine-hemmed cravats, and a waistcoat. His coat and breeches will come from a tailor's shop. We're working on it."

"Where are we getting the money for that?" Maddy asked. He knew he sounded snippy. He didn't mean to, but all their money put together wouldn't buy tailor-made clothes.

"Where do we get the money for anything?" Mama replied. "You didn't think your father would send you out into the world naked, did you?"

Maddy didn't know what he thought. Mostly, he thought that Beverly's twenty-first birthday was only three months away. Three more months until he never saw Beverly again.

Those three months were nothing but trouble.

First, Master Jefferson got sick. He went to soak at a famous hot springs for his rheumatism, and something in the water made great big boils break out all over his backside. Eston laughed when Mama first told them, but Mama said it wasn't funny at all. She said that during the long carriage ride home the boils had gone septic. Infections were serious. Master Jefferson might die.

Maddy didn't believe Master Jefferson could possibly die from something as undignified as boils on his backside, but as weeks passed he began to worry. All Master Jefferson could do was lie on his side in bed. It hurt too much to sit and he was too weak to stand. He couldn't write letters or talk to his visitors. After a few weeks he developed a fever. Mama said the infection had gotten into his blood.

"If he dies, what happens to us?" Maddy asked. "Will Beverly still leave?"

"Of course," Mama said. But she looked so worried Maddy wasn't sure he believed her.

Doctors came and went. Mama spent all her time at the great house, nursing Master Jefferson. He grew better, then worse, better, then worse. When at last he was out of danger, and starting to walk again, he looked like he'd aged ten years.

Then Burwell's wife died suddenly. Grief laid Burwell and his eight little children flat. The rest of Mulberry Row mourned too.

Then Charles Bankhead up and stabbed Mister Jeff. Charles Bankhead was the drunken fool who had married Miss Anne, Master Jefferson's oldest granddaughter. Everyone knew it was a miserable marriage. Charles Bankhead hit people when he was drunk, and he was drunk most of the time. He hit Miss Anne. Miss Martha and Master Jefferson worried that one day he would kill her. They begged Miss Anne to leave him and come back to Monticello, but she wouldn't, and no one understood why. She had little children. Maddy thought she'd want to stay alive.

Mister Jeff hated Charles Bankhead for hitting Miss Anne. Charles Bankhead hated Mister Jeff because he hated nearly everyone. They ran into each other in Charlottesville and got into a fight, and Charles Bankhead pulled out a knife.

A man from Charlottesville rode hard up the mountain just after dinnertime to tell them Mister Jeff had been stabbed, and was dying. Master Jefferson was still too weak to ride, but he called for his horse anyhow and galloped straight down to Charlottesville in the dark. Miss Martha fell to pieces worrying over her son, her father, and Miss Anne. Mama tried to comfort her, but Maddy knew Mama was anxious too.

Mister Jeff had been stabbed in the gut, which should have killed him, but it didn't. He was sick a long time. He'd been stabbed in the arm too. His arm never worked right again.

The sheriff drew up assault charges, but Charles Bankhead grabbed Miss Anne and their children and fled across the county line to escape arrest. Miss Martha begged Miss Anne to come home. She wouldn't.

If a woman won't leave the man that stabs her brother and leaves him for dead, there's no hope for her, Mama said. She said Miss Martha'd made a bad choice, marrying Mr. Randolph, and now her daughters were making bad choices too. "Harriet!" she said. "If a man ever hits you, even once, I want you to leave his house! That instant! You come back here if you have to, you hear me!"

Harriet said, "Yes, Mama. But I won't have to. If any man hits me, I'll knock him dead."

Maddy laughed, but not Mama. "Beverly," she said, turning on him, "you take care of your sister. You keep an eye on the kind of man she ends up with. You hear me? You've got to take charge since I won't be there. I want you both with good people—with kind people. You hear me?" Mama's voice choked. She wiped her eyes.

"Mama," Harriet said, "you taught us well. We'll do fine."

"I hope so," Mama said. "I hope and pray."

Beverly said nothing. The closer it came to the first of April, his birthday, the quieter Beverly became.

Chapter Thirty

Beverly's Twenty-first Birthday

On the last day of March, Beverly tried to give Eston and Maddy the kit violin. He polished it, tuned it, and played one final song. Then he put it into Maddy's hands. "You boys take care of that," he said.

Maddy choked and could only nod, but Eston said, "We don't want it. That old kit violin. You better take that violin with you, Beverly. Otherwise you'll have nothing to play."

"If I take it," Beverly said, "you won't have anything to play. How'd you like that?" Maddy enjoyed playing the violin, but he could survive without it. Eston, on the other hand, would die.

Eston lifted his chin. "Our father will get me another violin," he said. "A real one, a good one. I can't make a living playing music on an old kit violin."

Eston was not quite eleven. It was hard to believe sometimes, the way he talked like a old man. He looked just exactly like Master Jefferson.

"You aren't going to make a living playing music," Maddy said. "You'll be a carpenter, like the rest of us."

Eston narrowed his eyes. He said to Beverly, "I don't want your lousy violin."

Maddy couldn't believe they were arguing about a violin on Beverly's last day with them. He said, "Well, I do. You're just nuts, Eston, if you think somebody's going to buy us a better one. How much do you think violins cost? You know there's no extra money. Beverly'll make good money where he's going, he'll be able to buy himself a new violin."

Maddy didn't know where Beverly planned to go. He supposed Beverly had it figured out, but he didn't want to ask. It was safer if he didn't know. He also wasn't sure, even now, that he believed Beverly would be allowed to just walk away.

"There was money to buy Miss Virginia a new saddle last week," Eston said. "There'll be money for my violin."

"Arguing with you is like arguing with a tree," Maddy said. "Only a tree might get old and fall down." Eston wouldn't ever budge.

"You say that," Eston said, "but you keep arguing anyway."

"Oh," Maddy said, frustrated, "have it your way."

Beverly looked at the violin, then shut it up in its case, and slid the case back under the bed. "I'll fetch it in the morning," he said.

"You're really going?" As soon as Maddy said that, he wished he hadn't.

"Tell Uncle John he taught me well," Beverly said. "Tell him I'm grateful."

"Tell him yourself," said Eston.

"Eston, show some sense," scolded Harriet. She was knitting by the fire. Mama hadn't come in from her work yet, even though it was nearly dark and Beverly's last day.

"I'll send word," Beverly said. "Once I've found a place. A letter—"

"Send it to Jesse Scott," Maddy said. "We'll write back. We'll put Jesse's name on the envelope."

The door opened. Mama slipped in, her arms full. She sat on the edge of the bed and showed them what she'd brought.

A tailored white man's suit of clothes—a coat, and brass-buttoned breeches. A new pair of shoes, with brass buckles. A new felt hat. A knife that fit into a small leather sheath. A leather pocketbook. Mama opened the pocketbook and showed them the money inside. "Fifty dollars," she said. "With the shirts and socks and neckcloths I've made, it should be enough to get you on your way. Uncle John's set aside a box of tools for you. They'll be just inside the workshop door."

"And the violin," prompted Eston.

Beverly looked like he was about to cry. In the morning he slipped away. He took the violin with him.

He disappeared like a rock falling into a lake without a ripple. No one, not in the great house, not in the kitchen, not any-

266

where on Mulberry Row, so much as mentioned he was gone. Even little Peter Fossett acted like Beverly had never existed. The overseers didn't speak of him. Mama didn't speak of him. Harriet walked around with a closed expression on her face. Eston looked sad, but he held quiet too.

All Maddy's thoughts were of Beverly. Could he really pass for a white man? Was he somewhere safe? Was he frightened? Was he happy? The silence wore Maddy down like rough sandpaper on a board. "Uncle John," he said at last, when they were alone in the woodshop, just the two of them and Eston, "do you think Bev—"

"Hsst!" said Uncle John.

"But I just—"

"Not a word."

"But every—"

"Keep still," Uncle John said. "Less said the better. Trust me."

Maddy didn't understand why. Mama had promised nobody would try to catch Beverly. "We don't need folks from Charlottesville knowing our business," Uncle John went on. "The less they hear about any escaped slaves, the better."

"But he's not—"

"Hsst!" said Uncle John.

Eston looked over from the corner of the workroom, from where he was sweeping the floor. He winked at Maddy. Grateful, Maddy winked back.

On their way home that night, Maddy asked Eston, "Have you stopped thinking about him yet?"

"Nope," Eston said. "What do you think he looks like, free?"

"What do you think he feels like?" Maddy asked.

When they asked Mama, she said, "Someday, you'll know."

A week later, the laundry room in the north dependency caught fire. It spread to the laundry roof, then down the walkway toward the great house, fueled by a rising wind. Maddy joined everyone on the mountaintop, even Master Jefferson, who was still weak and thin, in beating the fire out with wet gunny sacks, brooms, and snow from the icehouse. Afterward, filthy and exhausted, Maddy slumped to the ground. Peter Fossett climbed into his lap. "That was scary," Peter said. "I thought it was going to burn up the horses." The stable next to the laundry had caught fire, but Wormley had gotten the horses out.

"I know," Maddy said. "Everything's okay now."

Peter nodded. "Wait 'til we tell Beverly." Then he clapped his hand over his mouth. "Sorry, sorry," he said. "Mama says we're supposed to pretend there wasn't a Beverly."

Maddy put his arms around Peter. "There was a Beverly," he said, "and there still is a Beverly. We'll stay quiet about him, but we won't forget."

Two weeks after Beverly left, only a few days after the fire, Mama came to the woodshop in the middle of the day, carrying something wrapped in a shawl. "It's for both of you," she said, setting the bundle on the workbench.

Mama unwrapped it. Eston sucked in his breath. It was a violin case. "Is it Italian?" Eston asked.

Maddy let Eston unsnap the case and lift the violin from its velvet bed. Eston's eyes shone. He stroked the violin's face and ran his thumb across the strings. "I've never seen this one," Eston said. "It's not the one he usually plays."

"It's the violin he played as a young man," Mama said. "The one his father gave him. Now he's giving it to you."

Eston sucked in his breath again. "To both of us," he said, very softly.

Maddy had a moment of understanding, of what Beverly, of what a good brother would say. So he said it. "No, sir," he said. "You'll have to let me play it, but you're the musician in this family. This violin belongs to you."

Chapter Thirty-one

Hailstorm

That summer disaster followed on the heels of disaster. It never rained. The blazing sun burned up the wheat, and then the other crops, one by one, until there was nothing to be sold. The grass turned crisp and brown. The hay crop failed.

The entire country fell into something called a panic. It meant no money anywhere. Banks failed, which meant, Mama said, that they shut their doors, and if you'd given them your money to keep safe, that was just too bad. Your money was gone.

Eston wanted to know how money could disappear. He went to his jar on the shelf and pulled out a penny. "It can't disappear," he said.

"Say you buy a farm," Harriet said.

"I won't," said Eston. "What would I do with a farm?"

"All right," Harriet said, shooting him a look, "say *I* buy a farm. Say it costs a thousand dollars, but I've only got a hundred dollars in cash. I pay one hundred, and get a bank loan for the other nine hundred. But my crops fail. I can't repay the bank what I owe. So the bank takes my farm, and they sell it to somebody else to get their money back."

"Who?" said Eston.

"They sell it to Joe Fossett."

"Mmm-hmm," said Eston. "'Cause he's got money."

"Only Joe Fossett, he's nobody's fool. He says the farm isn't worth a full thousand dollars anymore. Between the hard times all around and no crops growing, there's a lot of land for sale. The most Joe will pay for the farm is six hundred dollars. So the bank takes it. They gave out nine hundred and only got back six. Three hundred dollars disappeared."

Eston said, "The bank ought to wait and sell for nine hundred."

"They can't wait that long."

"Why not?"

"I don't know," Harriet said. "I'm not a bank. But that's what's happening."

Mama nodded. "Everyone's worried. Land isn't selling, and there isn't enough work for people to do."

They didn't say it, but they all thought of Beverly. They hadn't heard from him yet, and they were starting to worry. Beverly was a good carpenter, surely he could find work somewhere. And he had fifty dollars. A man could live a long time on fifty dollars.

Maddy figured the panic wouldn't hurt Monticello, because Master Jefferson would never sell his land. No planter would. Mama pursed her lips when Maddy said so.

"Master Jefferson signed a loan for Mr. Nicholas," she said. "That means he has to pay the bank back if Mr. Nicholas can't."

"Why'd he do that?"

"Friendship, I suppose. Mr. Nicholas asked him to. And Mr. Nicholas once signed a loan for your father, so your father felt he couldn't say no."

Since Maddy's first night at Mr. Nicholas's farm, on his first trip to Poplar Forest, he'd stayed there many times. It sure seemed prosperous. It was kept up much nicer than Monticello. "Why does Mr. Nicholas need a loan?" he asked.

Mama shook her head. "I don't know. It's for twenty thousand dollars, I do know that."

Eston burst out laughing. "Mama! You're making that up!"

Mama smiled back, but she didn't look happy. "I'm not, no, I'm not. Twenty thousand dollars." She stretched the words out. "Twen-ty thou-sand dol-lars."

Maddy knew Joe Fossett had over two hundred dollars saved. He made marks on his slate to help count: Twenty thousand dollars was Joe Fossett's two hundred dollars, a hundred times over. Maddy thought of a hundred men working as hard and saving as long as Joe Fossett had. He tried to imagine all that work turned into a piece of paper Master Jefferson could sign.

"It's as much as the government paid for Master Jefferson's library," Harriet said.

Eston sighed. "Too bad he doesn't have another one to sell."

It never once rained at Monticello that summer, but at Poplar Forest a fierce storm broke the drought—not just rain, but hail, big chunks of ice hurled from the sky. They crushed the meager crops flat and shattered the windows of the great house. The overseers wrote there wasn't a single one still whole.

Master Jefferson went there at once, with Miss Ellen and Miss Cornelia, Burwell, and Miss Fanny's brother Israel. A week later Master Jefferson sent for Uncle John. He wrote that he'd ordered new glass shipped to the nearest port on the James River. Uncle John should pick it up along the way.

Uncle John, Maddy, and Eston traveled three days in sweltering heat under a blazing sun. When they reached Poplar Forest the house looked as though it had sat empty and neglected for years. Tall weeds grew up around the front portico, and all the front windows were covered with boards. "Where's that rascal Israel?" Uncle John muttered. "Can't he at least cut the grass?"

No one came out to hail the wagon. Uncle John drove around to the stables, and asked a boy working there to unhitch and care for the horses. They looked into the empty kitchen, then found Hannah in the laundry next door.

"Oh, they need you in the great house," she said, the moment she saw them. "Burwell's that sick, nobody knows what to do."

Burwell lay in Maddy's bed, in the room on the lower floor. Usually he slept on a mat in the small room off Master Jefferson's bedroom. "Couldn't stay upstairs," he said. "Not when I can't stand up, and have to keep using—" He broke off, groaning, his hands pressed to his belly. Maddy didn't have to ask what he meant. The stench from the chamber pot nearly made him retch.

"Where's Master Jefferson?" Uncle John asked. He knelt beside Burwell. "Eston—get fresh water. Maddy—deal with that pot."

Maddy carried the pot to the privy. On his way back he ran into Miss Ellen, who was carrying a mug full of liquid. "Have you seen Burwell?" she cried. "I've got another dose for him—something Cornelia says Mama used to use. At least, she thinks so. We've tried everything. Grandpa's sent twice for the doctor, but he hasn't come."

The dose didn't help. Burwell gritted his teeth and groaned; his sweat soaked the blanket he lay on. "How long have you been like this?" Uncle John asked.

Miss Ellen said, "I don't think he's slept for two days."

Uncle John told them to leave him alone with Burwell for a while. Maddy and Eston followed Miss Ellen upstairs. "It's horrid here," she said. "The books grew mold after the storm."

Inside, the house smelled dank and stuffy. All the windows

facing north were broken. The dining room was entirely ruined, its wooden floor buckled, its plaster walls moldy, and its skylight beaten into an empty frame. The beautiful octagonal table Uncle John had made did survive the storm; Hannah had moved it to the parlor.

That night Maddy thought Burwell would die. He tossed and turned on the bed, sweating and groaning through clenched teeth. Uncle John sat beside him, wiping his face with damp cloths and trying to get him to drink.

In the middle of the night Maddy rose from his pallet on the floor. "Let me have a turn," he said to Uncle John. "You get some rest."

Uncle John shook his head. "I'll stay up with him," he said. "If it comes to the worst, I want to know I did all I could do."

In the morning Uncle John said, "Let's try a warm bath. A really warm bath might ease him."

Maddy went to the kitchen to ask Hannah's help. Israel was loading a breakfast tray for the table upstairs. "More bad news," he said. "Master Jefferson's sick."

Maddy's heart fell. If Master Jefferson was as sick as Burwell, he would die; he was too old to fight it. While Hannah put bathwater to heat, Maddy climbed the steps to see. Master Jefferson lay on his bed, panting a little, his face stiff from pain. "It's only rheumatism," he said. "My knees mostly. I'll get Ellen to wrap my legs in flannels. I'll be fine."

The warm bath helped; Burwell sank into something like

sleep. Israel went for the doctor again. Eston and Maddy began to replace broken windows.

"Will you serve dinner?" Miss Cornelia asked Maddy that afternoon. "Since Burwell can't, and Israel's gone."

It was the hottest day in the history of the world. Half the house lay sick in bed. Maddy thought Miss Cornelia and Miss Ellen might just once have been able to fetch themselves something from the kitchen, but no. They expected dinner served as usual. Maddy washed his hands, composed his face, and started to shuttle food from the downstairs kitchen to the table in the parlor. Part of the girls' old bedroom had been turned into a pantry, so at least he had a place to set the food down after he brought it up the stairs. He wished he had a dumbwaiter, like at Monticello, or about three more people to help him. When the table was finally ready, he called the granddaughters to sit down.

Miss Cornelia patted the sweat off her neck. "Is there ice today?" she asked.

Maddy didn't see how there could be. Poplar Forest didn't have an icehouse.

Miss Ellen nodded to Maddy. "Go check."

In the kitchen, Miss Hannah said that they bought ice from a neighbor's icehouse, a little bit every day, but that today's ice was gone. "Half of it melted on the way over here," Hannah said. "If you ask me, it's a waste of time. But those girls get fussy when the butter's melted, or the wine isn't chilled."

Maddy reported the lack of ice. Miss Cornelia pursed her

lips. He filled her empty water glass. "Oh, don't bother," she said. "I wanted something cold."

Someone knocked on the front door. Maddy answered it. A man handed him a packet of mail. Master Jefferson couldn't go anywhere without letters following him. He'd probably have mail delivered to his grave.

Maddy went through the boarded-up dining room and knocked gently on the door to Master Jefferson's bedroom. "Sir?"

"Come in," Master Jefferson said. Maddy opened the door. Master Jefferson looked puny, but nothing like as sick as Burwell.

"The mail," Maddy said, handing him the packet. "Shall I bring you some dinner?"

"No. The girls said they'd fix me a plate."

A little bell rang. That was the girls, calling Maddy to the parlor. "Could you give this plate to Grandpa?" Miss Ellen said.

Maddy took the plate back to Master Jefferson's bedroom.

Master Jefferson had propped himself up on a pillow. He was staring at a letter open in his hand, and his face was so perfectly still that for a moment Maddy thought he had died. He could swear Master Jefferson wasn't breathing. Maddy cleared his throat. Slowly, very slowly, Master Jefferson looked up.

"What's wrong?" Maddy asked.

"Nothing," Master Jefferson said. "Nothing." He closed the

letter in his hand, and set it atop the others on the pile. "I'm not hungry. Take that food away."

The letter turned out to be from Mr. Nicholas. The bank had asked him to repay his loan. He couldn't; he had no money left. Mr. Nicholas's money had disappeared. Since Master Jefferson had signed the loan, he would have to pay instead. The twenty-thousand-dollar debt belonged to him.

A day later the doctor finally arrived. He bled Burwell until Burwell nearly fainted, and gave him laudanum to make him sleep. Burwell survived.

Master Jefferson's rheumatism gradually improved. Uncle John, Maddy, and Eston repaired the windows, one by one. It seemed to take forever. For the first time Maddy was impatient to return to Monticello. He might get news of Beverly there. But when they finally reached home Maddy got the shock of his life.

Beverly had returned.

Chapter Thirty-two

Beverly's Story

The first thing Maddy saw as he came down Mulberry Row was that someone had shut the door to their room. He scowled. In summertime that room could heat up something dreadful. He yanked open the door.

Beverly sat on the edge of the bed. He looked up at Maddy with a sad half smile.

Maddy froze, his hand still holding the door. Eston bumped into him, then ducked under his arm.

"*Beverly!*" shouted Eston.

Maddy hoped everyone on Mulberry Row already knew Beverly was back, because if not, Eston had just told them.

Eston jumped forward and threw himself on Beverly. Beverly hugged him, hard. Then he turned to Maddy, who stood frozen from shock. "Aren't you glad to see me, Maddy?" Beverly asked.

"I don't know," Maddy said. "What happened?"

Beverly sighed. He sat down again, Eston clinging to his

arm. "I've been back three days. Haven't done much. Straightened the woodshop a little, worked on a cabinet—"

"Beverly."

"I didn't like it, Maddy. Being alone. I've never felt like that."

Maddy thought of all those roads, all the places between Monticello and Poplar he wanted to explore. Beverly didn't like freedom? Maddy didn't know what to think. Finally he asked, "What'd Mama say?"

Beverly shook his head. "She's about wore me out. She was so mad, for the first day she couldn't quit screaming at me. Since then she hasn't talked to me at all." Beverly sank his face into his hands. "She cried."

Maddy walked forward and hugged Beverly tight. Oh, he'd missed Beverly. He'd missed him so much, and he never wanted to see him again. His heart hammered. He didn't know what to think or say or do.

"She thinks I don't appreciate her," Beverly said. "She thinks I don't want what she's given me. It's not that. She won't listen. We're not doing it the best way, but Mama doesn't want to hear it. Neither does Harriet." Beverly sighed. "The women in this family wear me out."

Beverly was right. Neither Mama nor Harriet would speak to Beverly, or listen to a thing he had to say. For a few days Eston and Maddy just kept their heads down and hoped the storm would pass. Beverly went back to work in the shop. He stayed indoors and mostly out of sight. Maddy waited to hear what folks along Mulberry Row would say, but it was like Beverly was some kind of ghost. Nobody had said anything when he left, nobody said anything when he returned. Joe Fossett and Miss Edith and Burwell all looked like they could say plenty, but they held their tongues. The white overseers just passed their eyes over Beverly as though they couldn't see him.

Strangest thing ever, Maddy thought.

After a few days, when the hum of Mama's anger had begun to subside, Beverly told his story. It was evening. They'd propped the door to their room open with a chair, and Harriet sat on it, brushing out her hair. Mama sat on the other chair, near the empty hearth, and Beverly and Eston and Maddy sat on the floor.

"We're not doing it right," Beverly said. "We've got to have a story. We didn't know."

Mama looked at Beverly, but didn't speak.

"White folks are different from black folks," Beverly said.

Mama snorted. Harriet said, "That is such twaddle. You're as good as any white man—you *are* a white man—Beverly, I—" Harriet was getting wound up again.

"Harriet, *listen*!" Maddy said. He was suddenly furious. Why wouldn't they listen to Beverly? He'd been out there, he knew more than they did. "Nobody said you aren't going to get what you want. Nobody took anything away from you. You're not leaving here for another three years. Shut up and pay attention."

Harriet looked stunned.

"Thank you," Beverly said. "I repeat: White people are different. Not because they look different, not because they are born different. They're raised different." Beverly paused. "It's not the skin. The skin could be any color. We could all be purple, there'd still be a difference. Black people are either free or enslaved. They've got papers or they don't. If they're slaves, as long as they're doing what they're supposed to, nobody asks them questions.

"No white person wants to know who a slave is inside, what they enjoy, who their family was. A white person doesn't care if a slave is good at singing or had a brother they loved. A white person wants to know who they belong to and if they're where they're supposed to be.

"Now, if you're a black person and you're free, white folks don't care about your story either. As long as you've got papers, and you're doing something you're supposed to be doing, white folks don't care who you are. Where you're from. What your story is, who your folks are. None of that.

"And black people—"

"Which are you now?" Harriet interrupted.

Beverly looked pained. "I'm coming to that," he said. "I'm getting to that. You've been all over me for a week, and now you're going to listen. Hush *up*, Harriet."

Maddy had never heard the edge in Beverly's voice he heard now. He wouldn't have spoken for a dollar. Harriet rolled her eyes and looked ready to say more.

"Hush," Beverly repeated. "That's the problem. You all told me as much as you could about being white, but you raised me black. You couldn't help it. I know. Black folks, we know how sad our stories can be. We know better than to ask another slave who his daddy is—maybe nobody ever told him, maybe he was sold as a baby, maybe it's a white man and everyone's supposed to pretend they don't know. You can't ask another slave his story. Maybe it's so sad he's buried it deep, and he'll never tell it again. Black folks, they don't ask too many questions. They tell the stories they want to tell, and they forget the rest.

"White folks want to know everything."

Beverly passed his hand over his face. "I headed east," he said. "I thought I'd probably end up in Washington City, it's growing fast and they must need carpenters there. But one night on the way I stopped at a tavern. I ordered some dinner, and the man asked me what I did and where I was headed.

"I told him I was a carpenter going to Washington. Nothing more than that. I didn't know what all I was supposed to say, but I sure didn't want to say too much.

"He said he had a friend who was just desperate for a carpenter to help him finish building a house. The carpenter that had been working for him took sick. The man at the inn said this friend of his would pay me good to work for him a for few weeks, and anyhow I didn't want to go to Washington in the summer with all the malaria and the flies.

"It sounded like maybe a good idea. So the next day I

started working for this man. I worked hard for two weeks. Kept my head down. Got my pay on Fridays. But along about the middle of the third week the man started asking me questions. He said, 'Tell me your name again.'"

"I said, 'I'm Beverly Smith.' And he said, 'Whereabouts you from?' I was afraid to say Charlottesville, so I told him it was just a little town. He wanted to know what town. I told him Bedford."

Maddy nodded. "That was smart." Bedford was near Poplar Forest.

"He said his wife was from around that area, maybe she knew my people. He wanted to know who all I was related to."

"Did he really know people in Bedford," Harriet asked, "or was he just making that up?"

Beverly shrugged, spreading his hands wide. "How could I know? I think he was just making it up. I think he was trying to rattle me. He kept after me all that day, more and more questions, 'til I didn't know where to look or what to think. Then when I was packing up he looked at me and said, 'I think you're hiding something from me. I better not find out it's something bad.'

"So I took my tools and walked straight out of that town. Didn't go back."

Mama looked hot with indignation. "That man got what he wanted," she said. "He didn't have to pay you for your third week. Beverly, don't get spooked like that. You didn't have to tell him anything. Your life wasn't any of his business."

"I kept traveling down the road," Beverly said. "And everywhere it was the same. What was my name, who were my people? What was I supposed to say? That my father is the president, and my mother is his slave?"

Mama said, "I hope I raised you smarter than that."

Beverly looked up, and his eyes blazed fire. "You did. Believe me, Mama, if I told anyone I'd been born a slave I'd have been run out of town. If not worse. The only way to be white is to not *ever* have been black.

"But I didn't have a story. I felt so out of place. I wasn't ever good at lying. And I thought, my name is Beverly Hemings and my people live at Monticello. I'll just go on home.

"Besides, Mama, it isn't going to work to have Harriet show up three years from now, out of the blue. I could maybe keep quiet about myself and get along, but I can't have a sister without having folks we came from. Nobody would think she was a nice girl.

"And I was lonely," Beverly said. "I didn't know I could be that lonely. But that wasn't important, not really. I could have coped with being lonely. I came back to get a story."

As dusk fell the room had grown completely dark. Maddy could no longer see Beverly's face, or Harriet's, or Mama's. It was past time for Mama to leave for the great house, but she hadn't moved. From the open doorway Harriet spoke, low and firm. "Our mama and papa died of typhoid," she said. "We were so little we can scarce remember them. Our aunt Sally and uncle John raised us, only they weren't our aunt and uncle exactly, more like cousins, the only kin we had. Uncle John taught you carpentry. He died a few years ago, but you stayed on the farm, trying to be a help to Aunt Sally. Now she's gone, and with the price of land so low and crops poor and all, you had to let the farm go for taxes. Not that you minded—you like carpentry better anyhow, and I've always hoped to live in a city.

"So now you're seeking a job, and a nice set of rooms to rent. You've got a sister—me—staying back with friends for a few months—and as soon as you get settled you'll send for her. That's how it is, Beverly. That'll be our story."

"We've got three years," Beverly said. "I'll leave again a few months before you can, before you're twenty-one. You keep telling me our story, Harriet. You tell me until then."

Mama went away then, up to the great house. She kissed them all before she left.

Harriet lit the lamp. She turned to Beverly. "You better be brave enough to leave," she said. "Three years from now."

"I will be," Beverly said. "I promise."

"I'm not as strong as Mama," Harriet said. "I want children, and they will have to be white children, because I will never be strong enough to send them away."

Beverly gave Maddy a searching look. "What about you?" he asked.

Maddy nodded. He knew what Beverly meant. "I'm strong enough," he said. "I'll be okay alone."

Chapter Thirty-three

The Luckiest Boy

"Peter!" Maddy called. "Get back here!"

Peter laughed. He ran across the green lawn, looking back over his shoulder at Maddy. Maddy was all the time trying to make him sit down with that book. Peter wasn't going to do it, no sir.

Maddy chased him, as Peter hoped. Peter ran, squealing, but Maddy tackled him and rolled him over on the grass. "Spell your name for me," Maddy said.

Peter rolled his eyes and giggled.

Maddy tickled him. Peter squealed. "Do it," Maddy said.

"P-E-T-E-R," Peter said.

"Good," said Maddy. "Now *Fossett*."

"N-O-S-I-R," Peter said. He rolled to escape Maddy's grasp and sprang to his feet. "I gotta go!" he said. "It's almost time for the Eagle! I gotta go!"

Maddy let him go. He dusted his pants legs and watched Peter run barefoot across the grass. Worry hovered over the mountaintop like thick, dark storm clouds, but Peter Fossett was pure light.

Peter Fossett knew he was just about the luckiest boy in the world.

He lived at Monticello. That meant "little mountain" in Italian, Maddy said.

It was the most beautiful place in the world. He lived on the mountain's very top. From the front of his daddy's blacksmith shop he could see one direction, over the mountain to other mountains far away, and from the back of the shop he could see another direction, still over mountains and still far away, both directions as far as his eyes would work, and that was pretty far. Peter didn't think Monticello was a little mountain. He thought it was a great big mountain.

Maddy knew lots. He liked to tell Peter stories about other places, especially Poplar Forest, Master Jefferson's other farm. Peter enjoyed Maddy's stories, but he knew Monticello was really the best place, no matter what Maddy said.

Peter's daddy was the best blacksmith in the entire world, and his mama was the best cook ever. All the visitors who came to see Master Jefferson just couldn't believe how good Mama's food was. They filled their plates two and three times and rubbed their full bellies and licked their lips and said, "Could I have another muffin, please?"

Burwell told Peter white people were gluttons, but Peter knew he'd be a glutton too, if anybody would let him. Peter would love to sit in that dining room and eat all the muffins and ice cream he could hold. Lucky for him, his mama would sneak him a little taste, him and his little sister both, of anything she made for the great house.

Peter was seven years old, not old enough to work hard all day, but old enough to be useful. In the morning, he usually went up to the great house and helped old Burwell clear the breakfast plates away. Peter stacked them in the little box in the wall, and then he pulled on a cord and *whoosh!* sent the plates and the box down to the basement.

Once Peter climbed into the box himself. He rode down to the basement, and when his big sister Maria, who was fifteen, opened the door and saw him, she screamed. Then she laughed. But she told him not to do it again. He was such a big boy, what if he broke the box? Then they'd have to carry the plates up and down the stairs, and that would be a job.

Once the breakfast table was cleared, Peter took a little broom and swept around the fireplace in the dining room. Then he had a bit of time while Master Jefferson wrote his letters. Peter might go back to the kitchen, or he might visit Maddy and Beverly and Eston in the woodshop. He might even just sit down in the front hall and wait. If he did that he could listen while Miss Martha taught her younger children, all except the littlest one, George. Maddy was always after Peter to pay attention to Miss Martha's lessons, but

Peter didn't care about schoolwork the way Maddy did. He liked to be doing things. Sitting still with a book made him itch.

Maddy was always reading through his old primer or looking up words in John Hemings's dictionary. "But you're grown," Peter protested when Maddy tried to teach him. "I bet you didn't mess with books when you were a little boy."

Maddy said, "When I was your age, I messed with books all the time. I got Miss Ellen to teach me."

Miss Ellen was an old maid, twenty-six and still no husband. "She ain't going to teach me," Peter said. "She won't have a thing to do with me."

"She *isn't* going to teach you," Maddy corrected. "I know she won't. That was a long time ago; she's different now."

Peter hopped from one foot to another. "On Sunday, when James comes . . ."

"Yes?"

"Let's throw away that book and go fish."

In the mornings, when Master Jefferson finished his letters, Miss Sally would come out to the hall and say, "Peter?" in her quiet voice. Peter would run to the stables.

"It's time for the Eagle," he would yell.

The big boys who worked in the stable smiled at him, and old Eagle stuck his head over his stall door and whinnied. Eagle was Master Jefferson's riding horse. He was the best horse, and the smartest, and the sweetest in the world, and he was always glad to see Peter.

On his way into the barn Peter grabbed a handful of oats from the bin. He gave them to Eagle. Then he stood on a stool and brushed Eagle all over, head to toe. One of the big boys saddled Eagle, and helped Peter buckle the bridle.

Peter led Eagle to the great house. That was his very favorite part of the morning. When they came out of the stable Eagle always blew out his breath—*Phww!*—and lifted his head and pricked his ears. He looked as happy as Peter felt. But he never rushed or stepped on Peter's toes. Eagle had wonderful manners. He needed them. Master Jefferson was almost eighty years old, and not very steady on his feet. A fall from a horse would kill him. But Eagle was too sweet a horse to let Master Jefferson fall.

Peter walked Eagle up to the back porch and pushed him sideways so Eagle's body was right against the porch. He sat on the edge of the porch, holding the reins, and they waited for Master Jefferson. Eagle was always patient. He might sniff Peter's hands to see if Peter had more oats, but he never moved his feet.

Master Jefferson came out to the porch with his hat under his arm. He was tall and skinny and bandy-legged. He grew his white hair long, the way Peter's daddy said people did back in the old days, and he tied it with a scrap of ribbon. His breeches were always loose and his coat always flapped.

Master Jefferson settled his hat on his head. He took the reins. "Thank you, Peter," he said.

"Yes, sir," Peter said. He held on to one rein until Master

Jefferson's seat was safe in the saddle. Master Jefferson rode away singing. He was always singing.

After that Peter usually visited the woodshop, if he hadn't already. He wasn't going to be a carpenter when he grew up. He was going to be a blacksmith, like his daddy. But he liked visiting the woodshop.

"Morning, small fry," Maddy said when Peter came in. "How's Eagle today?"

"Prime," said Peter. He climbed onto the workbench and dangled his legs.

"Watch, now," said John, the head carpenter. "No splinters."

"I don't get splinters," Peter said.

John grunted. "Then you'll be the first boy that didn't."

"What are you making?" Peter asked Maddy.

"The same thing I was making yesterday," Maddy said.

"A table for Poplar Forest."

"That's right."

Peter liked the table. It had a wide top and fancy carved legs. The pieces weren't put together, but he could see how they would be. "Can I help?" he asked.

"I could use you over here," Beverly said. "Hold these for me." He brushed glue on the sides of two long pieces of wood. Peter pressed them together and held them tight while Beverly screwed on the clamps. "There! Thank you."

"How long until the glue dries?"

"Day or two. Depends on the weather."

"What are you going to do next?"

Beverly grinned. "How many questions are you going to ask?"

"Depends," Peter said. "How many are you going to answer?"

"You could get us something to eat," Eston said. "I'd answer a lot of questions if I wasn't so hungry."

Eston was always hungry. He was fifteen, taller than both of his brothers, and thin as a rail no matter how much he ate. Peter's mama said it was hard to get enough food inside a growing boy. Take Peter's brother James. He claimed he ate plenty over at Edgehill, where he lived, but he still looked scrawny. Every Sunday, Mama fed James a whole tableful of food, and packed more in a cloth for him to carry away, but he didn't fatten up at all.

Peter went to the kitchen and rounded up some scraps for Eston, and then he hung out in the shop and sanded some boards for fun. A noise on the road made him look out the window. "Visitors," Peter said.

"Something new," said Maddy. He was joking. They always had visitors.

In the afternoons Peter helped his daddy in the blacksmith shop. Daddy didn't talk much while he worked; he said talking led to carelessness, and you could never be careless around hot iron. He taught Peter lots, though. He was going to train Peter to be a blacksmith when Peter was just a little older, and then they'd run the shop together. When his daddy trimmed a horse's hoof, he held it up for Peter to see, both before the trimming and after, so Peter could learn how a hoof was supposed to be balanced, with all the trim lines straight. Peter worked the bellows and shoveled charcoal onto the fire. Sometimes his daddy even gave him a piece of scrap iron and let him heat it up and pound on it, to make his arm strong, but that was only if the shop wasn't busy.

Once the sun set, the workday was finished. Peter helped his daddy tidy the shop, and in the kitchen his sisters helped Mama wash dishes. The white folks ate their big dinner in the great house at three in the afternoon. After that, all Mama had to do was clean up from the big meal, make supper for the mountaintop workers, fix a little snack for the great house for the evening, and maybe bake cookies or set bread dough. Mama's kitchen filled up with workers right after the sun went down, but everyone ate fast, and pretty soon it was just Peter's family, all of them except for James. They always wished James was with them.

Mama banked the kitchen fire. They all went to the room next door, which was just for their family alone. Peter's big sisters talked with his daddy while Mama tucked Peter, his little sister, Isabella, and his baby brother, William, into the trundle bed and sang them to sleep.

One evening in early spring, Peter decided to go back to the kitchen early, before his daddy shut down the forge. He had just gotten there when Beverly came in behind him, carrying his violin.

Beverly, Maddy, and Eston all played the violin. Beverly

had a small one, Eston a bigger, better one, and Maddy played whichever he could lay his hands on. Maddy didn't mind not having his own violin. He said Beverly and Eston were the real musicians in the family.

"May I play a song for you, Miss Edith?" Beverly asked.

"Why aren't you working?" asked Peter.

"I left off early," he said. "Miss Edith, what would you like to hear?"

"Why'd you leave off early?" Peter asked. Nobody quit work early. It wasn't allowed. Eston did go to Charlottesville once a week for violin lessons, but Maddy and Beverly were too old for that.

Beverly didn't answer. Peter's mama smiled. She told him her favorite song, and he played it, right in the kitchen, sweet as could be. When he was finished, Peter's mama had tears in her eyes. Peter didn't know why. His mama never cried. "I'm going to fix you up some pie," she said. "A big piece of rhubarb pie."

"I'd like that," Beverly said. "Miss Edith, I'd like that very much. Thank you. Peter, what about you? Can I play something for you?"

Peter turned to Mama. "Why does he get pie?" At lunchtime she'd told him he couldn't have any. She said it was for tomorrow at the great house. "I don't want you to play for me," Peter said to Beverly. "Why would you play for me?" Beverly played for the house dances. Eston played for himself. Maddy played for Peter.

"I just thought maybe you'd like a song," Beverly said. "A song all your own. A gift song."

"I never heard of a gift song," Peter said.

Peter's big sister Betsy-Ann said, "I'd like a song." Beverly played for her, and then for Maria and Patsy and even Isabella and William, and then he played a little song that he said was for Peter whether Peter wanted it or not. Then Beverly took the pie that Peter's mama had wrapped up in a cloth. He put it in his shirt. He bowed deep to Peter's mama, a fancy bow like a white man would do, and he left with his violin tucked under his chin. Peter could hear him walking down Mulberry Row, still playing.

Beverly played songs for everyone. He played for hours. Late into the night, from Miss Sally's room one door down from Peter's family's, Beverly's music poured onto Mulberry Row.

Maddy came to their door. "Mister Joe," he said, "Miss Edith. Beverly wants to know if he's keeping you all awake. Because he'd like to keep playing if he's not."

"Tell him keep on," Daddy said. "We're enjoying the music. We don't mind."

Peter minded. He couldn't sleep and it didn't make sense. Beverly never played this late.

"Why isn't he quiet?" Peter asked. "It's night."

Mama shushed him. "I think it's pretty," Maria said.

"That's because you're sweet on Beverly," Peter said.

"Fat lot of good it does me," Maria shot back.

Mama said, "Both of you, hush."

Eventually Peter fell asleep. In the morning he ate breakfast, helped in the dining room, and brought Eagle up to the house. Master Jefferson set off on his usual ride, humming his usual tune. Peter went down to the woodshop. Maddy and Eston were working there, but not Beverly.

"Is Beverly sick?" Peter asked. Maybe that was why he'd acted so strange about playing the violin.

John gave Maddy a look Peter didn't understand.

"Come here," Maddy said to Peter. "We better talk private."

Peter scooted over to the corner. Maddy sat down next to him. "Do you remember when Beverly went away for a while, three years ago?"

"No," said Peter.

"Well," said Maddy. "He's gone again. Only this time he's not coming back."

Peter stared at Maddy. Maddy stared back at him. Peter started to cry. "Like James," he said. "Oh, no. Like James." Mama and Daddy never talked about it, but Peter's sisters had told him how James got taken away.

Maddy hugged him. "No, not like that," he said. "It's not like James. James went away because he had to. Beverly went away because he wanted to. It's happy, not sad."

That didn't make any sense to Peter. Maddy looked sad, and besides—"People can't just go away because they want to," he said. "They can't do that." People had to do as they were told. Mama had to listen to Miss Martha, Maddy had to listen to John, and everybody had to listen to Master Jefferson.

James had been sold. It was terrible and hard to understand, but Peter knew it was true. "Who bought Beverly?" he asked.

Maddy smiled, an odd, faraway, sad-and-happy smile that frightened Peter a little. "Nobody bought him. He went away free."

"Free of what?"

"Free," Maddy repeated. "Free to do whatever he wants. He won't have to listen to anybody unless he wants to."

Peter thought about that. "Except Master Jefferson," he said.

Maddy said, "Not even Master Jefferson. Beverly's gone away from Master Jefferson. He won't see Master Jefferson ever again."

"He's not coming back on Sundays?" James said.

"No," Madison said, with the same funny smile but with a catch in his voice like he might cry. "He's not coming back. He's got his story straight and he'll never come back again."

Eston came over and put his hand on Maddy's shoulder.

Peter said, "You mean he'll never see *you*?"

"He'll never see me," Maddy said.

"He'll never see his mama?" Peter started to cry again. He was sorry he hadn't wanted Beverly to play for him. He was sorry he hadn't said good-bye. "Why would he leave?" he sobbed. "He'll miss his mama."

Maddy hugged Peter. "Shh, now," he said. "It's okay. It's good, it's happy. And we've got to be quiet about it. Okay? But it's happy."

"It doesn't feel happy," said Peter.

Eston said, "It doesn't feel happy, but it is."

Maddy said, "You'll understand when you're bigger. But right now, just trust me. And don't talk about Beverly. Okay? If you have a question, or you need to talk about him, you come to me. Just me, or Eston if you can't find me. You can talk to the two of us about Beverly, but not anybody else."

"Not even my mama?"

"Not even her."

"Not even my *daddy*?"

Maddy scratched his forehead. "I guess you could talk to your daddy," he said. "I don't want to say you can't. But I think it's better if you just talk to me."

"Okay," Peter said. "Maddy?"

"Yes?"

"I have a question."

"Go ahead."

"How come Beverly gets to be free, but James didn't?"

Maddy shut his eyes and then opened them. "That's a very hard question," he said. "I know the answer, but I can't explain it just now."

"It's not fair," Peter said.

"No." Maddy took his hand and led him back to the workbench by the window. "It isn't fair. Here. You hold this board so I can measure it. Then I'll mark the spot, and I'll show you how to use a saw."

Maddy had never let Peter saw a board before. It was harder than it looked, and Maddy had to help. After that Peter swept the floor without being asked. No one spoke. Usually the woodshop rang with laughter and singing and jokes. The silence hurt Peter's head.

"Maddy?" he whispered at last.

"Yes?"

"I still don't think it's happy. And I still don't think it's fair."

"It isn't fair," Maddy said. "Don't you ever let anybody make you believe that it's fair."

"You going to be free someday?"

"I hope so," Maddy said.

Peter nodded. "Me too. I think it sounds pretty fine."

Chapter Thirty-four

Harriet Turns Twenty-one

Peter tried to put thoughts of Beverly and freedom out of his mind. He had work to do. Eagle was shedding his winter coat. Peter stood on a stool and scraped the thick hair off him for hours. Eston and Maddy planted two rows of cabbages. Peter earned a penny picking worms from the baby plants. He held horses for his daddy while they were being shod, and licked the bowl when his mama made gingerbread.

He kept busy so he wouldn't have too much time to think. Thinking made him wonder, first about Beverly and James, and then about himself. Wondering made him sad and scared.

"Daddy," he finally asked, when he and his father were alone in the blacksmith shop. "Could I be sold someday?"

His daddy froze for a moment with his hammer in the air above the anvil, then brought the hammer down, hard, on the iron he was shaping. "Yes," he said.

"Oh." Peter felt like his father had hit him in the gut. He guessed he should have known. It had happened to James. Peter had never thought about it before.

Peter's daddy set his hammer down. He held his hands out, and Peter went to him. Daddy put his big hands on either side of Peter's face, and looked straight into Peter's eyes. "It's a terrible, terrible thing," he said. "I will do everything I can to keep us together and safe. I promise you. I will do all I can, and your mama will too. But we couldn't protect James, no matter how hard we tried. It's terrible, terrible, but it's the truth.

"I'd rather lie to you," he continued. "If I thought it was right, I'd tell you a lie and let you feel safe just a little while longer. But it's not right, and I won't do it. I want you to know I will never lie to you. You can always trust everything I say."

It was terrible to think about even from the strength of his daddy's arms. Peter shuddered. Daddy held him tighter. "I'm sorry," Peter's daddy said.

Three months after Beverly left, Peter was going into the kitchen when he saw Mr. Bacon, one of the overseers, drive a farm wagon up Mulberry Row. Mr. Bacon pulled up just past the kitchen and got down. Peter stopped in the doorway to see what was going on.

Mr. Bacon knocked on the door of Miss Sally's room. The door opened, and a fine-looking young woman wearing a hoop dress came out. Peter thought it was one of Miss Martha's girls, but he couldn't tell which—her face was shaded by her big straw hat. She held a carpetbag in her gloved hands. Mr. Bacon took it from her, helped her onto the wagon seat, and settled the carpetbag by her feet.

Peter stared. He was sure he knew her—he recognized the set of her shoulders and the way she carried herself—but he didn't know her name. He'd never paid much attention to Miss Martha's girls. What was one of them doing in Miss Sally's room? "Ma—" he said. Mr. Bacon started the horses. The wagon went down the row and disappeared around the bend.

"Mama," he said, "a white woman just came out of Miss Sally's room."

"Leave it," Mama said. She was chopping greens, a big heap of them, her knife flashing through the pile.

"But Mama, a white woman. Looked like one of Miss Martha's girls. Mr. Bacon drove off with her. Mama"—she didn't seem to be paying attention—"shouldn't I go get Miss Sally?"

"You should not," Mama said. "Fetch some wood. The stoves are running low."

"But Mama—"

Her knife never quit moving. "Peter, shut your mouth and go away. And stay away from Miss Sally. She knows all about that lady on the wagon. She doesn't want to talk to you."

Peter shut his mouth. He fetched wood. He looked at the stern set of his mother's face, and decided to go find Maddy.

The woodshop was empty. Finally Peter tracked Maddy down in one of the lower farm fields, mending fence.

"This woman came out—this woman who looked like—" As Peter began to speak, the truth suddenly hit him straight upside the head. He fell backward onto the grass. "That was Harriet," he said. Harriet was Maddy's big sister. She looked almost white even when she was dressed as a slave. He looked up at Maddy, stunned. "That was Harriet, leaving."

Maddy's face was even more expressionless than Peter's mama's. "Yes," he said. "It was." He turned away and knocked one of the ends of a new fence rail into place.

Peter couldn't believe he hadn't recognized Harriet right away. But the difference between Harriet wearing homespun and a headscarf and Harriet wearing a hoop dress and lady's hat was astonishing. "It's going to be another thing we can't talk about, isn't it?" he said. "That's why Mama shut me up."

"It's safer if we don't talk," Maddy said. "Safer for Harriet. I want Harriet to be as safe as she can."

So did Peter. He liked Harriet. She was one of his sister Maria's best friends. "She went off with Mr. Bacon," Peter said. Mr. Bacon was a short old man, with a wide flat face like a badger. "She's not taking up with him?" That was a horrible thought.

"No," Maddy said. "He's giving her a ride into town, that's all." Maddy sighed and ran his fingers through his hair. "He's putting her on a stagecoach bound for Philadelphia."

"She's going to Philadelphia!" Peter'd heard of that place. It was far, far away. A great big city.

"No," Maddy said. "She's not."

Peter waited for him to explain, but he didn't. Peter watched Maddy pound fence rails for a while, then said, "I suppose I might go ask my daddy. He tells me the truth."

Maddy's face looked tight and smooth, like one of those head statues Master Jefferson had. Like it was carved out of stone. He didn't say anything.

Peter waited some more. "Please tell me," he said.

Maddy sighed. He sat down next to Peter. "A lady can't just walk away," Maddy said. "Or ride off on a horse, or go anywhere on her own. A lady has to travel respectably, or she isn't a lady anymore."

Peter had never thought of Harriet as a lady. He guessed she was, but he'd never thought of her that way.

"So we had to send her off that way," Maddy said. "With an escort, someone to buy her stage ticket and put her on properly. But we don't want Mr. Bacon to know where she's really going. He might decide to tell somebody, or to go after her himself. Harriet's going to get off that stage in a day or so and switch to another one. She's not going to Philadelphia." Maddy sighed. "She's going to live with Beverly."

The grass tickled Peter's legs. The wind whipped his shirt. Sheep lay in the pasture with them, chewing their cuds and watching them warily. "You know where Beverly is?" he asked Maddy.

Maddy nodded. "He's in a city. He's all right. He has a job, and a place for him and Harriet to stay."

"How do you know all that?"

"He wrote a letter."

Peter frowned. "I didn't know you got a letter." He should. News like that traveled all up and down Mulberry Row.

Maddy said, "It's a secret, Peter. He sent the letter to Jesse Scott."

Peter turned this over in his mind. "Where's he at? What city?"

Maddy frowned. "I'd better not say."

Peter pouted. "Why not?"

"The less people know, the better," Maddy said.

"My daddy tells me the truth," said Peter.

"So do I," Maddy said. "The truth right here is, I know and I'm not going to tell you. Keeping a secret is not the same as telling a lie."

It wasn't the same, but Peter didn't like it. On Sunday, Peter told James all about Harriet, and about Maddy keeping secrets too. He told the whole story right in the middle of the kitchen, and he didn't care who overheard.

James stopped eating. He took hold of Peter's hand and walked him down to Miss Sally's room, where Maddy lived. James stuck his head inside.

Miss Sally wasn't there, but Eston was playing his fiddle and Maddy was lying on the bed.

"I just heard," James said. Eston kept playing. Maddy nodded.

"Don't you worry," James said. "Harriet's smart. She was born smart. She'll do fine."

Maddy blew out his breath. "Hope so," he said.

Peter tugged on James's hand. He wanted James to ask where Harriet went. Instead James spoke to Eston. "How long now until you turn twenty-one?"

Eston kept playing his music. He said, "Five years, two weeks, and one day."

James smiled. "I'd be counting like that too."

Eston played another flourish. "But I won't be leaving town," he said. "I figure I'll just stay."

"You're leaving," Maddy said.

"Probably not," Eston said. "Miss Virginia hired me to play for her dance next week. Five years from now I ought to get fiddling jobs pretty much all the time. Nobody minds a fiddle player being black. I figure, I can just stay here."

Maddy looked angry. Peter wondered why. "You'll go be with them," he told Eston.

"I won't," Eston said.

James laughed. "What's that you used to say?" he asked Maddy. "A tree, it might get old and fall down, but Eston won't never budge."

Maddy got up from the bed. He smacked Eston's backside and picked Peter up by the arms. "It's a nice day," he said, throwing Peter over his shoulder and tickling him until he howled. "Let's enjoy it."

That night, before he walked back to Edgehill, James took

Peter aside and told him to leave Maddy alone. Whatever secrets he wanted to keep belonged to him, and to Miss Sally and their family. Peter wasn't to poke in Maddy's business. "But—" Peter said.

"No buts," James said. "That's how it is." They were in the kitchen. Mama was sitting down to a cup of tea, trying to catch her breath. Patsy and Isabella were washing dishes, and Maria was packing a bundle of food for James.

"Maria's not leaving, is she?" Peter asked.

Mama frowned at him. Maria tightened the knot on the bundle with her teeth. "If I do," she said, "it won't be on a stagecoach wearing a hoop dress."

A few weeks later, on a Sunday, Maddy came to their room looking for James. He sat down between James and Peter, and his smile lit the room like daylight. "Eston went to Jesse's for his lesson," Maddy said. "Jesse had a letter. She's safe. They're together, and they're doing fine."

Every day that summer, Peter searched for worms in Maddy and Eston's cabbage patch. He scooped them up in his hands and fed them to his mama's hens. In the fall, when Maddy and Eston sold a hundred cabbages to Master Jefferson, they paid Peter a quarter for his work. He took it to his daddy. "Put this with the money," he said.

"What money?" Daddy said.

"The money under the bed," Peter said. Daddy had a

whole jar full of money, saved up in a secret cubby dug into the floor beneath the bed.

Daddy laughed. "I didn't know you knew about that money," he said.

"You put my quarter with it," Peter said. "It's my wages. It goes with yours."

Daddy closed his fingers around the quarter. "All right," he said. "All right, son. That's what I'll do."

Chapter Thirty-five

As Long as Master Jefferson Lives

That fall, Master Jefferson returned from Poplar Place determined to improve the great house at Monticello. He planned to tear down the wooden steps along the back porch, build new brick steps, widen the portico, and build new, grander columns.

Peter thought it sounded exciting, but Maddy shook his head. "A couple new coats of paint, that's what the great house needs," Maddy said. "A cistern that doesn't leak, a better laundry, new cabin roofs. Master Jefferson's always more excited about creating something new than taking care of what he's already got. This place looks like a pigsty."

It was true the great house looked shabby and run-down. But, Peter thought, it had always been that way.

Maddy and Eston tore down the old wooden steps in a single day. Peter helped haul the pieces away. Then John and Maddy widened and leveled the bare ground where the old steps had been, measured it, and marked where the new steps would be with sticks and string. Master Jefferson came out to see. He, John, and Maddy discussed the new steps for a long time. Peter grew bored. He went to the kitchen and then to the forge.

The next day, John showed Peter how to mix up a kind of mud called mortar that dried hard and wouldn't wash away. He showed Peter how to use a trowel to slap mortar onto a brick, and how to lay the bricks on the ground in a long straight row.

"Stop," Maddy told him, "that's sloppy." Maddy wanted the bricks lined up perfectly straight, with exactly the same distance between each brick, and exactly the same amount of mortar on each one.

Peter didn't see why that was important. "Because details matter," Maddy said. He made Peter go study the outside walls of the great house, and the outbuildings, and the kitchen. "They're all built the same way, aren't they?" Maddy said. "All in straight lines, with even spaces. That's because details matter."

"I'm going to be a blacksmith," Peter said. "My daddy—"

"Agrees with me," Maddy said, grinning. "You go ask him, small fry. Ask him if he has to get a horse's shoes exactly right, or just pretty close."

Peter scowled. Then he had to laugh, because Maddy was right. Peter knew what his daddy would say.

On the bottom layer of the steps, where the bricks would be covered by the ones above, Eston scratched something into the smooth surface of the mortar.

"What's that?" Peter asked, coming up behind him.

Eston jumped like Isabella caught stealing a cookie. "Just my initials," he said. "Just for fun."

Peter studied the scratch marks. Eston looked at him. "That's a Q and a K," Eston said. "Stands for Eston Hemings."

Peter nodded. "I knew that."

Eston laughed out loud. "Peter, my name does not begin with Q. That's an E you're staring at. Don't you know your letters yet?" He looked around quick to be sure they were alone. "Hey, Maddy," he said, "we forgot to teach this boy to read."

"I've been trying," Maddy said.

Eston said, "We'll have to try harder. Else we might run out of time." He put a stick into Peter's hand.

"I don't want to," Peter said.

"Sure you do." Eston helped him scratch P and F into the mortar. Maddy put his initials in too, and then they covered the letters with bricks before anyone could see.

That afternoon Master Jefferson came out to check on their progress. He was standing on the old part of the portico, leaning over, and all of a sudden he just sort of tumbled, the way Peter's baby brother, William, did sometimes. Master Jefferson fell so slowly Peter thought he'd catch himself, but he didn't. Eston rushed forward, but not in time.

Master Jefferson landed on his left arm. Peter heard a loud crack. Master Jefferson sat up, with Eston's help, and his arm bent where it shouldn't have. Peter realized the noise had come from Master Jefferson's arm breaking. He felt sick. Master Jefferson groaned. Eston and John lifted him to his feet. Master Jefferson cradled his arm.

Burwell ran out from the great house. "Peter!" he yelled. "Run tell Davy Hern to go for the doctor."

"No need to fuss," Master Jefferson said. His face was pale, nearly gray. He swayed. Eston caught him. Peter ran for Davy Hern. By the time he'd returned to the great house, Master Jefferson was inside and the door closed tight.

Peter hesitated on the portico. Eston had gone back to working on the steps. "We'd best stay outside," he said to Peter. "There's plenty of people taking care of him. Mix some mortar, will you?"

Peter mixed mortar and watched Eston lay bricks.

"Is he hurt bad?" Peter asked.

"I don't know," Eston said. "Broken arm, you saw that. I didn't see any bones sticking out, which is good. But at his age anything could be bad."

The doctor reset the broken bones, splinted them, and gave Master Jefferson laudanum for the pain. News of the accident spread fast. Before nightfall there were double the usual number of visitors, all of them eager for the details of Master Jefferson's accident. Newspapermen came to write about it.

Miss Martha forbade them the house. "The president has a slight fever, but is resting comfortably," she said. "Thank you for your concern." She shut the door in their faces, dismissing them.

A few of the newspapermen didn't leave. They wandered down Mulberry Row instead. Peter tailed them. He was curious about newspapermen. They came to the blacksmith shop, where a group of overseers and townsfolk stood gossiping while their work was being done, and one of the newspapermen asked Peter's daddy how he liked having Mr. Jefferson for a master.

The pack of white men fell silent, waiting for Peter's daddy to answer. Daddy straightened up from his anvil, because he never talked and worked at the same time. He paused a moment, and then said, "As long as Master Jefferson is alive, his people know we'll be treated just fine."

It was a fine answer, Peter could tell. All the men relaxed and smiled. The newspapermen wrote the answer down. "Glad to know you appreciate him," one said.

"Yes, sir," Peter's daddy replied.

Later, after all the men had left, Peter said, "What's *appreciate* mean?"

Daddy put down his hammer and said, "It means, we know we've got it good."

Peter thought about that. "We've got it good, then?"

"Better than some," Peter's daddy said.

Peter thought some more. "As long as Master Jefferson is alive."

"That's right. That's exactly right. You have hit upon the crux of it."

His daddy set to making spoons from a pot of pewter he had melted on the forge. He ladled the pewter into the spoon molds, slow but not too slow, so the mold would fill without any air bubbles, and the pewter would harden in one piece, without layers. When he finished filling the molds he put the ladle back into the melting pot, and Peter knew it was okay to speak again. "So what happens," he asked, "when Master Jefferson dies?"

His daddy took a deep breath. "That is an important question," he said. "I do not know the answer." He opened each mold and popped the still-hot spoons onto the edge of the forge. One had a chunk missing out of the handle, where air had been trapped in the mold. Daddy shook his head, and threw the misshapen spoon back into the melting pot with his tongs.

Peter waited. He knew his daddy had more to say.

"There's the farms, they're worth something," Daddy said. "That's on the one hand. On the other hand are the debts, and folks talk like those are terribly high. Miss Martha might be the one to inherit, but it might be Mister Jeff or Mister Jeff plus some of the other grandchildren. Whoever it is, they get the good with the bad, the property and the debts. It's hard to say how it's going to work out. I asked Miss Sally once; she said she didn't think he'd written a will.

"That's a piece of paper," Daddy said, before Peter could ask, "that says what you want done with your things after you die. If he dies without a will, merciful heavens, we'll have a mess on our hands."

Peter looked at the row of gleaming spoons. "People don't die from broken arms," he said.

His daddy shrugged. "A man his age doesn't need a reason to die."

Master Jefferson didn't die, but Peter guessed the accident must have shook him up, because not too long afterward, he gave Poplar Forest away.

Maddy and Eston told Peter about it, one day in the woodshop. Master Jefferson's grandson Francis Eppes, who they said was Miss Maria's boy, had gotten married, and Master Jefferson gave him the whole of Poplar Forest as a wedding present.

"Why Francis Eppes?" Peter asked. He knew a swarm of Master Jefferson's grandchildren, but he didn't know anyone named Francis Eppes.

"I guess Master Jefferson wants to divide things between Miss Martha and Miss Maria," Maddy explained. "Miss Maria was his daughter too. She died back when Beverly was a little boy. Francis was her only child that survived."

"But how come he gets all of Poplar, just him?" asked Peter. He was helping them sand some boards. He liked to sand wood. "Mister Jeff works here and lives here. When he got married, nobody gave him his own farm." Mister Jeff worked hard—harder than the overseers, harder than any of the other white men on the farm.

Maddy shrugged. Eston said, "I guess it was just what Master Jefferson wanted to do. He's always paid for everything for Miss Martha's children, and he never paid for anything for Francis."

"He didn't have to," Maddy explained. "Francis's daddy does pretty well."

Peter knew Miss Martha's husband didn't do much. Everyone knew that. He ran Edgehill, but James said it wasn't a profitable farm. "So he's splitting his property between his children," Peter said.

In a flat voice Eston replied, "Some of them."

"Oh, right." Peter waved his hand. He forgot sometimes that Maddy and Eston were Master Jefferson's children too.

"What do you—" Maddy started to ask him.

"I think I'd leave that alone," Eston said, cutting Maddy off.

"Will you still get to go there?" Peter asked. "Will Francis Eppes need carpenters at Poplar Forest?"

"I doubt it," Eston said. "If he does, it won't be us."

"I'm sorry," Peter said.

Maddy sighed. "It was my favorite place in the world."

Maddy and Eston told Peter it was past time he learned to read. They brought out their battered old primer, and every time he came by the woodshop they opened the thing up and stuck it under his nose, and made him repeat, *ay, bee, cee.*

Peter's mama and daddy and even James said he needed to learn to read, but Peter would rather sweep the shop. "You're not trying," Maddy said. "You're not even letting the letters sink in."

"Maybe I'm stupid," Peter said.

"Maybe you're not." Maddy shut the book with a sigh. "Maybe you are too young. We can hold off a bit, still, but you've got to learn. You've absolutely got to learn to read."

It seemed to Peter that for a long time then, everything on the surface stayed the same. Nobody left, nobody took sick, nobody was born, nobody died. The sun shone bright on the mountaintop. Eagle whinnied when he saw Peter in the mornings, and Master Jefferson, his arm healed, rode away humming a tune.

Yet somehow Peter could feel a change, like a shifting in the pattern of the wind, or a melody from Eston's violin sliding into minor key. The happiness on the mountaintop began to feel strained around its edges. Peter thought that if he were a horse, he'd be standing at the highest point of the pasture, looking all around him between mouthfuls of grass.

"Is something wrong?" he asked Maddy at last.

Maddy was heading down the mountain to put in a new gate on one of the outlying farms. Peter's daddy had forged the hinges for it. Maddy borrowed a farm wagon, and Peter helped him hitch.

"Is some—" Peter began to ask again.

"Sst," Maddy said. He jerked his head sideways, toward an overseer walking to the blacksmith shop. Peter shut his mouth. When the horses were hitched Maddy heaved the gate into the wagon bed. He motioned to Peter to climb aboard.

Once they were away from Mulberry Row, Maddy asked, "What do you mean? Wrong in what way?"

Peter squirmed. "Just everywhere. Just not right. Something's not right." He struggled to think of a reason. "Miss Martha's unhappy." Peter knew that was nothing new.

Maddy sighed. "I think I understand what you mean, but it's not anything in particular, not any new thing. The money problems are worse than ever. Yesterday a merchant from Charlottesville came to the front door of the great house. He wanted payment for his past due bills, right then and there, in cash. That's never happened before."

"Did he get paid?"

Maddy shook his head. "Master Jefferson didn't have the money. He acted all astonished, that someone in his position would be dunned by his creditors, but the man didn't back down. He went away angry. He'll tell the whole town."

"How do you know all this?" Peter asked.

Maddy shrugged. "Burwell told Mama. Mama told me."

They rode for a bit.

Maddy didn't say anything else. Peter thought about the

story, but it didn't seem enough to him, to explain the feeling of worry he had. One little tradesman wanting to be paid? That wasn't a big problem.

The next day Peter went to his daddy. It was Sunday, so Daddy didn't have to work, but he'd fired up the forge and was making pot hooks out of scraps, to sell.

"Something's wrong," Peter said.

Daddy blew out a big deep breath like the bellows.

"I know it is," Peter said, "I just don't know what it is."

Daddy smiled at him. "You're a smart boy," he said.

"Yes, sir."

"So you can see, Master Jefferson's getting older. He's not going to live forever."

Peter leaned against his daddy's leg. He wished his daddy gave out hugs, the way his mama did. "You said that before," he said.

"Yes, I did," Daddy said. "But the longer he lives, the closer he comes to dying. I guess everyone's worried because they don't know what will happen then. We're worried, and up at the great house, Miss Martha and her family are worried too."

Tap, tap, tap. Daddy pounded the side of the pot hook perfectly flat, then grabbed one hot end with his tongs and twisted it into a perfect curve. Peter stepped out of the way so Daddy could douse it in the water bucket. "But Maddy said it was about the money."

Daddy nodded. "Sure. If there were plenty of money, nobody would be worried."

Peter laughed. "But we have plenty of money," he said. "We've got that whole big jar!"

"That's true," Daddy said.

"How much is in that jar?"

"Three hundred sixty-five dollars and eighteen cents."

Three hundred! Peter laughed again. After a moment his daddy laughed too. Peter never realized they had as much as that. He guessed he was wrong to be worried. They didn't need to worry, not with three hundred sixty-five dollars and eighteen cents.

Chapter Thirty-six

Freedom Fighters

The year Peter turned nine, three important things happened. His baby brother Daniel was born, the University of Virginia opened, and the Marquis de Lafayette came to visit from France.

Peter cared a whole bunch more about Daniel than any university or marquis. Daniel's birth made Mama tired, but Maria was seventeen now, and she took charge of everything. She made sure that the kitchen ran okay, and that Patsy and Betsy-Ann took care of the little ones, Isabella and William. "And you, Peter," Maria told him, "you're old enough to take care of yourself, so don't you give me any trouble."

This made Peter mad. "I know how to behave," he said. "I have jobs to do."

"Well, you make sure one of them is fetching water and wood," Maria said. "I don't want Mama having to walk for anything, and I don't want us running short in the kitchen. I've already had Miss Martha down here twice, complaining because I burned the muffins and messed up the eggs."

Nothing Peter could do would make Maria a better cook, but he knew better than to say so.

When James came to see the new baby on Sunday, he brought a woman with him. Her name was Mary. She had high cheek-bones, dark skin, and very soft eyes. She smiled at Peter's mama, but hardly said a word.

James said, "Mama, Mary and I are getting married."

Mama kissed them both, and said she was glad. Peter scratched his toes. He watched Mary try to play with William, who was two. Mary wriggled her fingers and poked William in the belly. "Goo—chee!" she cooed.

Peter said, "He hates baby talk. He thinks it's dumb."

Mama said, "Peter!"

Mary just grinned, and James laughed. He held baby Daniel in the crook of his arm. "I remember holding you like this when you were little," he said to Peter.

"Nah," Peter said.

"Don't 'Nah' me. I held you all the time."

"Why'd you stop, then?"

James scooped Peter up with his other arm. "I didn't stop. See? I can still hold you just like I used to."

Peter wriggled in James's grasp. When James didn't let go,

Peter leaned forward and whispered in his ear, "Why you got to get married?"

James whispered back, "I don't have to. I want to."

Peter glanced at Mary. William had run away from her, but Isabella had climbed onto her lap. "She doesn't look like much," Peter said.

"Neither do you," James said, "and I still love you."

After James got married they didn't see him every week. Mama said it was only natural that sometimes he and his wife might want to spend their day off alone. "I don't see why," Peter said. "You cook better. He ought to come here to eat."

Mama laughed. "If James is smart, that's something he'll never say."

Master Jefferson's school, the University of Virginia, opened down in Charlottesville. Peter was surprised by all the fuss people made about it. Maddy said Master Jefferson had planned the whole thing, had pushed the state government to make it happen—Peter didn't understand that part at all—and had even designed some of the buildings.

"It's his last big achievement," Maddy said. "He's spent years on it. He's proud. And it's a good thing—education is a wonderful thing. This school is just as fine as the ones up north in New England. It's as good as William and Mary."

Peter said, "Could you go to that school?"

Maddy frowned. "Don't be foolish, Peter. You know better."

The school was for white men only, for rich white men who already knew how to read but wanted to learn some more. Peter snorted. "If it's not for us, what do we care?"

Maddy said, "I'm not telling you I care. I'm telling you why other people care. You don't need to care about the university, but you should care about education. What you learn can't be taken from you."

Peter rolled his eyes. He'd finally learned his alphabet, but he didn't love reading, and the last thing he wanted was Maddy pulling out the primer again. Fortunately, Maddy was too busy. The roof of the great house had been leaking awhile, but it had finally gotten so bad Master Jefferson decided to have it fixed. All summer Maddy and John and Eston replaced the old, rotten wooden shingles with new shingles covered in tin.

Miss Virginia was angry that Master Jefferson was spending money on a new roof. She wanted his money spent differently. She was getting married at Monticello in September, and she wanted John and Maddy to fix the peeling paint and rotten walkways and windowsills instead. Miss Martha told her they couldn't afford new paint.

"That's ridiculous," Miss Virginia said. "If we can afford a roof, we can afford paint."

Miss Martha sounded impatient. "We can't possibly do both. New paint won't help us if the roof caves in."

Miss Virginia rolled her eyes. Peter felt sorry for her new

husband. "Of course we can do both," she said. "I don't understand what you're talking about. Oh, and I want a new piano for a wedding gift. Grandpa's old one is so worn out it's nearly useless."

"Certainly," Miss Martha replied, but Miss Virginia's wedding came and went, without paint, walkways, or a new piano.

The Marquis de Lafayette arrived in November. He was visiting Monticello as part of his first trip to America since the Revolutionary War, fifty years ago. Everyone at Monticello was in a tizzy about him, and Peter didn't understand why. He didn't even know what a marquis was.

"Some kind of French gentleman," Peter's mama said.

"Like a duke," said Miss Sally.

"What's a duke?" Peter asked.

Dukes were nobility, Miss Sally said. They were big shots who owned lots of land, and people had to do what they said.

"Oh," Peter said. "You mean they're masters."

Miss Sally was old, older than Mama, but she was still pretty when she laughed. "No," she said. "Not masters."

"But you said—"

She waved her hand. "Everything's different in France."

She told Peter that the marquis loved freedom. He had come to America all on his own as a young man, to fight in the war against England. "Without him we never would have won," she said. "He was as important to us as Master Jefferson was.

"I saw him once," she added. "At a party in Paris I took Miss Martha to. He was very handsome, tall, elegant, and strong. He was a wonderful dancer."

Miss Martha insisted the whole house be turned out, even cupboards and cabinets the marquis would never see. Burwell muttered his way through the wine cellar and storerooms, and Peter's mama planned and practiced the finest meals. Miss Sally cleaned and mended Master Jefferson's best suit of clothes, and said she would make him wear it too. No one painted the house, Peter noticed. But Wormley raked the dead leaves from the front lawn, and John replaced the most obvious of the rotten windowsills. By the day of the marquis's arrival, Monticello was looking pretty fine.

Everyone gathered at the front of the great house, waiting for Master Jefferson's landau to bring the marquis from Charlottesville. Some of the Charlottesville people followed it up the mountain. Peter could hear them coming, laughing and cheering and singing songs. On the front porch Master Jefferson steadied himself on his cane.

The landau pulled up to the house. Israel Gillette jumped down and opened the door. Peter saw a long stockinged leg come out of the carriage and slowly reach toward the ground, and then a hand grip the doorframe, and then, finally, an enormously fat man ease himself through the narrow doorway.

He was entirely bald, and as round and pale as a dumpling.

He looked up toward the house, his fat chin wobbling, his eyes watering in the sun. Master Jefferson leaned forward. His eyes watered too, and his lips moved. His skinny legs shook. He took an uncertain step forward with his cane.

Peter waited for the marquis to come out of the carriage behind the fat man. But the fat man didn't move. He stared up at Master Jefferson, and Master Jefferson stared down at him. Finally the fat man croaked, "Jefferson?" and Master Jefferson said, "Lafayette?"

Then they both burst into tears.

Peter never saw grown men cry before. He didn't know what to think. The fat old marquis hobbled up the front walk. Master Jefferson hobbled down the porch steps. They looked at each other from a few feet away, and then they fell onto each other's shoulders and bawled. Peter had to look away. Miss Martha had tears streaming down her cheeks, and so did old Miss Sally. The marquis and Master Jefferson tottered up the steps and went into the parlor. The crowd cheered and wiped their eyes, and then, to Peter's relief, began to leave.

Peter found Maddy. He said, "I don't understand this at all."

Maddy took Peter's hand. "Come with me." They went through the side door of the house. Maddy peeked into the entrance hall. It was empty. He led Peter inside. He picked Peter up and held him in front of one of the glass-framed squares on the wall, the one with writing in it instead of a picture.

"Read that," Maddy said.

"You know I can't. Besides, the writing's squiggly."

Maddy sighed. "You are working on your reading and writing, aren't you?"

"Some. But I can't read that."

"Okay." Maddy set him down. "Just listen. Part of it says, *We hold these truths to be self-evident, that all men are created equal, that they are endowed by their Creator with certain unalienable Rights, that among these are life, liberty, and the pursuit of happiness.*

"Master Jefferson wrote that," Maddy said. "It's why our country fought a war. It's why Lafayette helped."

"Say it plain," Peter said.

Maddy said, "We think all people are equal, that God gave everybody the right to live, be free, and try to be happy."

Peter looked up at him. "If Master Jefferson wrote that, how come he doesn't believe it?"

"He does believe it," Maddy said. "At least, he thinks he does."

Miss Sally and Miss Martha hurried past, but neither of them spoke to Maddy or Peter.

"But it says all people are free," Peter said. "Not all white people. Right?" He frowned at the paper. "Read it again."

"*We hold these truths to be self-evident,*" read Maddy, "*that all people are endowed by their Creator with certain unalienable rights, that among these rights are life, liberty, and the pursuit of happiness.*"

"It does say all people," Peter said.

Maddy sighed. "Yes. It does."

"What does that first part mean? *We hold these truths to be self-evident?*"

Maddy paused. "That means—it means, this is so true everybody ought to know it. It's plain truth. It's obvious."

"But people don't know it," Peter argued.

"I didn't read it to you to tell you that," Maddy said. "I read it so you'd understand what those two old men were crying about. They believed this a long time ago, when almost nobody else did, and Master Jefferson wrote it down, and they made a whole new country around it. And now they're so old they're almost dead, and they're crying for what they did a long time ago."

"But they didn't really do it," Peter said.

Maddy shook his head. "I know," he said. "But they think they did."

Chapter Thirty-seven

Extra

Master Jefferson was sick most of the following winter. He improved a little in time for Miss Ellen's wedding at the end of May. Miss Ellen was marrying a wealthy businessman from Boston. She would be moving there to live.

"I feel like I'm deserting a sinking ship," she said to Miss Martha, the week before the wedding. "I feel like a coward, running away." She and Miss Martha were at the breakfast table. Peter was sitting on the floor in the corner, waiting to clear.

"I'm thankful your situation at least will be secure," Miss Martha said. "It's one consolation in the face of our impending misfortune."

Miss Ellen said, "Grandpa says it will get better."

Miss Martha nodded. "He always thinks so. But I don't despair. If we have to, we can sell some of the extra Negroes."

Peter frowned. He must have misheard. *Negroes* meant

black people. Surely Miss Martha hadn't said that. Extra people? Who did she think was extra? She could sell some extra furniture—they had plenty of that. Or extra livestock, there were baby calves and lambs. Or some of the books or china or wine—lots of extras there.

Maybe she hadn't said *Negroes*. Maybe she had said *clothes*. The word *clothes* sounded like *Negroes*. Some of the extra clothes. Miss Martha and her family had more clothes than they needed, that was sure.

Peter sat back on his heels. Surely Miss Martha had said *clothes*. And why would she need to sell anything? Master Jefferson was still alive.

"I don't know," Maddy said, when Peter asked him about it. His worried expression made Peter feel worse. "They must be in more trouble than we know. I thought they'd be able to manage, while he lived." He shook his head. "Pay more attention next time, okay? And tell me whatever you hear. Like my mama says, keep your mouth shut, your eyes and ears open." Maddy went back to work. After a while he spoke again. "I never thought Miss Ellen would marry."

"Why not?" Peter never thought about Miss Ellen at all.

"Something she told me, a long time ago."

"She used to talk to you?" Peter said.

"When I was a little boy. Look here, Peter, you need to get serious with this primer. You hear me? I want you to get serious about learning to read."

"I hear you," Peter said, but he rolled his eyes.

. . .

In August, Maddy and Eston traveled to Poplar Forest one last time, to replace the roof on the house there the way they'd done at Monticello. Master Jefferson stayed home. He was too weak to make the trip.

The flood of visitors continued unceasing, even as Master Jefferson declined. Miss Martha tried to always answer the door herself, so that she could turn strangers away, but if Master Jefferson heard the door he would totter out to the hall and invite everyone to spend the night. He couldn't preside at lengthy dinners anymore. He was always tired, but he needed laudanum to get to sleep.

"Daddy?" Peter asked. "Are we going to be okay?"

"I wish I knew," Daddy said.

The Marquis de Lafayette visited again before he returned to France. Peter begged Burwell to let him help serve in the dining room. He loved the sight of the long table loaded with the best food his mama could make, and with china and crystal glasses that glittered in the light. The diners toasted Lafayette, and Jefferson, and freedom; they cheered and raised their glasses high. But Master Jefferson lay in bed, too sick to attend. He and Mr. Lafayette wept again when they said good-bye.

"What do you mean, no piano?" Miss Virginia's angry voice filled the hall. "Mother! You promised this time!"

Miss Virginia and Miss Martha were sitting in Miss Martha's little parlor. Peter was waiting in the hall, to see if Master Jefferson wanted Eagle. On his good days he sometimes still rode.

Miss Virginia had been whining about a piano for months. Peter was sick to death of hearing about it. He supposed Miss Martha was too.

"Jeff tells me he spent the money elsewhere," Miss Martha said. "I thought he'd set it aside for the piano, but he says he didn't, and it's gone." After a pause, she added, "He says we can't afford a new piano."

"How ridiculous!" Miss Virginia huffed. "I refuse to believe it. He simply doesn't care about my needs. I know our situation is bad, but I must have a decent instrument if I'm to have any hope of keeping up my skills. Think of all the time I've invested in learning to play. The old piano is hopeless. It's inadequate."

"I agree," Miss Martha said. "But Jeff seems to feel that any indulgence, however small, is too much for us now. I'll tell him again how important it is."

In the hall, the door to Master Jefferson's bedroom creaked open. Peter jumped up. "Eagle?" he whispered to Miss Sally.

Miss Sally shook her head. Peter nodded. He went to the stables, and turned Eagle out to grass for the day.

In the kitchen Peter told Miss Sally and his mama about Miss Virginia and her piano. Miss Sally shook her head. "That girl is worse than a two-ton mosquito," she said.

Miss Sally told Peter's mama that Master Jefferson couldn't pass water. His water was getting blocked up in him, and that caused terrible pain. The Charlottesville doctor was bringing them tubes made from rubber gum, which could bend without breaking, to stick inside Master Jefferson and let his water out.

Peter's mama shook her head sympathetically. She seemed about to say something when Peter's little sister Isabella came in. "Miss Martha said to tell you twenty-six for dinner today."

Mama looked at Miss Sally. "When will it end?"

At first the gum tubes helped. Then Master Jefferson got an infection from them. It was terrible to get infections up inside of you.

Night and day, either Miss Sally or Burwell stayed at Master Jefferson's side. They sponged his forehead to bring his fever down, and fed him broth Peter's mama made. He survived.

Christmas came. With Master Jefferson sick in bed, no one felt like celebrating. Peter thought of what his daddy had said: As long as Master Jefferson lived, all of them would be just fine. As long as Master Jefferson lived. *Please don't die*, he begged Master Jefferson in his head. *Please don't die.*

Miss Virginia borrowed money for a piano from a friend of Master Jefferson's. Her brother Jeff argued hard against it, but she shouted him down. She wrote to Miss Ellen in Boston to find a good piano and have it shipped to them.

"I told her we didn't want to spend more than two hundred and fifty dollars," Miss Virginia told Miss Martha.

Peter perked his ears. Two hundred and fifty! He never dreamed pianos cost so much. No wonder Mister Jeff didn't want to buy one.

He still wished he knew for certain what Miss Martha had said that day—selling Negroes? Old clothes? He told himself over and over that *Negroes* didn't make sense. If Miss Martha sold the workers, there would be no one to grow crops on the farms. Then there'd be even less money.

Negroes, old clothes. She'd said Negroes. In his heart, Peter knew.

Worry lived on the mountaintop. The cold winter winds blew it back and forth, around the edges of the doorways and down the chimney draughts. Mister Jeff's face stayed creased and his fists clenched tight. Master Jefferson, up again and walking gingerly about the house, never smiled. When folks knocked on the door now, they were more likely to want money that was owed them than to meet the president.

Burwell said there was a heap of debts, from little ones to wine merchants and tailors to big ones like the one left over from Mr. Nicholas. Nobody knew their total, except maybe Master Jefferson. "And I doubt he does," Burwell said. "He doesn't want to know."

One winter night Peter went up to the great house with a cup of hot spiced wine his mama made for Master Jefferson. He scratched on the door of Master Jefferson's room and handed the cup to Miss Sally. "He's sleeping," Miss Sally whispered. "Tell Miss Edith thank you. I'll give it to him when he wakes."

Instead of taking the stairs to the basement, Peter stepped through the parlor onto the back portico. The new brick steps were still unfinished along one side. Master Jefferson had forgotten them. Peter looked across the broad lawn, peaceful under the moonlit sky, and there, standing beside the north pavilion, was Master Jefferson.

He stood hatless, his back to Peter, his coat open and one hand on his hip. Peter knew Master Jefferson had no business being out on a cold night. He'd get sick and die for sure. "Master Jefferson!" Peter called. "Hey—Master Jefferson!"

Master Jefferson didn't turn around. He'd grown pretty deaf in the past months. Peter ran forward, still calling. He had nearly reached him when the man finally turned—but it wasn't Master Jefferson. It was Eston.

"Oh!" Peter said. "I thought you were Master Jefferson."

Eston looked down at him and smiled. "No. He's in bed, I hope."

Eston was tall, over six foot, the tallest man on the mountain besides Master Jefferson. He was thin, and he moved in the same loose way Master Jefferson did. Peter had never realized before how exactly they resembled each other. "You look just like him," Peter said.

"Mmm," said Eston. "Stars are pretty tonight, aren't they?"

"Yes." A gust blew, and Peter shivered.

"Come on," said Eston. He put his hand on Peter's shoulder. They walked across the lawn, back toward the kitchen. "He's my father," Eston said. "Master Jefferson."

"I know," Peter said. "Everyone knows that."

Eston smiled. His smile looked like Master Jefferson's too. "I thought it was a secret," he said.

"Not really," Peter said.

Chapter Thirty-eight

Waiting for
the Fourth of July

One spring night, Master Jefferson dreamed of a way to make enough money to save them. Peter listened to him tell Miss Martha about it at breakfast the next morning. Master Jefferson's face shone like a boy's.

He would hold a lottery, with the farm as a prize. No one would pay a high price for his land right now, but surely hundreds, even thousands, of people would pay a small price for a chance of owning it.

"The house too?" Miss Martha asked. "Monticello?"

No, Master Jefferson said, his face falling a little. Not Monticello. Surely not. He could never sell Monticello. But he would be willing to sell his farmland, if only it would bring enough to clear his debts. If enough lottery tickets sold—

tens of thousands, perhaps even hundreds of thousands, given the size of the nation—it might be that he could pay all he owed and even have money left over, for Miss Martha to live on after he died. Lotteries were illegal, but that didn't bother Master Jefferson. He wrote Congress immediately to ask them to make an exception.

Miss Virginia's new piano arrived before Congress replied. Miss Virginia hovered anxiously as the carters unpacked it; as soon as they were finished, she sat down to play. Master Jefferson came in to listen. He said, "That's a lovely instrument. If our lottery succeeds the way I hope it will, I may buy one like it for myself."

Miss Virginia looked puzzled. "But you don't play the piano, Grandpa," she said.

The idea of the lottery seemed to buoy Master Jefferson. His health improved. He started riding again, every day, at first only short walks around the mountaintop road, but gradually longer ones until he sometimes stayed out for an hour. He even trotted a little. Miss Martha fussed, but Miss Sally smiled when Peter brought Eagle to the house. In the saddle Master Jefferson looked spry.

But it didn't last. The rubber gum tubes and the careful nursing and even the lottery weren't enough. On the sixth of June, a bright, clear day, Master Jefferson's hands trembled as he took Eagle's reins from Peter. He looked so feeble Peter hesitated to let go.

Miss Sally, who had come out with Master Jefferson, put her hand on Eagle's shoulder. "Maybe you should rest," she said, "and ride tomorrow."

Master Jefferson looked at Miss Sally. "I think I need to ride today," he said.

He came back early, exhausted. Miss Sally shouted for Peter to take the horse as Burwell carried Master Jefferson into the house. Master Jefferson went to bed and didn't get up again that day.

"Don't bring Eagle anymore," Miss Sally told Peter the next morning. "He won't ride again."

For a few weeks Master Jefferson could sit up sometimes. He wrote a few more letters and once in a while had something to eat. Miss Sally, Miss Martha, and Burwell made sure he was never alone.

Congress allowed the lottery, but only if Monticello itself was part of the prize. The great house would go to the lottery winner.

"If it pays the debts, that will be enough," Miss Martha said. "I know I can always find a home among my children."

But the lottery failed. So few tickets sold that eventually Mister Jeff canceled the whole thing. Some people and even some state governments sent Master Jefferson money out of charity, but no one, it seemed, wanted Monticello.

Peter couldn't tell if that was a good thing or a bad thing. He'd been scared at the thought of Monticello changing hands, but everyone around him seemed more upset that it wouldn't happen. As long as Master Jefferson is alive, Peter repeated to himself, we'll all be fine. Master Jefferson had been sick so many times before. He had always gotten better. Surely he would this time too.

One morning in the woodshop John Hemings asked Peter to bring him a board. Peter took one out of a group of fine, straight boards leaning against the back wall.

"Not those," John said. "I'm saving those."

"What for?"

John took a deep breath. "For when I make his coffin."

Master Jefferson had finally written a will, Miss Sally said. She didn't know what it said, but she knew he'd written it. Miss Sally seemed happy about that, beneath her sorrow.

"Daddy," Peter asked, "if Master Jefferson dies, what are we going to do?"

Daddy looked him in the eye. "When he dies," he said, "we're going to work hard and stick together as much as we're able. We'll do our best, the same as always."

By the second of July, Master Jefferson no longer ate or drank. He no longer spoke, and opened his eyes only if someone shook him. Peter wasn't allowed near him, of course, but Maddy got the details from his mama.

"He wants to live until the Fourth," Maddy said.

Maddy explained that July 4, 1826, was fifty years exactly

after July 4, 1776, which was the day the constitutional delegates signed the Declaration of Independence that Master Jefferson wrote, and the country America was born.

Some other old man named Mr. Adams, who was president even before Master Jefferson, was dying too. He lived a long way away. Peter had heard of him because he and Master Jefferson used to write letters to each other all the time. "They're both trying to stay alive until the anniversary," Maddy said. Peter didn't see why.

If not for the worry on the mountaintop, everything would have been so beautiful. Summer was in full bloom. The garden burst with fruit and vegetables. Ripening peaches hung golden from the trees. Grass shimmered green in the fields. When Peter visited Eagle in his pasture, the horse whuffled hello and came eagerly to get whatever treat Peter brought him. Eagle smelled so good in the sun.

Without the worry, it would have been wonderful, but Peter felt like no one other than him even noticed the sunlight or the warmth or the green crops growing. All over the mountain, everyone was holding their breath, waiting for Master Jefferson to die.

July second passed. On the afternoon of the third, Master Jefferson woke for a moment. He seemed unhappy, and tried to speak. Burwell shifted his pillows. Master Jefferson nodded, and closed his eyes.

Miss Sally told them that, in the kitchen.

Much later, Peter heard that just before old Mr. Adams died, on the night of July the Fourth, he opened his eyes and said, "Jefferson survives." But by then it wasn't true. Master Jefferson died at ten o'clock in the morning, July 4, 1826.

His will gave Poplar Forest free and clear to Francis Eppes. Monticello, all the property there, and every single debt went to Mister Jeff. That hardly seemed right. Mister Jeff had always worked so hard. But the debts had to go to someone. Someone had to pay.

The will gave Burwell his freedom immediately. It gave Joe Fossett, John Hemings, and John's "two apprentices" their freedom from exactly one year after the day Master Jefferson died, or, in the case of the apprentices, on the day they each turned twenty-one. The apprentices were Maddy and Eston, of course, but Master Jefferson didn't write out their names.

Joe Fossett and John Hemings were given the tools they used. Master Jefferson's will also asked the legislature of Virginia to allow all five freed men to remain in the state, instead of leaving it immediately once freed, as Virginia law now demanded.

When Peter's daddy heard the news, he buried his head in his hands.

"What's it mean?" Peter asked. The look on his father's face frightened him.

"Next summer I'll be a free man," Daddy said. "Also Burwell, John, Madison, and Eston."

"And Mama too?" asked Peter. "And us?"

Daddy's face looked like it might break. He took a long, terrible breath, and then he folded his arms around Peter and held him tight, just as Peter always hoped he would. But he didn't speak. Peter felt a wave of overwhelming dread.

"What's going to happen?" Peter asked. "Will Mister Jeff be master now?"

"That won't matter," Daddy said. "They're going to take all the money Master Jefferson owes, and put that number on one side of a scale. Then they'll turn every last thing he owns into money, put it on the other side of the scale, and try to make the two sides balance."

"What if they don't?" Peter asked.

"They won't." Peter's daddy looked angry now. He looked furious. "Not from all I've heard. But that's not our problem. Our problem is that Mister Jeff will have to sell everything Master Jefferson owns. He'll have no choice."

"Sell Monticello?" Peter asked.

Daddy spat in the dirt by the forge. "I don't give a fig for Monticello," he said. "I suppose they'll sell it. The big house, the fields, the farms, the furniture."

He turned toward Peter. "They'll sell the people."

"Which people?" Peter whispered.

Daddy didn't answer. Peter understood.

Him. His mama. His brother and sisters. Everyone, except his daddy, Burwell, Maddy, Eston, and John.

Never before had he thought of himself as a slave.

Chapter Thirty-nine

Washington, D.C.

Beverly subscribed to a weekly newspaper. He unfolded his copy, and read the bone-chilling words in black and white: "Executor's Sale. Will be sold, on the fifteenth of January, at Monticello . . . 130 valuable Negroes . . . believed to be the most valuable for their number ever offered at one time in the state of Virginia."

So this is what it comes to, he thought. Never a visitor turned away. The finest food in the country on the table every night, the finest imported wine—the grandchildren decked out in silk dresses, the favors done for friends. One hundred thirty people to be sold. Beverly had read that the total debt exceeded a hundred and fifty thousand dollars.

One hundred thirty valuable Negroes. Beverly knew most of their names.

"Dear?" his wife asked. "Is something wrong? You look—shaken."

Beverly folded the paper and rose from the breakfast table. He kissed her cheek as he stood. His wife was the meekest of women. She rarely asked him anything, which was something he treasured about her. Now he forced himself to speak lightly. "Merely my continued astonishment at our namesake's demise."

She laughed, because it was a little joke they shared, that Beverly's last name, and now hers—Jefferson—must bode some connection, however far-off, forgotten, and distant, with the great patriot. "Perhaps it's as well we aren't related," she said. "Someone might come asking you for money."

One hundred thirty persons to be sold.

Beverly paused just inside the dining room door. "I'll be in the shop all day, but after I close I might step over to Harriet's for a moment," he said. "You won't mind?"

"Of course not, dear. Tell her I hope she's feeling well."

Beverly hesitated. "I know you'll think this is foolish of me. I'm sure it *is* foolish—but I might go to that auction. To Monticello."

His wife furrowed her brow. "But why?"

"I don't know. I just think I'd like to be there."

"But it's such a long trip," she said, "and whatever household goods they're selling will be far too grand for us. Certainly more than we can afford. Unless—surely you're not thinking . . ." She paused, and bit her lip. Beverly knew what it cost her to confront him. "Beverly," she said. "Perhaps I haven't expressed myself fully on one particular subject. As your wife I must bow to your wishes, I know, and I realize you'll soon need more help in the shop, but I can not—I really can not—agree—" She broke off, and looked at her lap.

"What are you talking about?" Beverly asked.

"I will not own slaves," she said in a rush. "I hope you're not thinking of bidding on a person. I won't have it. I think it's wrong."

Beverly crossed the floor in two steps and kissed her full on the mouth. "No," he said. "No. It's not that. I'd just like to see this place they talk about. Monticello. Who knows what will happen to it now?"

"No," said Harriet. She anchored her needle into the small breeches she was sewing, put her hands on her lap, and glared at him. "No. Are you insane, Beverly? All it would take is one person—*one*—to recognize us, and it would be us up on that block. We don't have papers—we're still probably written down in the estate book. We weren't in the will. We are still his legal property."

"No one would—"

"Beverly." He saw she held her hands not on her lap, as he'd first thought, but cupped protectively around her swelling belly, her second child. "Anything you do endangers me. And my children. And yours, when you have them."

A wail came from one of the back rooms. Harriet glared at

Beverly as she got up. She returned carrying a sturdy blond little boy. "Look who's up from his nap," she said. She joggled the baby and said to him, "Look who's here. Your uncle Beverly."

The baby's sleepy face lit into a beautiful smile. He held his hands out to Beverly.

Beverly took him and swung high in the air, then brought him back down to kiss him. Then he turned back to Harriet. "I just keep thinking—Mama. The will didn't mention her."

"It hardly could, could it?" Harriet returned to her sewing, her needle darting swiftly through the fabric. "It didn't even mention Maddy or Eston by name. Mama's fine. You know she is, she has to be. Miss Martha will be too afraid of the truth getting out to treat Mama poorly. We'll send them another letter. Maddy will let us know if they need help, help we can give them." Harriet paused to move a pin. She looked up at him. "I'd give anything to see them," she said. "Anything but my babies. That's final."

Beverly paced across the little room, bouncing his nephew in his arms. "I'm going to send money through Jesse Scott," he said. "Ten dollars, more if I can manage it. Not for Mama—for the rest of them. Jesse will know how to use it."

Harriet nodded. "I've got a bit saved up," she said. "I'll give it to you—but you'll mail it, won't you? Please."

"Yes," Beverly agreed.

Chapter Forty

The Graveyard

Maddy was already twenty-one when his father died, so he was legally free the day the will was read. He wasn't quite sure what to do with himself, however. Eston was only nineteen, and Uncle John wouldn't be free for a year. Maddy kept going to the woodshop, even though none of them had work to do.

A few weeks later Miss Martha opened the door of the shop. She stood in the doorway without coming in. "We're closing the house," she said. "I'm going to Boston with Tim and George. The others are moving in with Jeff."

Miss Martha looked strange and severe in her stiff black dress. John, Maddy, and Eston stared at her. None of them knew what to say.

"Shut this place down," she said. "Eston, John, you can have your time. I told Sally she could have hers. Find her a place down in Charlottesville. Find yourselves work down there.

Take the tools, the wood. Do what you like. Only"—here she fixed Maddy with a fierce glare—"don't be spreading lies about my father. Do you hear me? Make no trouble for me, and I'll make no trouble for you."

Maddy heard her. Before the week was out, he, Eston, and Mama were settled into a little house near Jesse Scott. John moved to a cabin down the mountain that Miss Martha gave him—alone, since Miss Martha took his wife with her to Boston. They all found carpentry work at the new university.

Now it was the day before the auction. At the great house, auction personnel were cataloguing furniture and preparing for the sale. Maddy avoided the house on his way up from town. He went first to the graveyard on the far side of the mountaintop, near where the woods began. Even from there he could hear clangs coming from Joe Fossett's anvil in the blacksmith shop. Maddy shuddered. Joe was working half to death.

It was bitter cold. Snow blanketed the ground. The sharp wind scudded drifts against the gravestones, except for Thomas Jefferson's. That one grave had been brushed clean, and a small shining pile of holly lay upon it. Mama's work, Maddy knew. She climbed the mountain two or three times a week to tend the grave.

He heard a noise behind him. Turning, he saw Peter Fossett a little ways away. Peter looked thin and cold; shadows underlined his sad eyes. "Peter!" Maddy went to him and hugged him. "I was coming to see you next."

Peter didn't say anything. Maddy took off his own scarf and wrapped it around Peter's neck. He wished he had mittens to cover Peter's hands. "Tomorrow—" Maddy said.

"Daddy can't bid on us," Peter said, his voice high and trembling. "He's still a slave until July, and slaves can't own property, so he can't bid. But he gave all his money to Jesse Scott. Jesse's going to bid on us for Daddy."

Maddy nodded. He held Peter's shoulders. "I know. Me and Eston and Mama, we gave Jesse all the money we had. It wasn't much, but it might help." Maddy knelt in the snow, and pulled something from his pants pocket. "I came to see you special, though, because I have some things just for you." He pressed a small flat object into Peter's hands.

"That old primer," Peter said, looking down.

"Miss Ellen gave me this primer," Maddy said. "I've always treasured it. Words are powerful things. Learn them and you'll have their power. Only keep it a secret—white people don't like for us to read."

"My daddy's going to try to buy us," Peter said. "With Jesse Scott. And if he can't buy me—if he runs out of money before he gets to me—he's found a nice white man to buy me, who says he'll let my daddy buy me back later on."

"That's good," Maddy said. "That's real good, I'm glad. But you listen to me. There isn't such a thing as a nice slave owner. Slavery is bad. It's evil. All slave owners are bad. If a person would own another person, you can't trust a word they'll say, so you be careful, you hear me? That's why I'm giving you this too." He opened Peter's hand, and pressed two quarters into it.

"A long time ago your brother and I caught a bird, and sold it to my father for fifty cents apiece," Maddy said. "I always felt bad about it. I gave Jesse the rest of the money I had, but I'm giving this fifty cents to you. You keep it secret, and you hang on to it. Get one of your sisters to help you sew it into your clothes. You never know when you're going to need it.

"I'm in Charlottesville. I will always help you with anything I can," Maddy said. "But sometime you might need that money. You hang on to it."

Peter nodded. From Mulberry Row a woman's voice called, "Peter! Pee—ter!"

"That's Mama," Peter said.

"You better go," Maddy said. "I love you, Peter Fossett."

Peter started down the path, then turned. "You all going to be here tomorrow?" he asked.

Maddy shook his head. "No. Think we should?"

Peter shook his head too. "Eston looks just like him. You all better stay away."

Maddy turned back to his father's headstone. *Author of the Virginia Statute on Religious Freedom and the Declaration of Independence,* it read. *Founder of the University of Virginia.* That was what Master Jefferson—no, Thomas Jefferson, Maddy corrected himself—had wanted written there. That was how he wanted people to remember him.

The champion of freedom, Maddy thought, who owned

slaves. Who lived his life so that at his death one hundred thirty people must be sold.

Maddy heard a loose shutter banging against the side of the worn-out great house. He reached down to touch the holly on the grave. It was fresh, and so were Mama's footprints in the snow at the grave's edge. At her age Mama had no business climbing this mountain in the cold. She did it anyway. Despite everything, Mama loved him. Maddy hoped that someday he would too.

Chapter Forty-one

The End

The night before the auction was savagely cold. Icy air seeped into Peter's family's room from the walls and ceiling and floor; it blew in under the door and around the windowpanes. Daddy built the fire high, but the cold remained and seemed to deepen the coldness in their hearts.

For months they'd known the auction was coming. They'd watched the preparations being made. Daddy had worn himself out. He'd worked every job he could for wages, but he didn't have enough money to buy them all. He'd tried to broker deals with some of the white men in Charlottesville, so that at least they would all stay nearby. The auction had been advertised in newspapers across the nation. If a stranger from the Deep South—no, Peter wouldn't think of that. He drew his knees up sharp and huddled closer to his sister Isabella.

They were all on the one bed for their last night together.

Peter, Mama, Daddy, Maria, Patsy, Betsy-Ann, Isabella, William, and Daniel. And the new baby, the baby Mama was carrying in her belly, the baby Mama had told them about only a week ago. It was crowded, but Peter wanted to be crowded. He wanted to be surrounded by his family forever.

Daddy said, "You all remember this. No matter what, we are a family. We belong together. I will not stop working until we can be together. Do you hear me?"

Before he could help himself, Peter whispered, "James."

James wasn't with them. James and his wife, Mary, belonged to Mr. Randolph, so they weren't being sold in the auction.

"James," Mama said, "we will have to worry about some other time."

"I want you to understand," Daddy said. "All of you. I have to bid on Mama first. The babies—William and Daniel—they'll go up with her. That's how it's been arranged.

"Jesse will do all he can," Daddy continued. "He's got all the money we could scrape together, between us and all our friends. He'll bid on Mama first—he's got to get Mama.

"Maria after that, then Patsy, Betsy-Ann, Isabella, and Peter."

Isabella, who was seven, started to cry. Mama held her tight.

"It has to be like that," Daddy said. "Bella, Peter, do you understand? I love you with my life. I love you equal, every one of my beautiful children, I love you all the same, but I've got to get the girls first, and I've got to get the older ones safe before the younger ones. Do you understand? Peter?" Daddy's voice was pleading.

Peter understood. Since slave marriages weren't legal, Mama wasn't safe. Some slave owner—some white man—might want Mama to have babies she didn't want to have. Or Maria—or any of them. Except Peter, because he couldn't have babies.

It was, Peter thought, the hardest thing to think about in the world.

Peter felt like the floor was opening up beneath his feet, like he was falling, falling. He was last in line. Who would protect him?

"I won't ever rest," Daddy said. "I will never rest in my life until we are all together again. Free and together. We are family no matter how far apart we are, but someday, I promise you, someday we will live like one. All of us free."

The words gave Peter something solid to stand on. "I'll help you," he promised. "I'll work too. I won't ever stop."

Maria asked, "How much money do we have?"

Daddy drew in a deep breath. "I don't know exactly. I think it's around five hundred dollars."

"And they said Mama was worth three hundred twenty-five," said Patsy. The auctioneers had come around with paper and pencil, and looked at all of them, and written numbers down. What they were worth.

Peter had been appraised for the same amount as a decent pig.

He wished he could find that funny.

"If Mama goes for that much . . ." Maria's voice trailed off.

She was next, so she might be safe. Mama would be sold with the little boys, and she was a trained cook. The paper said Mama was worth a lot more than Maria.

"I hope we can do pretty well," Daddy said. "But if not, you keep your chins up. I've made all the deals I can. So long as you get bought by the right people, I'll be able to buy you back once I get the money raised."

Peter knew what Daddy'd said before, that a white man's promise wasn't necessarily worth the spit that sealed the handshake. Daddy said, "We've done the best we could do."

Morning came. The wind howled, and the rising sun seemed unable to warm the frigid air. An endless row of horses and wagons and people streamed up the mountain, white people, cash in hand. It seemed like everyone in the world wanted to buy something from Monticello.

The morning passed without Peter knowing how. He couldn't eat. He couldn't talk. He couldn't even seem to feel the cold.

Suddenly Mama stood on the block with Daniel in her arms. William clung to her skirts. Mama stood tall and proud. The auctioneer, a white man, told her to smile.

"Let them see your teeth!" To people watching he said, "This one's still got her teeth!" He thumped Mama's shoulder, hard. From the edge of the crowd Peter cried out. Maria slapped her hand over Peter's mouth.

Mama opened her mouth wide. She didn't smile. She showed her teeth.

"You can also see she's an excellent breeder!" the auctioneer continued. "Birthed eight living children, and young enough for more! You'd turn a handy profit on her in just a few years. Better yet—folks, this is hard to believe, but I have it on very good authority that she's been trained in the art of French cookery. Ever since Thomas Jefferson left the president's mansion, this wench has cooked his every meal! All up and down the Albemarle I've heard raves about the food at Monticello, and now here's a chance to have that food served at your very own table—and get these two fine boys into the bargain, with more coming if you know how to get them! What am I started at? What am I bid?"

So many people put their hands into the air. So many numbers. Peter shook. His sisters' hands steadied him. So many people bidding on Mama—how would Daddy ever win? Larger and larger numbers, until at last they slowed. The auctioneer dropped his hammer. "Sold, for five hundred and five dollars. To Mr. Jesse Scott."

Peter's heart leaped with relief and horror. Maria sobbed. Mama and the babies were safe. But five hundred and five dollars! Jesse would have nothing left.

Peter's sister Maria stood on the block.

Sold, to a man whose name Peter didn't hear.

Patsy.

Sold. To Mr. Charles Bonnycastle.

Betsy-Ann.

Sold. To Mr. John Winn.

Isabella.

Sold. To someone else entirely.

Wormley's wife, Ursula.

Sold.

Their children: Joseph, Anne, Dolly, Cornelius, Thomas, Louisa, Caroline, Critta, George, Robert, and Burwell.

Sold.

Davy Hern.

Sold.

His wife, Fanny.

Sold.

Their children: Ellen, Jenny, Indridge, and Bonnycastle.

Sold.

At last Peter climbed onto the tall wooden block. The wind cut through his pants, stockings, and coat, seared his arms and legs. He bit his lip hard so he wouldn't cry out, and tasted the metallic tang of blood.

He was too cold to shiver. He could hardly see. The bidding started, but he couldn't hear the numbers. He couldn't hear anything but the wind.

Someone moved to stand in front of him. It was his father, looking straight into his eyes. That look sent strength into Peter. Whatever else happened, he would be Joe Fossett's son.

He heard the hammer fall.

Sold.

Afterword

Every time I have written a piece of historical fiction, I have been asked afterward which parts of my book were really true. The answer for this book, like the story itself, is complicated.

I believe Thomas Jefferson was the father of all of Sally Hemings's children. So does almost everyone else who's investigated the subject—and there has been a lot of careful research done, including what DNA testing could be done without actually digging up Thomas Jefferson's body. If you want to read further, the "Report of the Monticello Research Committee on Thomas Jefferson and Sally Hemings," which can be found online at www.monticello. org, is a good place to start.

Every named character in this book comes from history—their ages, situations, and relationships to each other are all historically documented. Most, though not all, of their actions in this book are also historically documented. However, we really know very little about them. We know what they did, but not how they felt; where they worked, but not how they spoke or what they said.

For example, we know that Beverly Hemings left Monticello right around the time of his twenty-first birthday. We know that he returned a few months later, and that he left for good three years after that. But we don't know why he returned. We don't know anything about what happened to him during the months he was gone; we don't know how he felt about leaving his family, or how they felt about seeing him again. I've had to, as best as I am able, put myself in Beverly's shoes—to imagine, if I were Beverly, what could make me go back to Monticello. And if I were Sally, or Maddy, or Harriet, how would I react when he did?

As another example, we know that Maddy was taught to read and write by one or more of Jefferson's grandchildren. We know that Miss Ellen was the most scholarly grandchild, and we know that Maddy later named one of his own daughters Ellen. We don't really know whether it was Miss Ellen who taught Maddy—that's an educated guess.

We know that Miss Cornelia gave John Hemings a dictionary. We know that Peter Fossett secretly carried a primer he treasured with him to his new master's house after the auction. We don't know where Peter's primer came from; when I wrote the scene where Maddy gives it to him, I was making that up.

We know James Fossett became the property of Thomas Randolph around the time of his eleventh birthday, but we don't know why. We don't even know whether he was sold or was given away.

Different people might draw on the same facts I did and come up with a very different story. That's okay. This is Beverly's story, and Maddy's, Eston's, Harriet's, and Sally's. It is Peter Fossett's story, and Joe Fossett's, and James Fossett's. It is Thomas Jefferson's story, and Martha Jefferson Randolph's, and Burwell's and John Hemings's and mine. I have done what I can with what we know now. I've told all the truth I can find; so far as I know, nowhere have I written anything that couldn't be true—that contradicts something we know for sure.

But history changes; that's part of the wonder of it. Even during the three years I have been writing and researching this story, historians have uncovered new information in old letters, census records, and long-buried documents, and I've had to revise my story accordingly.

Madison Hemings, the overseer Edmund Bacon, and Peter Fossett all left personal recollections of their lives at Monticello. Maddy's tells us that Harriet and Beverly both married white people, and had children. Neither ever told their new families about their past. They are lost in history; though Madison said they lived in Washington, D.C., he and Eston died without revealing the names Beverly and Harriet lived under.

Madison and Eston stayed in Charlottesville with their mother until her death in 1835. They then moved to Ohio, which had become a free state. Both married light-complexioned free black women and had families. Among Maddy's eleven children were sons named after his brothers and himself, and daughters named Sally, Harriet, and, as I said before, Ellen. Although Maddy never passed for white, some of his children did.

In the early 1850s, Eston, his wife, and their three children moved to Wisconsin, changed their last name from Hemings to Jefferson, and passed into white society. Eston was a professional violinist whose signature tune was Jefferson's favorite, "Money Musk." I don't know where or how Eston acquired his violin. Thomas Jefferson was known to have owned at least five violins; three of them, including his expensive Italian violin, can be traced after his death.

Joe and Edith Fossett and their children Daniel, William, and Betsy-Ann (whom Joe was eventually able to buy), along with Lucy and Jesse, who were born after the auction, moved to Ohio around 1840. Peter escaped slavery when he was thirty years old, and joined them. He became a Baptist minister and a conductor on the Underground Railroad. We don't know exactly what happened to Patsy, but she may have run away from her new owner after the auction: She is listed in the 1850 census as living free in Cincinnati. Peter is said to have forged a pass allowing Isabella to run away, but we don't know if she succeeded; she does not seem to have reunited with her family. Neither did Maria; we don't know what happened to her.

Historians believe James Fossett married a woman named Mary. Nothing else about his adult life is known.

Most Useful Sources for Further Study

The best place to go first for more information about Thomas Jefferson, Sally Hemings, and the other people in this book, is the website Monticello.org. It's a huge site, with lots of information tucked in odd corners—I particularly used the Plantation Database and the Digital Family Letters Archive.

Monticello itself is a fascinating place to visit, as is Poplar Forest, Jefferson's retreat home.

The books I found most useful are listed below. A more comprehensive list of sources can be found on my website, www.kimberlybrubakerbradley.com.

Betts, Edwin Morris, ed. *Thomas Jefferson's Farm Book*. Rev. ed. Charlottesville, VA: The Thomas Jefferson Memorial Foundation, 1999.

Gordon-Reed, Annette. *The Hemingses of Monticello: An American Family*. New York: W. W. Norton & Company, 2008.

———. *Thomas Jefferson and Sally Hemings: An American Controversy*. Charlottesville, VA: The University of Virginia Press, 1997.

Lanier, Shannon & Jane Feldman. *Jefferson's Children: The Story of One American Family*. New York: Random House, 2000.

Stanton, Lucia. *Free Some Day: The African-American Families of Monticello*. Charlottesville, VA: The Thomas Jefferson Foundation, 2000.

———. *Slavery at Monticello*. Charlottesville, VA: The Thomas Jefferson Foundation, 1996.

Webster, Noah. *American Dictionary of the English Language*. Facsimile copy of the 1828 edition published by the Foundation for American Christian Education, Chesapeake, VA, 1995.

———. *The Original Blue Back Speller, 1824*. Facsimile copy published by the Vision Forum, San Antonio, TX, 2009.